THE LAST PRINCE OF ATLANTIS CHRONICLES

BOOK II
BATTLE FOR THE CROWN

THE LAST PRINCE OF ATLANTIS CHRONICLES

BOOK II
BATTLE FOR THE CROWN

LEONARD CLIFTON

THE LAST PRINCE OF ATLANTIS CHRONICLES
BOOK II BATTLE FOR THE CROWN

Library of Congress Control Number: 2020910102

Print information available on the last page.

Rev. date: 06/02/2020
To order copies of this book, contact: www.leonardclifton.com

This Book Series was Created for The Dreamers. Dream Big. "Hail Atlantis!"

CONTENT

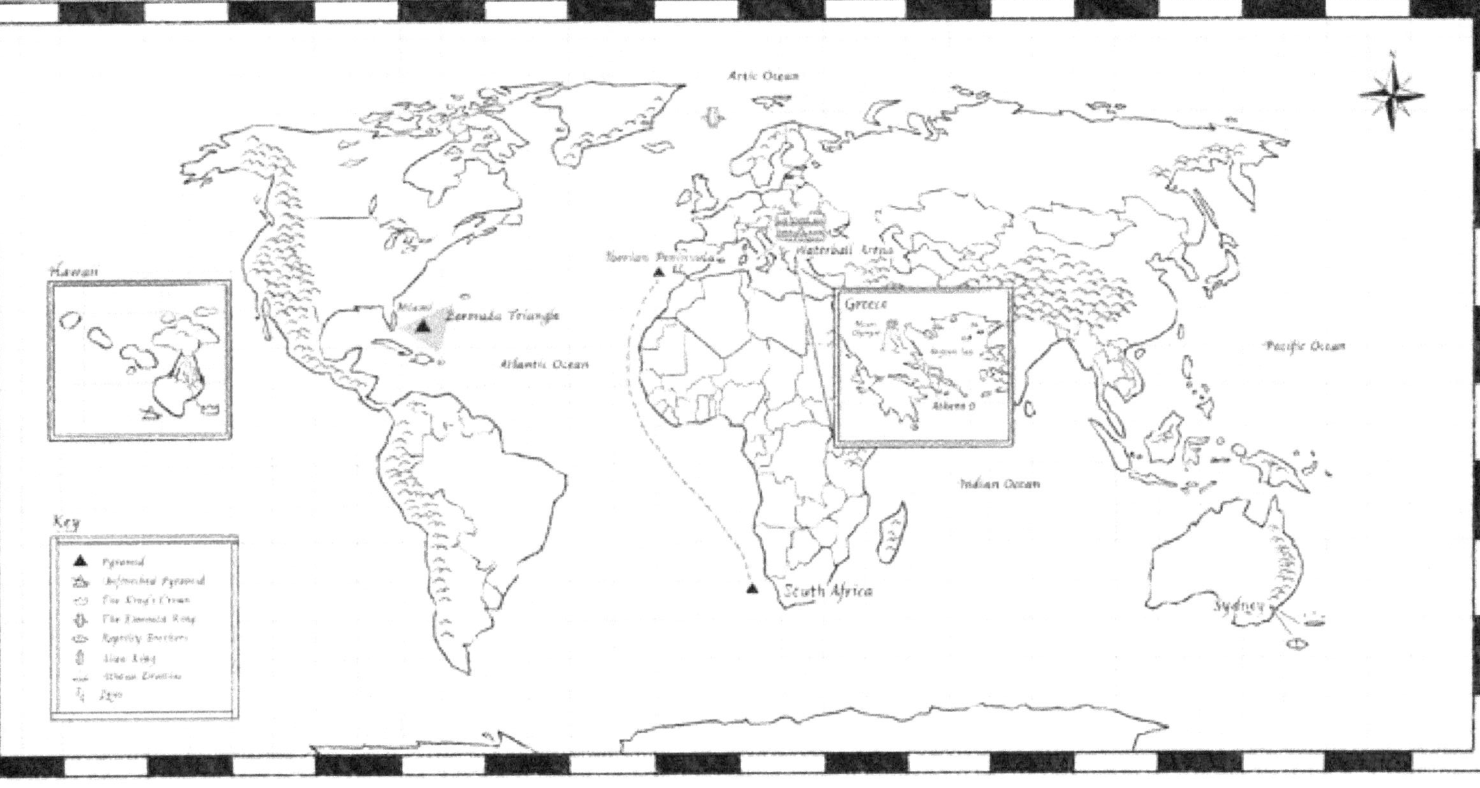

Artic Ocean
Hawaii
Miami
Bermuda Triangle
Atlantic Ocean
Iberian Peninsula
Greece
Athens
South Africa
Indian Ocean
Pacific Ocean
Sydney
Key
Pyramid
Unfinished Pyramid
The King's Crown

CHAPTER ONE

ALLEN IS BEING WATCHED BY ANDROMEDA

Zeus touches my forehead and says, "Andromeda, now you know everything I know regarding my Goddaughter and the Atlantean, including everyone around them. Good and bad."

He grabs his lightning bolt and says, "Keep me informed."

I reply, "Don't worry, Zeus. I will."

He disappears in a flash returning to Mount Olympus. I look around the one-bedroom apartment with a large TV hanging on the wall, walk into the kitchen, and open the stainless-steel refrigerator. "Zeus loves Greek yogurt a lot," I whisper. The refrigerator stores yogurt and Greek wine. I grab a glass out of the cupboard and pour a glass of wine as I observe the earth tone walls and modern books and magazines lying on the glass coffee table. I take a sip of wine and sit down on the reclining sofa. My body sinks into the comfortable cushion, as I grab the remote control and say a spell to make Zeus' TV magical. The modified TV will allow me to watch everyone I now know about from Zeus. I whisper, "It's time to see what's going on with the Atlantean. I'll watch everyone closely including the Atlantean's adversaries."

I turn on the TV watching Allen King and everyone at my granddaughter's (Athena Dranias) mansion in Miami, Florida. It's Monday morning, and Tyrone McCoy's funeral is set to take place after school. Uncle Zadok has prepared a special breakfast for his nephew,

Allen, (Allen's girlfriend) Athena Dranias, Allen's best friends he considers as brothers, Francisco Gomez, Jake O'Connor, and Zadok's wife, Aoki. The teenagers are superheroes, known as the Atlantean Superhero Ballers and the acronym ASB. The long marble breakfast table is brimming with delicious food (pancakes, waffles, scrambled eggs, turkey bacon, fruit salad, and fresh squeezed orange juice). Zadok wants to cheer them up, in addition to the cowbell; he's installed an intercom in the dining room and speakers throughout the mansion, which allows him to announce to the teens that their meals are ready.

Zadok yells into the intercom, "Okay, boys, and girls, it's breakfast time!" He rings the cowbell *(ding, ding, ding!)* and shouts, "Come and get it while it's hot! Let's eat ya'll."

Feeling a little somber in their black mourning suits, the teens file into the dining room and silently take their seats around the table. Aoki looks at them and says, "Wow! All of you look elegant!"

The teens politely say, "Thank you."

Zadok says, "This is something new for me, so please be patient. Let us all bow our heads and pray." As an Atlantean, Zadok worships the Alien Elders, and like all Atlanteans generally. Atlanteans do not make a habit of praying in public. But out of respect for Tyrone's mother and grandmother, he feels compelled to acknowledge their God.

Zadok prays, "Oh Heavenly Father, I thank you for every person sitting at the table. I pray that they make it safely out the front door, to their classes, and to their friend Tyrone's funeral. Lord, I ask you to continually bless Annie Mae and Tyretta McCoy as they grieve during this horrible time. Amen."

The family echoes, "Amen." The teens feel as if the prayer bestowed some instant blessing upon them.

Allen smiles at Uncle Zadok and applauds. The teens cheer for the man who's been there for them as their friend and father. They gather around him in a giant group hug and shower him with kisses.

Zadok mock-grumbles, "Alright! Alright! Let's stop that and eat."

Francisco jokes, "This is a great breakfast, Unc. What are you trying to do, get us all fat? My chica won't like that."

Zadok laughs and rubs his big belly. "There's nothing wrong with a little fat." He kisses Aoki, who runs her hand over Zadok's stomach and kisses it, leaving a lipstick stain on his T-shirt.

Athena exclaims, "Oooooh, sexy! I can't wait until my King has a belly. By that time, we'll be watching over oodles of grandchildren and great-grandchildren. I'm going to kiss Allen's belly when we're old fogies propped up on the couch in the royal entertainment room."

Allen laughs and brags, "You can kiss my six-pack now, and the big belly later… if I ever have one. Remember Princess, Atlantean warriors look the same when they're over two-hundred- years-old, as they do when they're forty, or even twenty, for that matter!"

Reminiscing, Zadok says, "Look out now! When I was fighting in World War II…"

The teens roll their eyes.

"Here we go," Aoki says giggling.

Zadok punches his stomach and boasts, "I was solid back then! A sledgehammer couldn't knock me down."

Aoki teases, "Honey, a sledgehammer couldn't knock you down now."

Jake stifles a laugh and says, "Uncle Zadok, you're what we call an OG. You're the Original Gangster."

Zadok admonishes with a stern look, "There's nothing nice about being a gangster. I'd rather be the Original Atlantean Warrior."

The teens and Aoki raise their juice glasses and cheer, "Here, here!"

Allen, Athena, Jake, and Francisco decide to drive their cars to school that morning. For the first time since Tyrone's death, they feel like being independent. They also want to race each other to school.

Before Francisco hops in his car, he challenges Athena. "I know you have your souped-up car, sis, but you can't beat my all-American Camaro. They don't call it a muscle car for nothing! Let's see if you can out race me." He jumps in and peels out of the driveway.

Athena smirks. "I can beat you, gangster boy!"

Jake says nonchalantly, "Since your cars may be a little faster than mine, I'm taking an alternate route none of you know about." The gang laughs at Jake's comment.

Traffic is lighter than usual, even though Athena left two minutes later, she is able to get behind Francisco and tailgate him. Suddenly, she kicks her car into fourth gear, switches lanes, pulls up alongside Francisco and smiles at him. She shifts into fifth gear and accelerates like a missile, leaving him in the dust.

Francisco punches his steering wheel and using his crystal necklace, shouts telepathically, *Not so fast! I have something for your ass!* He lifts a switch close to his steering wheel making red flames burst out of his exhaust. Francisco's Camaro looks like a rocket ship as he quickly passes the socialite's vehicle.

With a tone of superiority, Athena transmits, *Okay, Mr. Francisco Gomez, if that's the way you want to play it, let's play.* She hits a blue button next to her stereo. The computer voice in Athena's car counts down to racing mode. "Three, two, one."

She has green lights for the next seven blocks ahead. Athena waves to Francisco as she passes him and takes the lead. Grinning to herself; she straps on another seatbelt that crosses the one she's wearing, creating an X across her body. The tires grip the road as the engine roars, and exhaust plumes momentarily blind Francisco, who's already a block behind Athena.

Athena crosses four streetlights within six seconds flat. She has three more to go. She fights the g-forces as her hand moves in slow motion toward the blue button. She releases it and quickly slows down as she cruises through the last traffic light and into the school parking lot. She squeals into a parking space, stops on a dime and punches her fist on the ceiling of her car, yelling telepathically, *Victory! Don't you ever challenge an Aussie to a race, especially a Greek one!*

With admiration, Francisco says telepathically, *Damn, sis. You could be the next great female racecar driver. I thought Allen was a badass. I see why you guys are together!*

Athena gets out of her car as Francisco pulls into the parking spot next to hers. She pretends she's brushing dirt off her shoulders, saunters over to his window and motions for him to open it, which he does. She leans in and says, "Thank you, Fran my man, for being a fan."

Francisco's eyes light up as he gets out of his car and proclaims, "You're one down-ass chick!"

Athena bursts into laughter and mimes a three-point jump shot. "And you better believe it, because I'm balling."

Francisco covers his face and shakes his head, mumbling, "Oh, my God, what have we created? You went from being a socialite to an urban girl in two point one seconds flat... faster than your whip."

"I got it like that," replies Athena smiling victoriously.

Francisco can't take it anymore. "Sis, please... keep your composure, alright? And remember, you're the classy alias you created to hide your true identity. In high school, you are, Audrey Monroe and not some road-hog gangster warrior. You're freaking me out right now, so please... stop the lingo."

Audrey puts her arm around Francisco. "Alright, G."

Allen and Jake pull up.

"I beat Allen here," brags Jake.

Allen grins sarcastically. "Dude, I let you."

The mood instantly changes when they notice Josh driving into the parking lot. They see that the star quarterback, Josh Stone is wearing his best friend, Tyrone McCoy's jersey.

CHAPTER TWO

ALLEN AND JOSH BECOME CLOSER

Josh is wearing dark shades to hide his sad eyes and the fact that he was crying on his drive to school. As he emerges from his car, Allen notices that he has two new tattoos on his right arm. On his forearm is inscribed *TYRONE #87 FOREVER*, and on his right bicep is tattooed an image of an Indian warrior sitting in a crouched position with a Gargoyle that resembles Destroyer rising out of the mist behind him.

Allen telepathically says to the ASB, *Look at the tattoo on Josh's right bicep.* They're all stunned.

Audrey responds telepathically, *We shouldn't read too much into it just yet, maybe it's nothing. Time will tell.*

Josh nods his head toward Allen, Athena/Audrey, Francisco, and Jake as he walks past with Mercedes on his arm. The Teen Warriors reciprocate and head nod back at him.

Athena's shocked by Josh's friendliness, and exclaims telepathically, *Wow! Now that's a change.*

As the ASB walk to their lockers, they notice students passing out flyers with a picture of Tyrone and the time of the funeral. Everyone's in a melancholy spirit, holding and hugging each other, crying and whispering. Two girls start arguing. "Tyrone was my man, Monica!" shouts the Columbian American girl.

The Brazilian American girl yells, "No he wasn't, you skank!"

They are at the point of pulling each other's hair when Principal Jenkins steps between them. "Stop all of this nonsense and get to class."

He says over the loudspeaker: "Attention, students! There will not be any fighting. I know we are all grieving. Violence is not the way to solve things. After the funeral, we will have counselors if you feel you need to talk to someone about your grief. We're here for you. I was a student at this school just like you are now. We're all Pirates, and we will be here for each other. So please get whatever you need in your lockers and go to class. There will not be any tardiness today. Thank you."

Allen sits at his desk in history class and watches Josh walk in with Mercedes.

Telepathically, Athena/Audrey remarks to Allen, *They seem to be back to their normal selves.*

I agree, they look like nothing ever happened, Allen telepathically replies.

Josh passes Allen and says, "Hey, Allen, how are you?" He extends his hand to Allen, who grasps it and they shake. Josh winks and says, "It's a pleasure meeting you," as if they were meeting for the first time.

Allen smiles at Josh. "The pleasure is mine."

Josh nods. "No, it's mine, really." He takes his seat.

Allen opens his hand to find a piece of paper with Josh's phone number on it with a message asking Allen to call him whenever he has time… maybe once the funeral's over, and things have gone back to normal. Allen enters the number into his cell phone.

Mrs. Ramirez walks in. "Good morning, class. I know you all experienced a tragedy on Halloween, last Friday night. Today we're not going to talk about history. We're going to discuss how you're feeling about what happened. Anyone would like to open the discussion?"

Mercedes raises her hand, fighting back the tears. "It's really hard, Mrs. Ramirez. I talked to Tyrone before he was killed. It's unfortunate… and the scariest thing. No one has a clue about who the killer is. That monster costume he was wearing looked real, it's still freaking me out. This guy could come back and kill someone else."

Mrs. Ramirez nods. "I understand how you feel, Mercedes. I was mugged years ago when I was in college. I was afraid for months, imaging that the person who assaulted me was lurking behind every tree. It took me almost a year to get over that fear. I don't know what to tell you, Mercedes, but you should do whatever it takes to feel safe again. If you feel like you need to be able to protect yourself, maybe you should take a self-defense class…"

Another hand goes up. The class looks at the shy, tall skinny teenager, who's always been a little scared of Josh and his football buddies. In an angry outburst, he blurts out, "All I remember is seeing Josh standing next to Tyrone right before he was attacked."

Josh leaps out of his seat and shouts, "What are you talking about? I wasn't near Tyrone. Everyone saw the video!"

In a soothing tone, Mrs. Ramirez says, "Josh… calm down."

Josh yells, "No, I won't! Tyrone was my friend! No one will ever understand how much I truly cared for him! He was like a brother to me." Josh cries blue tears. The students watch Josh in shock, and then Josh's eyes start to turn red. One student's jaw drops as he points at Josh.

Another student says, "Josh, you have blue tears coming down your face, and your eyes are turning red like when you fought Allen."

Josh runs out of the class. Allen chases after him.

Mrs. Ramirez yells, "You two come back in this classroom right now!"

Athena asks Allen telepathically, *Do you want me to come with you?*

Allen replies telepathically, *No, I'll handle this.*

He grabs Josh, who turns around and says, "Allen, what's happening to me man? I'm… I'm freaking out here!"

Allen whispers, "Let's go somewhere and talk about it."

Teachers from other classrooms open their doors and peer into the hallway to see where the commotion's coming from.

Allen whispers with urgency, "To the bathroom, quick."

As the bathroom door closes behind them, Allen summons a rainbow cloud, grabs Josh's arm and teleports with him to the Bermuda Triangle. They hover in the cloud just above the ocean's surface.

Astonished and thrilled, Josh whispers, "Everything you told me is true, isn't it?"

Allen nods. "Yes. It's not a dream, Josh. This is real. We're part of the same bloodline."

Standing in the rainbow cloud looking down into the ocean below, Josh notices two dolphins swimming in circles. They talk to Allen, and he proudly introduces them. "Josh, meet Jumper and Dance II." Allen reaches through the cloud to pat his friends.

Allen gestures to Josh cheerfully. "You should try it."

Josh extends his hand out, but for some strange reason Jumper bites him. Josh pulls his hand back and yells, "Ouch! You dumb-ass dolphin!"

Allen says in a surprised tone of voice, "Josh, I'm… sorry about that. Jumper has never done that before."

Josh apologizes, "I'm sorry, Allen. I just reacted to the bite. It's okay. It's not my day anyway."

Allen looks at the dolphins, and they look back at him with expressions of remorse before swimming away.

Allen ponders. *I wanted to show Josh the Atlantean Kingdom, it might not be a great idea after seeing how Jumper reacted to him. Who knows how my grandfather Leon would react? I think General Lionel might not have a problem with him, but King Leon most definitely would.*

Allen says, "Josh, I'm here for you like I said before. We're family. I noticed you have two new tattoos… and one of them appears to be a Nomadic Indian with a Gargoyle rising out of the mist like a genie."

Josh gasps and replies, "It's a long story. I'm trying to help myself get rid of the monster in my life. This is my Indian ancestors' tribal tradition that should help me conquer my demons."

"I understand. Are you… feeling better now?" asks Allen.

Josh nods. "Yes, thank you."

Allen asks again with concern, "Are you sure your hand is, okay?"

His nephew laughs a little. "Yeah man, thanks for asking, and besides, I'm a star quarterback. I think I can handle a little dolphin… a really big dolphin bite."

They laugh lightheartedly.

Allen whispers, "Okay, let's sneak back to campus. I'm sure Mrs. Ramirez will be okay with us missing a minute or two." He looks at his watch. "Wow! A whole class I guess."

In a matter of seconds, Allen teleports them back into the bathroom. Mrs. Ramirez's class has ended. They run back into the classroom to grab their things. Mrs. Ramirez is still in the class. She says, smiling at them, "Your lady friends grabbed your backpacks for you."

The teens apologize.

She says, "Don't worry about it. Everyone's dealing with Tyrone's passing in their own way. One thing I'm happy to see is that you two are friends now."

Allen and Josh politely say, "Thank you."

"Things happened, and we found out we have more in common than not," explains Josh.

Allen nods and smiles in agreement.

Mrs. Ramirez says, "Well, Josh, your eyes aren't red anymore. I know it's painful. You two will be okay."

Josh happily replies, "Thank you."

They walk out of the classroom and downstairs being met by Athena/ Audrey and Mercedes. As if they were twins, Allen and Josh simultaneously exclaim, "Thanks for grabbing our bags for us." They look at each other and laugh with their girlfriends. Josh gives Allen a dap on the fist and strolls off with Mercedes to find his friends in the lunchroom.

Athena gives Allen a peck on the lips. "It took Tyrone's death to bring you two together. I hope it stays that way. I think it's good to have another person of your kind… close to it anyway. Josh Stone cried blue tears; can you believe that?"

Allen replies as he scratches his long, thick dreadlocks, "Yeah, its wild isn't it."

The Party Boys are playing music in honor of Tyrone. One of The Party Boys says over the microphone, "Here're a couple of songs Tyrone loved." They play Drake's "Started From The Bottom," and Nipsey Hussle's "Grinding All My Life."

Some of the girls and guys who knew Tyrone are wearing T-shirts with his number 87 and dancing together. Francisco, Jake, Allen, and Athena sit together watching.

Jake rubs his stomach. "Hey, any of you guys hungry? Feel like making a quick teleportation pit stop back at home?"

Allen and Audrey nod no.

Allen says, smiling, "Let's stay here and enjoy the memories we have of Tyrone. The guy we never really knew personally. But one thing I do know, he was a great cocky-ass football player."

Francisco grins and reminisces, "He sure was, wasn't he, bro? At least he knew what he wanted to do with his life before he passed away. There's nothing like not having a dream. It's like wandering around in the forest not knowing which way to go."

Audrey's impressed. "That's a great analogy, mate."

Francisco puts his hand on Allen's shoulder. "Now I sound like Uncle Zadok. Jake and I didn't have a dream at all until you and Athena put it into perspective. I love helping to save the world, and I'll continue to do that. But you know what, bro. I'm going to become a stockbroker when I graduate college."

Jake exclaims with excitement, "You know what I think I'll do once we graduate high school and college?"

The ASB look at Jake asking with enthusiasm, "What would that be?"

Jake smiles and says, "I want to buy the bar Your Last Resort and fix it up and put Jack Um specials and some of Uncle Zadok's dishes on the menu. He looks at Athena and says, "That is if I receive permission from the lady in disguise after you get the restaurants going down in the Land of Oz."

"Thank you, Jake… I think that would be a great idea for you," Athena replies.

Jake smirks. "Absolutely, there's nothing like the beach and having great times with old friends and new ones… and plus, the best part about it is. I'm going to start putting it in everyone's mind. And by the time I graduate college and buy the place, word of mouth will have spread. Free advertising… letting everyone know. I can see people saying, 'Hey, Jake, I can't wait for your new bar to open once it's renovated.'" Jake laughs, "Who knows, I might hire those two jerks Franny and I beat up last summer."

Francisco says, "Now that would be turning the other cheek. We have great hearts, Jake, my boy."

Jake replies, "We do, don't we?"

At the end of the school day, the ASB hang out together during PE. Becky Honeycomb watches Jake doing jumping jacks and jumps her way next to him. Flirtatiously, she coos, "Hi, Jake, how are you today?"

Jake says in his Southern drawl, "I'm fine, darlin'." Jake notices her braces are gone. Becky looks stunning with her clear pearly white teeth. "Becky, there's something different about you."

She bats her eyes at him. "Maybe one day we could go out for pizza if you like."

Jake winks and replies, "Sure, that sounds like fun."

Becky says, "I know you have a girlfriend because I saw you with her at the Halloween dance. She's really pretty, but we still can be friends, can't we?"

Feeling like a stud, Jake says, "Sure we can, darling' I don't see anything wrong with that."

Francisco whispers to Jake, "Damn, bro... she had an extreme makeover, and it wasn't just her braces. She's beautiful, Jake... and what's up with you saying darlin' like you're at some country western concert? Yee haw!"

Jake chortles in reply, "Whatever, Franny panny... but yeah, dude, I can't believe it's her."

Allen and Athena both say, "Wow, Jake, you have a looker there."

Athena says admiringly, "She's Cinderella. Don't forget about your girlfriend?"

Jake smiles big and says, "Don't worry about me, sis. I'm just being friendly."

PE ends and the teens meet in the parking lot. They hop into Allen's Range Rover to join the funeral procession. A police escort leads the students to the First Baptist Church in Miami.

CHAPTER THREE

DROGAN PUTS ATHENA UNDER HIS SPELL

Drogan Reptilly clutches the plastic wrapped remains of his dear brother's tail and the body of the hideous Gargoyle, Invincible. He has radioed a helicopter to pick him up in the dinghy he used to escape his sinking yacht. He lies in a fetal position, shivering in the cold wind as the little boat bounces along in the choppy ocean water. Drogan whispers to himself, "I will avenge my brother's death and destroy the Atlantean by any means necessary." The helicopter finally arrives, and Drogan's personal rescue team scoops him up and his gruesome package out of the water.

The pilot immediately transports Drogan to his secret biogenetics engineering facility-sequestered miles below the surface of the Earth, just outside of Miami. The scientists freeze the remains of the Gargoyle and preserve Damon's tail.

Barrington says, "The blood sample from the Atlantean may be useful now with the blood from the Gargoyle's dead body and Damon's tail."

Drogan asks, "Do you think you could somehow create synthetic hot blood out of the blood cells from the dead Gargoyle and my brother's tail… and then replace my cold blood with the synthetic blood?"

Barrington laughs diabolically. "Absolutely, Mr. Reptilly. The transfusion should give you hot blood… and make your skin more of a Caucasian flesh tone rather than albino. You will still have red hair, but your eyes may change to blue thanks to the Atlantean blood sample you gave me."

Drogan grins from ear to ear. "How long will it take for the blood to be ready?"

Barrington can't contain his excitement. "Very soon! I've been working on the experiment for years! Sorry if I'm overeager…to make sure the blood is right, I need another blood sample from you, to make sure you won't have any side effects."

Drogan gripes, "I don't care about side effects. There will be no drawing of my blood. I want this cold blood out of me and your synthetic hot blood flowing in my veins as soon as possible! I'll have the power of the Gargoyle and the evil spirit of my brother. I'll then summon the Gargoyle Destroyer through Josh Stone and make him my servant, or he will die."

The evil scientist chortles, which causes the slight hump on his back to protrude. "Yes, sir, I'll have it ready for you in twenty-four hours."

Drogan pats Barrington on his head, as if he were a dog. "Barrington, you've served me well, as my evil scientist. The spy cologne you created to seduce the marks for all of my spies and the recent spies like Vicki Stacks and D Sparks, has made me very wealthy."

Barrington replies, "Thank you for the compliment, sir."

Drogan says, "You will be handsomely rewarded after the Earth becomes my permanent playground. The Atlantean's beautiful girlfriend will become my bride. Her powers cannot resist the new potion… together we'll spawn a new generation of superior Hybrid leaders."

Drogan worries to himself: *The Greek Gods will undoubtedly miss her. I'll figure that out later once I'm infused with the Gargoyle's power.*

Barrington uses a lab rat to see if it'll survive after he drains its blood and replaces it with the synthetic blood. Barrington howls in a state of pure evil bliss. "It's a success! Yes! The rat's eyes changed to a crystal blue color."

While Barrington is performing his experiments, Drogan relaxes in a lounge area adjacent to the lab where he listens to Beethoven while eating a light dinner of lab rat in a salad sprinkled with feta cheese.

Barrington bursts in on Drogan's dinner screaming, "Boss, the… the syn… the… the synthetic blood is a success!"

Drogan exclaims, "Well done, Barrington!" He quickly gulps down his rat and follows Barrington into the lab. Barrington straps him down on the gurney.

Drogan yells, "Let's get a move on it, Barrington! I have a Greek Goddess to tame!" He glances across the room at the cages of rats, cobras, and baby crocodiles. He smiles and licks his lips.

The scientist replies with an evil grin, "Right away, Drogan, sir." He inserts needles into Drogan's arms, legs, and neck.

Drogan yelps from the pinch of the needles, but grimaces and shouts, "Woohoo! Let's get this party started!"

Barrington pushes a button and watches as the red-hot synthetic blood travels from a clear glass container through a hose into another tank, where it is cooled down before it replaces Drogan's own blood that is pumping out slowly like molasses and being collected in another clear container. The new hot blood flows into Drogan's body. He jolts, writhes, and yells, "Arrrghhh!"

Barrington apologizes. "I'm sorry, sir, bite down on this so you won't bite your tongue off."

Drogan shouts, "You id—"

Barrington immediately jams a plastic stick between Drogan's teeth. Drogan's body stiffens, and he shakes feverishly for what seems to be an eternity. The last bit of synthetic blood flows into his body as Barrington scans the monitors to check Drogan's heart and brain wave patterns. He notices Drogan's body is growing in mass and his facial structure changing as his teeth become more fang-like. Barrington smiles as he observes that Drogan can protract and retract his new fangs like a vampire. As soon as the transformation is complete, Drogan will be able to control the new enhanced features. Drogan's eyes change to blue, and he finally stops shaking and becomes calm.

Barrington quickly removes the straps and takes the plastic stick out of the remodeled Hybrid's mouth. Drogan leaps up and looks at his reflection in a mirror. The entirely new person he sees throws him off for a moment. He sheds a single tear and whispers as he touches his face. "I look like a normal human." Drogan's demeanor changes. He is happy with the transformation and proclaims, "You've done an excellent job, Barrington! You will be well rewarded personally… and I will fund any project your evil heart desires."

Barrington bows his head. "Thank you, Mr. Reptilly."

"Call me Maximilian, better yet, call me Max," replies Drogan.

Barrington proudly says, "As you wish."

Drogan says, "I want you to refine the potion in the spy cologne for me again. I've got to get that Greek babe to fall in love with me ASAP." Drogan turns on his heel, marches out of the lab with a smirk and announces, "Revenge will be mine!"

Tyrone's funeral is at full capacity with people packed in the pews and crowding the aisles. Tyrone is propped up in an open casket, looking peaceful and elegant in a white suit and tie. Uncle Zadok sings "Amazing Grace" with the choir, which has some members of the congregation murmuring, "Thank you, Jesus. Thank you!" and others-silently weeping.

Allen whispers to Athena and the guys telepathically, *What in the hell is Uncle Zadok doing singing in church?*

Ms. Tyretta is draped over her son's casket, wailing as she kisses his face. She repeats over and over, "Oh, God! Why, my baby! Why!"

Two deacons approach Ms. Tyretta and gently hold her steady as she continues to sob. When her sobs finally subside, they guide her back to her seat in the front row.

A minister approaches the podium at the front of the altar, waits until the last strains of "Amazing Grace" fade out, clears his throat and intones, "Good afternoon. I'm Pastor Daniels. I knew Tyrone from the time he was five-years-old. He used to come to Sunday school with his Bible and a little plastic football." He starts to laugh, which ignites a chain reaction of laughter that ripples through the audience.

One of the Sunday school teachers blurts out, "Bless his little heart."

Ms. Tyretta laughs through her tears and chimes in, "My baby sure did. You couldn't pry that little plastic football out of his hands."

Pastor Daniels continues. "Today's going to be a celebration of Tyrone's life."

A large television screen behind the podium comes on, and the audience is treated to a lovingly compiled pastiche of short video clips interspersed with still photos of Tyrone playing football and hanging out with friends and family. When a clip of Tyrone and Josh playing football flashes by, Josh breaks down and weeps silently in Mercedes' arms.

Allen isn't sitting next to Josh, so his crystal necklace doesn't have an impact on his eyes. Josh cries clear tears, not blue tears. He wipes his eyes and stands up. The entire church applauds as he makes his way to Ms. Tyretta. They hug for a moment, before Josh walks up to the casket and places a photo of himself and Tyrone as little kids, posing together when they were on the Pop Warner football team, inside the coffin.

Josh walks to the podium and stands uneasily, with his head down and one hand in his jacket pocket, while he tells a story about the first time, he and Tyrone played football together. "When Tyrone and I were in the first grade, we used to play football on the playground. We didn't ride on slides or climb monkey bars. All we ever talked about was how we were going to be the next great football legends. I remember throwing a huge football with both my hands and Tyrone would say, 'If you're going to be a quarterback, you have to throw harder than that with one hand… not two.'"

The audience laughs, and Josh becomes more confident and animated. "I said to Tyrone, 'Okay then, Tyrone.' He was only five feet away from me. I threw the ball hard. He didn't grab it in time… it slipped through his hands, hit him in the mouth, and knocked out one of his baby teeth. He was so mad at me… he started crying and screaming, and I just said to him, 'Tyrone, if you're going to play football you have to catch the ball and not cry.'"

Again, everyone laughs, but Josh becomes serious. "Tyrone and I had something in common. We both loved football with every breath we took." Josh starts to cry. "I'll never forget you Tyrone, and I appreciate you catching all those balls I threw to you this season, which helped me get into the University of Florida. I'm going to miss you, my brother." Josh cries harder. Ms. Tyretta and Aluna step up to the podium to comfort Josh, then Aluna guides him back to her seat toward the rear of the church.

Everyone watches them as they wend their way through the crowds of people still clustered in the aisles. Sitting in the back of the church near Aluna is Drogan, who is not wearing his characteristic black shades, and can be seen blinking back a tear or two. Though he looks like a handsome gentleman in his impeccably tailored black Armani suit, he's nothing but a wolf in sheep's clothing. Athena catches Drogan's eye, and he smiles sadly as he nods his head toward her. She nods and smiles back, noting his glistening and somewhat arresting blue eyes.

The memorial service ends and as everyone slowly walks to the front of the church to pay their last respects to Tyrone, and his family.

Athena and Allen walk by Drogan, who has sprayed himself liberally with the new, much more potent spy cologne. Athena notices him, nods again and then gets a whiff of the cologne. She looks into Drogan's blue eyes and feels inexplicably intoxicated by his presence. As she and Allen pass him, Athena turns her head back to stare at him. Francisco and Jake notice the strange encounter, but decide not to say anything telepathically to her, knowing that Allen would likely pick up on it.

Drogan stares into the casket for a moment, then approaches Ms. Tyretta to give her his condolences. Drogan's spy cologne makes Ms. Tyretta and every other woman in the church stare at him as if he were a movie star. He shrinks into himself so he can avoid detection when he slips his business card into Athena's hand on his way out of the church. Athena is standing behind Allen, who doesn't notice the interaction.

Drogan has sprayed a bit of the cologne on the card, to make sure Athena stays in his thrall. Athena takes the card and looks surreptitiously at it. The front of the card is embossed with Drogan's alias (*Maximilian Coastal, Fashion Designer*) and his Miami and Melbourne phone numbers. When Athena turns it over, she sees that he has written a note: *Hi Beautiful, You must be the famous socialite, Athena Dranias. Please call me. I would love to talk to you about your design ideas for a new swimsuit line. Sincerely, Max*

Athena sniffs the card, smiles to herself and slips it into her purse. Jake and Francisco catch the entire scene.

Jake says to Francisco, "That guy looks strangely familiar."

Francisco whispers, "Strangely familiar like what? Being tall with dark hair and good looking. He probably has a lot of loot?"

Jake teases Francisco. "Are you getting hot and heavy over this guy now?"

Francisco smirks and says, "No way, bro! Geez. I'm just metrosexual... which means I can compliment a guy who has a bit of swag... but I agree with you, Jake. We should keep an eye on him. We can't tell Allen unless there's something to tell."

Jake gives Francisco a dap on the fist. "Agreed."

They stare at the guy as he gets into his limo.

The Teen Warriors drive together to the cemetery in Allen's Range Rover. As they pass through the ornate gates of Miami's most exclusive final resting place, Allen says to Athena, "You did a wonderful thing, sweetheart. It was so generous of you to take care of this for Tyrone and his family."

Athena sighs and says, "It was the most appropriate thing to do."

They park and join Zadok and Aoki. As they walk with the crowd to the gravesite, Allen whispers to Zadok, "We didn't know you were going to be singing, Unc."

Zadok says, "After watching the news about Tyrone, I went to Ms. Tyretta's home to offer my condolences. It turns out that she, Anna Mae, and I have some things in common… we all love the music of Marvin Gaye, Stevie Wonder, and Al Green. All that good soulful music was happening long before your hip-hop stuff became popular. Don't get me wrong, nephew. I adapt to the trends. Hip-hop is here to stay, but I'm a soulful brother who loves jazz, blues, and good crooning music."

Allen nods with respect. "I understand."

Everyone gathers around Tyrone's grave, and the pastor says the final words, "Ashes to ashes and dust to dust."

Jake and Francisco look around for the guy Athena was talking to.

"He's not here," Jake says with relief, "but I still want to ask Athena what's up with her and that guy when Allen's not around."

Francisco sighs. "Good luck with that, they're always together."

Jake says, "When the time is right, I will."

After the burial, the ASB are together again, riding in Allen's Range Rover back to school to pick up their cars. They stop next to a limo at a red light. The limo's tinted windows descend, revealing the Star Island Twins.

They ask Allen, "Where are our boyfriends?"

Francisco says to Allen, "We'll catch you later, and don't worry about our cars at school. We'll have the twins drop us off later to pick them up."

Allen gives his friends a thumbs-up. "Okay, guys."

Francisco and Jake jump out, and Allen looks at Athena and says, "It was a delightful funeral, wasn't it?"

Athena's still feeling dazed and confused by Max and reacts with annoyance to Allen's voice. "What? Oh, I'm sorry… I have so much on my mind… I'm thinking about a charity event I want to put on soon."

Allen asks lovingly, "Do you want to talk about it, sweetie?"

Athena looks out the passenger window while rubbing her fingers over the embossed business card hidden in her purse. "Hmm… no, not right now. I think I need to go for a drive by myself, so I have the space to think about everything."

Allen nods. "I understand, princess. You have quite a few things on your mind."

"Yes… thank you for understanding."

Allen senses a change in Athena but doesn't say anything as they continue to drive in uncomfortable silence. He drops Athena off at her car in the school's parking lot, and she follows him back to the mansion. They park, and Athena runs upstairs to her bedroom in the west wing while Allen walks upstairs to his bedroom in the east wing. They don't utter a word to each other.

Zadok walks in with Aoki, who is listening to him sing "Oh Happy Day," a famous gospel song. Even though Zadok doesn't go to church, he knows all the renowned gospel songs. He can hear a song once and know it as if he'd sung it his entire life. Zadok's a walking music library of pure soul.

Aoki says, "Honey, I'm going to make us a drink and unwind with you in the Jacuzzi."

Zadok sings to her, "That sounds mighty fine, baby…"

Athena walks downstairs quickly after having changed into a pink halter top, short black skirt, and six-inch stilettos. She's wearing her hair down and looking seductively gorgeous.

Athena catches Zadok's eye. "Well look at you. You look like a supermodel. Where are you and my nephew off to?"

Athena doesn't pay Zadok any attention; she walks past him and says in a sharp tone as she heads out the door, "I'm running late for a business meeting."

Zadok turns his wheelchair around and watches Athena smiling devilishly to herself as she struts to her car. Zadok mutters to himself, "Teenagers, once you think you have them figured out, they change on you." He forgets about Athena when he sees Aoki approaching with two glasses of wine.

She hands him a glass, they clink and say, "Cheers."

Aoki asks, "Was that Athena I just saw running out the door looking stunning as ever?"

Zadok shakes his head and says, "Yeah, and Athena looked like she was going out on a date, but she said she was late for a meeting..."

Aoki shrugs and says, "It's probably nothing."

Athena calls Max from her car to suggest they get together for a bite to eat.

Max/Drogan says to Athena, "I'm so happy you called, Ms. Dranias. I knew it was you."

Athena giggles like a little schoolgirl. "You caught me off guard, Mr. Coastal. I go by an alias when I'm at school. I'm Audrey Monroe around my classmates."

The Hybrid grins and says, "You have to tell me all about it. Could you meet me at the Casa Blanca Hotel in, let's say, twenty minutes?"

Athena revs her engine and brags, "I can be there in ten minutes, handsome."

Max whispers, "That's great to hear. I have a private dining room reserved for us so we can speak freely about our joint business venture."

Athena blushes and says flirtatiously, "I'll see you soon, Max."

Drogan shudders with excitement as he says goodbye. He admires himself in a gilt mirror hanging on the living room wall of his ocean-view penthouse suite. He says into the mirror, "This is going to be fun," and then stares at himself for another minute. He declares with authority, "I am Drogan the new Invincible," then blows a kiss to himself.

Feeling brand new, Max goes downstairs to the lobby. The place is vibrant with attractive women and men attending a party being thrown by a famous soccer star from Brazil. Max has a cabana by the pool, but he'd rather have his meeting in a more private and exclusive section in the hotel. Athena Dranias could be his new bride, which is far more rewarding than a pool party filled with supermodels and famous athletes.

Athena enters the Casa Blanca Hotel looking fierce in her black shades. She strolls through the front lobby like she owns the place. Max sees her and tells the maître d' to escort her to the back of the private section of the restaurant overlooking the ocean. They can converse while gazing at the beautiful people below.

Max rises from his chair and kisses Athena's hand. "It's a pleasure meeting you again, Ms. Dranias."

Athena blushes. "Thank you, Maximilian."

He pulls out her chair, and the waiter asks, "Mr. Coastal, would you and your beautiful friend like a glass of wine or sparkling water?"

"I'll have water please," says Athena.

Max says, "Make it two sparkling Italian waters please."

Athena's impressed. "Oh, you like the Italian?"

Max speaks a few words in Italian.

Athena blushes. "You speak Italian very well."

Max smiles. "Ms. Dranias, you are full of surprises."

Athena giggles coyly. "So are you, Max Coastal. You like Italy?"

Max says with passion, "I love Italy, especially Milan. However, I also love going to the Greek Islands. Do you go to your native land often?"

"I don't go as much as I'd like."

"Then maybe this summer we could go together."

Athena thinks about it. "I'd love to, but there's an important thing I have to do this summer with friends."

"Sounds intriguing," says Max.

The waiter comes back and pours the sparkling water. "What would you like to have for your dinner… madam, sir?"

"I'll have a chicken Caesar with a sprinkle of feta cheese please," replies Athena. Max smiles and blushes a little. Athena is curious. "What's so funny, Maximilian?"

Max says to the waiter, "I'll have a lab ra… I mean, I'll have exactly what the exquisite lady is having, but hold the chicken, and I'll have extra feta cheese, please."

Max looks at Athena and says, "I love feta cheese."

Athena's cheeks turn red as she touches Max's hand. "Do you now, Max? I do too."

He whispers, "You were saying something about this summer… you're doing something important with your friends?"

Athena answers nonchalantly, "Yeah, I have to go on a rock-climbing expedition in Hawaii… for research purposes."

Max smiles wide and asks, "That sounds very interesting. What type of research?"

Athena blurts out, "I have to look for rare rocks near a crescent-shaped volcanic crater and I'm looking for an undiscovered island close by."

Max ponders. *I think I know exactly where they'll be looking for the gold crown.* He suppresses his glee and asks, "You're going on the expedition around what time this summer? I'd love to take you to Greece or Italy. We could search for new inspirations for a swimsuit and fashion line."

Athena talks like she's intoxicated by Max's charisma (when in fact it's his spy cologne). Slurring her words, a bit. "I think… I think… I'm sorry… my head. I think when the summer is right at its peak."

Max doesn't pry anymore about the summer. He asks, "What made you decide to come to Miami after having such great success in Sydney?"

Athena smiles. "I made new friends, and I thought it would be a good change for me. I don't know now, Maximilian… after meeting you. So why are you here? You grew up in Melbourne?"

Max nods. "Yes, I did. I have a manufacturing company there. We make things like textiles and fabrics for companies in the fashion industry. I want to branch out now… and I'd especially love to work with someone who is as fashionable, talented, and lovely as you. I couldn't resist giving you my business card at the memorial service."

Athena turns red and asks, "What made you decide to go to the memorial?"

Max looks sad and says, "I saw the news footage of Tyrone's horrific death. It really broke my heart. I thought the young man would have had a promising career." Max looks out the window at the famous Brazilian soccer player taking selfies with supermodels and sports stars. He points out the window and says, "Tyrone probably would have been right over there in a few years, living a great life."

Athena notices Max's muscular physique. She leans over the table and touches his bicep. "You look like you could be an athlete yourself."

Max grins and nods. "Yes, I consider myself a renaissance man."

Athena coos, "Has anyone ever told you that you look like a Hollywood leading man?"

Max blushes.

"You're turning red, Max. Are you shy?"

He whispers bashfully, "I'm not used to receiving compliments from an exquisite lady like you."

Athena asks, "Now I am curious. Why don't you have a special girl in your life, Mr. Coastal?"

Max says from the heart, "I've been waiting my whole life for the perfect lady to be by my side. So we can live a beautiful and promising life together. Do you have… anyone special in your life?"

Athena blushes and says, "To be honest I feel a little confused right now. I thought I had someone special in my life until I met you. I've never met anyone as intriguing as you."

Max blushes. "I am flattered. Could we meet another time?"

"Absolutely! How about tomorrow?"

Suppressing his excitement, Max asks, "What time is good for you?"

"After school…" replies Athena.

Max smiles. "Perfect, then we'll meet tomorrow late afternoon. I have a house on Star Island, we can meet there."

Athena thinks about it and says, "That sounds great, but I would actually like to meet here again if we could. Gazing at the attractive people inspires me… but it also makes me miss my beloved Australia and Greece for some reason. However, Miami is bringing something new out of me, enticing me to create. I'll have sketches for you."

"Okay, we shall meet here tomorrow, say four p.m.?"

"Perfect!" Athena kisses Max on his cheeks French style and leaves the table. She dances through the throngs of models and professional athletes as she makes her way to the front exit. Drogan stares longingly at Athena. Through gritted teeth, he whispers, "I will have you Athena. You are the love of my life. I'll ruin the Atlantean's plan. He'll never be King. I'll be King of a new Atlantis and Athena, my darling, you will be my queen."

CHAPTER FOUR

ALLEN AND ATHENA ARE FALLING APART

Meanwhile, Jake and Francisco are having a great time hanging out with the Star Island Twins at their home. Suzy says, "Our parents are gone on business in Cairo for a few months."

"That's very cool," says Jake.

Samantha nods. "Yes, it is...our father builds casinos in exotic places. He's working on designing a fleet of riverboat casinos, and our mother is accompanying him. They know that we are responsible enough to take care of ourselves, so here we are. How do you like our home?"

Francisco looks around and says, "I admire what I see. Your casa is very beautiful, chicas. The place looks like an Aladdin-themed home... I love the exotic rugs and huge Moroccan vases."

Suzy smiles. "Thank you."

The guys stare in awe at the ceiling of bas-relief clouds in a clear blue sky with a huge painting of Aladdin and Princess Jasmin on a magic carpet. Suzy proudly says, "My father is dressed as Aladdin and my mother is dressed as Princess Jasmine."

Jake exclaims, "I think that's the most enchanted painting I've ever seen."

Samantha grabs Jake by his arm. "Thank you, handsome. My parents love Aladdin. I'm surprised our parents didn't give Suzy and me Arabic names. We're as American as apple pie."

Jake whispers to himself, "And a little ditzy too."

They walk out back to the dock. The twins show the boys their custom-made hundred-foot yacht.

Samantha smiles and points. "Here's our yacht, Suzy and I named it Star Island Twins. We will hang out on it later."

Francisco and Jake say, "Awesome."

They continue strolling along the walkway to their pool and Jacuzzi. The guys see pink flamingos walking around the yard and a yellow parrot sitting in its cage.

Francisco walks up to the parrot, who squawks, "Loser… Loser!"

Francisco yells back, "Who are you calling a loser, jailbird!?"

The parrot shouts, "Ha, ha! You're a loser!"

Francisco yells back like they're two kids arguing. "Ha, ha!"

"The parrot doesn't like you, Francisco," says Jake with a grin.

The bird looks at Jake and squawks, "Slacker, slacker!"

The teens laugh.

"Don't pay Spartacus any attention… our dad trained him to say those things to any guys we might bring around. We're his precious daughters, he's a little protective of us," says Suzy.

Jake and Francisco nod and Francisco says, "Okay, I get it…."

The twins say at the same time, "You want to go for a swim?"

Jake and Francisco shout, "Sure!"

Jake looks concerned. "But we don't have any clothes."

Samantha smiles. "Don't worry, we know your sizes."

Suzy grins mischievously. "When we were at your house a while back, we snuck into your rooms and found out your sizes."

The guys walk into the pool house to change into their bathing suits while the twins run back inside the house to put on their bikinis. In the pool house, the guys find matching white shorts, tank tops, and boat shoes, with their names embossed in gold. The guys put on their clothes and laugh at each other.

Jake yells, "Hey, we look like twins! We're matching, bro… It's a little creepy, but hey, the girls have great intentions."

"I say they do. You have to feel like a happy camper, playboy. You have Samantha <u>and</u> Becky Honeycomb jocking you," replies Francisco.

Jake nods. "Yeah, it's a good time for us. I hope things are still good with Allen and Athena. She was very flirtatious with that guy."

Francisco feels a little sad. "We'll just keep an eye on her whenever we can."

The girls come out in their designer bikinis. Francisco grabs Suzy and dives in the deep end with her in his arms. Jake and Samantha dive in together a second later.

A butler appears and asks, "Would everyone like to have dinner inside or outside?"

Samantha replies, "We will have our meal on the yacht."

Francisco smiles and says, "Great idea."

The teens merrily eat their chicken sandwiches and French fries; they notice a speedboat passing by.

The girls light up and yell at once, "That's the new guy who just bought the house three homes away from us!"

Francisco whispers, "Hey, Jake, that's the guy from church."

Jake gasps. "I can't believe it… it's crazy to bump into him again."

They watch him dock his boat and leap out and onto the dock with one step. Jake and Francisco look at each other and Jake mutters, "Who does he think he is… James Bond or something?"

Samantha coos, "He looks like a supermodel."

"I agree, Samantha, he's pure perfection," says Suzy.

Francisco asks the twins, "How long have your new neighbor been living there?"

Suzy thinks about it. "Only a week or two… we've never spoken to him. We wave at each other whenever we lay out on the boat."

They finish their meal before the twins have their driver take them to their cars at school.

Athena is floating on cloud nine when she arrives home. Allen's downstairs hanging out in the entertainment room and notices Athena running upstairs. He ponders. *Athena is dressed like she was out on a date*

instead of a charity meeting. Then again, my girlfriend is a socialite and is always fashionable. He smiles to himself.

Allen telepathically asks, *Athena, where were you earlier?*

Athena doesn't answer. She takes off her crystal necklace and throws the chain inside her dresser drawer.

Athena, my love, why aren't you answering me?

Allen mumbles, "Something's wrong."

He goes upstairs and knocks on Athena's bedroom door, but she doesn't hear him. She is in the shower.

Allen walks in and knocks on her shower door. "Athena?"

Athena yells, "What are you doing!? You startled me! Get out! I'm taking a shower."

Allen apologizes. "I'm sorry for interrupting your shower."

Athena continues to shout, "Thank you for respecting my privacy!"

Allen walks out and mumbles, "What's going on with my Greek Goddess girlfriend?" He goes downstairs as Zadok and Aoki come in from the Jacuzzi.

Uncle Zadok notices that Allen seems unhappy. "What's going on with you, nephew? Why are you looking so sad and lonely?"

Allen shouts in confusion, "I don't know what's going on, Uncle Zadok! Athena yelled at me; she's never done that before… ever!"

Uncle Zadok replies in a calm voice, "Who knows what she's going through, give it some time. I'm sure Athena will come around."

Aoki says, "Sometimes a teenage girl's hormones can change, and they get a little moody. Just give her some space. Okay, nephew?"

Allen smiles, feeling a little better. "Yeah, maybe you're right, Aunt Aoki."

Zadok says, "You'll be all right, neph. You want me to make you something to eat?"

Still sulking a little, Allen says, "No, I'm not hungry."

Francisco and Jake walk into the mansion, but Allen doesn't acknowledge them, just turns around and walks back upstairs.

Jake shouts, "Hey, Teen Warrior, what's up?"

Allen doesn't look back, mumbles as he ambles towards his room, "Nothing, guys, just tired."

"Boys, I'm concerned, do you know what's going on between him and Athena?" asks Uncle Zadok.

The guys nod and reply in unison, "No, not really, Uncle Zadok."

"Keep an eye on him and let me know if he continues to act this way. It's not good for him. I know he may still be grieving Tyrone's death. I hope he'll be all right."

Jake and Francisco say, "Sure thing. We'll watch out for our brother."

They decide to knock on Athena's bedroom door and see if she's inside. Athena is giggling on the phone, and the guys hear her say, "I had a lovely time with you today, Maximilian. I can't wait to see you tomorrow after school, back at the Casa Blanca Hotel around four."

Jake whispers, "Athena is talking to another dude."

Francisco whispers, "It has to be that guy who lives close to our girlfriends. I'm pissed... Athena is two-timing on our brother."

"There's nothing we can do but follow her at the Casa Blanca tomorrow. We can go with the twins, which will make it easier for us to get into that hotel. That way, we'll see what's going on," says Jake.

They hear Athena humming a song as she walks back into her master bathroom. Francisco cracks her bedroom door open and notices Athena's purse lying open on the dresser. He runs in, rifles through her bag and grabs the business card Drogan gave her. He quietly closes the bedroom door behind him, and they run back downstairs where Aoki greets them.

Aoki walks toward Francisco, who is hiding the spiked business card in his hand. "Hmmm... Franny, you're looking good." She seductively rubs Francisco's chest and murmurs, "*Ooo*, you *sexy* teen boy, I want to teach you some new tricks."

Francisco whispers in shock, "Aunt Aoki, what's come over you?"

Uncle Zadok shouts, "What *the hell* is going on!?"

Francisco stutters, "Uh... no... nothing, Uncle Zadok."

Aoki squeezes Francisco's butt as he leaps away and runs outside. "I need to run to my car and grab my backpack."

Jake blurts out, "I have to go with him."

Aoki coos, "Hurry back, Franny."

Zadok's jaw drops in shock.

Aoki suddenly comes back to herself, and says, "I have a slight headache." She looks at Zadok and yells, "What's your problem!?" then storms off to their bedroom.

Zadok ponders. *What the hell's going on with these women up in here?*

Outside, Francisco says to Jake, "Bro, there's something on this card, like a love perfume, or something."

Jake nods. "I know. Did you see how Aunt Aoki acted towards you? She wanted you right then and there on the stairs."

Francisco remarks, "I'm a little creeped out, she's hot for an older lady, but… ugh, no way! That's Uncle Zadok's woman. What can we do? We have no proof of what this good-looking Hollywood hunk of a guy has done to Athena."

"I wish we could figure out who this guy is," mumbles Jake.

Francisco replies, "Well, they'll be having lunch tomorrow around four at the Casa Blanca Hotel, right? You go with the Star Island Twins without me and meet them there. I'll sneak in his house and see what I can find out."

Jake says, "That could be risky, bro. We don't know if this guy has any bodyguards or wild pit bulls running around."

Francisco boasts, "Look, bro. We battled crocodile bodyguards, Hybrid Reptilians and Gargoyles. What's a little pit bull going to do to Francisco, The Don, huh?"

"You have a point there. We'll act like everything's normal and figure out who this James Bond-looking guy is."

The guys do a warrior's salute, pounding their fists on their chests while chanting out loud. "Atlantean Superhero Ballers!"

Francisco says, "We have our own little spy mission."

Jake nods as he grins. "Yeah, dude. This is going to be cool."

The guys walk back into the mansion as Athena comes downstairs smiling. "Hi, everybody."

Francisco asks, "Hey, Athena. How was your day?"

Athena replies with a nonchalant shrug. "It was good after the funeral. I had a charity meeting about a project I might do. It feels weird that

Tyrone's funeral was only a few hours ago and now it feels like a brand-new day. I see different things happening in my future."

Jake says, "Really, then I guess that's good."

Uncle Zadok asks, "Are you feeling okay, Athena? Allen doesn't look so happy."

Athena yells, "I'm fine! Stop agitating me! Allen needs to relax, and I need to breathe a little if that's okay with all of you!"

The guys say at the same time, throwing their hands up in the air like they're being held hostage, "Hey, it's fine with us."

Athena walks to the kitchen and grabs a soda before heading out to the pool.

Jake says to Francisco, "Maybe you better slip the card back into her purse."

"Okay, bro." He runs into Athena's room, puts the card back into her purse, and quickly strolls back downstairs without getting caught.

Zadok goes to his room to see if Aoki is okay.

She apologizes. "Baby, I'm so sorry. I don't know what came over me. I felt this urge that was uncontrollable."

Zadok says lovingly, "It's okay, sweetheart. There's nothing to worry about. At first, I thought it was the attack of the female hormones." He laughs.

Aoki giggles. "You're, my Z Bear. And you'll always be."

Zadok whispers with affection, "I love you, my darling."

CHAPTER FIVE

JAKE AND FRANCISCO SAVE THEIR SUPERHERO FAMILY

The next morning, Uncle Zadok makes the teens turkey bacon, croissants, oatmeal, and scrambled eggs. He's also prepared a sumptuous fruit platter and a variety of freshly squeezed juices. He rings the cowbell and yells into the speaker, "Come and get it while it's hot!"

Francisco and Jake race downstairs foaming at the mouth, starving for the delicious meal. They arrange themselves at the table next to Zadok and Aoki. Everyone notices that Allen and Athena haven't come down yet. An uncomfortable silence descends over the breakfast, as they exchange worried looks.

Allen finally strides in as if nothing is wrong, and sings out, "Good morning," plops down at the table and eats breakfast.

Uncle Zadok glances at Jake and Francisco, waits for Allen to look up from his plate and asks nonchalantly, "How're you feeling today, nephew?"

"I feel good," replies Allen with a grand smile.

Zadok beams back and crows, "That's great! Glad to see you have a good appetite! You need a hearty breakfast so you can study hard and keep those grades up."

"We're all doing pretty well," says Jake.

"Yeah, Uncle Zadok, turns out we didn't need a tutor," says Francisco.

Zadok says, "I'm happy to hear that. But remember, you shouldn't be too proud to get one if you ever feel you need help."

Jake says, "Uncle Zadok, you know how smart Allen is… he always helps us if we need it."

Allen nods and smiles at them. They try not to react to Athena as she walks in behind Allen, wearing a skimpy white miniskirt, tiny midriff-baring top, and thigh high, patent leather spike-heel boots. Uncle Zadok's eyes bulge out, but he says nothing. Allen takes a sip of his juice; he notices that everyone is suddenly quiet. He turns around and gasps.

Athena smirks at him. "What's your problem? You wouldn't be where you are if it weren't for me." Athena looks at everyone, and yells, "None of you would never be in this mansion if I didn't allow you to live in it. Look at all of you! Two former orphans who act like they're the kings of Miami and a crippled old man who wishes he had a singing career. And you, Alien King, you're looking for some non-existent crown in the hope of restoring some long-abandoned kingdom!" Athena takes a bite out of Allen's croissant and shouts, "This croissant is just like you. It tastes old, stale, and soggy." She throws it back on Allen's plate screaming, "I'm moving out of here first thing tomorrow morning!"

Everyone's completely shocked. Allen's eyes turn blood-red. He's angrier than anyone's ever seen him. No one utters a word. Allen takes off his necklace and emerald ring and tosses the jewelry at Uncle Zadok. "Here, uncle, you want Atlantis more than I do! Why don't <u>you</u> become King and bring <u>your</u> legacy back!" He storms out of the house.

Uncle Zadok is tearful. Allen's words cut through him like a knife. Zadok picks up the necklace and ring, and whispers solemnly, "I'll put these in his mother's golden box and keep it in my room for him until he's ready to continue his quest."

"We'll look out for him and Athena as much as we can," reassures Jake.

Francisco says, "Allen left his backpack upstairs… I'll go grab it and take it to him at school."

Jake says to Francisco telepathically, *It's up to us, amigo, to keep the Atlantean Superhero Ballers intact. We're falling apart like a house of cards.*

Francisco responds telepathically, *Let's stay in communication at all times during and after school.*

Jake transmits, *Agreed.*

They go to school in separate cars, and as they walk on campus, they observe a crowd of students dancing to music the Party Boys are playing. They see Athena dancing with the two girls who were fighting over Tyrone. One girl twerks in front of Athena as the other dances seductively behind her.

Principal Jenkins walks up, and the crowd disperses. He looks at Athena with disappointment on his face and says, "Young lady… Miss Monroe… please put a jacket on. Your outfit is not appropriate for school."

Athena winks at the principle. "How about I extend my skirt?" She makes a spectacle of pulling it down to her knees and brags, "It's a one of a kind skirt I designed myself. I call it the accordion skirt…" With a devilish smile, she says, "You see… all better now."

Jake transmits to Francisco, *This isn't looking so good... our sister is wild beyond belief right now! Luckily, Allen didn't see her weird performance.*

The bell rings, and Jake and Francisco walk inside. They find Allen standing by his locker looking sad and confused.

Francisco hands him his backpack and says, "Here's your backpack, bro."

Allen whispers, "Thanks, Fran. I appreciate it," then walks away without saying anything else. Jake and Francisco exchange a disheartened look.

"What can we do?" asks Jake.

Francisco shrugs. "I don't know… we will figure something out."

Allen walks into history class late. With his head down, he mumbles to Mrs. Ramirez, "I'm sorry I'm late."

Mrs. Ramirez says in a stern but compassionate voice, "Mr. King, I understand why you're upset, but the funeral's over. It would be best to move on with your life… for your own good."

Allen mutters, "Yes, ma'am." As he sits down, he notices that Athena is wearing Glam Girl Warrior Princess makeup on her eyes.

Allen whispers, "Audrey, what are you doing?"

She giggles in reply. "I'm giving these idiots a hint of who I really am… Glam Girl Warrior Princess… without the prince." She laughed out loud catching Mrs. Ramirez's attention.

Mrs. Ramirez says, "Please, Ms. Monroe, don't disrupt the classroom."

Mimicking Allen, she parrots, "Yes, ma'am," as she stealthily passes him a note.

Allen sits in his desk, unfolds the note and reads: *I found another man, Alien King. He's a normal handsome, rich man who doesn't need anything from me. You have fun trying to find the crown without me, loser.* Allen crumples the note and glares at Athena.

Josh whispers to Allen from behind, "Allen, are you okay?"

Allen snaps, "I'm fine! Mind your own business, nephew!"

Besides Athena no one in the classroom knows who Allen is talking to.

Josh whispers again, "Calm down, bro. I'm here for you."

Allen jumps up, faces Josh and yells, "You're here for me! You're not even here for yourself. What are you going to do without your dead receiver, huh?"

Josh pounces on Allen and hits the love-battered warrior several times.

Mrs. Ramirez yells, "Stop fighting in my classroom!"

Josh is stronger than Allen now simply because Allen's not wearing his ring and necklace. Josh punches Allen hard in the eye, knocking him on his butt.

Mrs. Ramirez shouts, "Allen King, to the principal's office now!"

He shouts back, "What about Josh!?"

Mrs. Ramirez screams, "Do I look stupid to you!? You provoked the whole thing!"

Athena points and snickers as Allen scrambles up off the floor and storms out of the classroom. He doesn't go to the principal's office, but straight to his Range Rover.

Furious, he peels out of the parking lot and runs a red light. As he screeches through the intersection, he's rammed by a Mack truck. Unconscious, he's cut out of his SUV and taken by ambulance to Miami Memorial Hospital. As the doctors and nurses begin to treat him, Allen comes to and asks, "Nurse, could you please call my Uncle Zadok and tell him that I'm in the hospital."

The nurse nods. "I will do that for you."

She calls Zadok, who immediately contacts Francisco and Jake telepathically. *Boys, I don't know what happened but Allen's in the hospital.*

The guys reply, *Oh no.*

Jake transmits, *We will go to the hospital as soon as we find Athena.*

Francisco and Jake can't find Athena to tell her about Allen. Her car is gone, but they think they know where she might be. The guys take off to the hospital to see Allen, and for the first time, they see the Atlantean Prince bruised and battered. He's awake but has a broken arm and a few bruised ribs. Without his crystals, his abilities are normal like the rest of the mortals on Earth.

Although, he's happy to see his friends, Allen declares, "I don't want to see Athena ever again. I'd rather be a longshoreman working on the docks like my brother did. Leroy lived a simple life."

Zadok is being wheeled in by Aoki as he hears Allen say this. He blurts out, "You don't mean that, nephew!"

Allen shoots back, "Yes I do! I don't ever want to enter that house again. She's made me so angry. I'd rather be homeless! So please, everyone… just let me rest." He turns his back on his family and pretends to fall asleep. The boys, Zadok and Aoki leave sadly, at a loss for words. They don't know what to say to Allen.

A little while later, Josh enters Allen's hospital room. Allen looks at him with tears in his eyes and says, "I'm sorry, Josh. You're the one person in this world I didn't ever want to hurt. It seems like everyone around me is hurting me. Well, my girlfriend, I mean."

Jake nods. "I understand, no worries, man. I've been where you are right now except for the broken arm. How is your eye?"

Allen compliments. "You have a pretty good right jab."

Josh nods and smiles. After a moment, he says, "I really mean it from the heart. I hope you don't plan on throwing away what could again be a great kingdom."

Allen looks at the wall and mutters, "What's a kingdom without a queen? Without Athena, I'm nothing."

Josh says with confidence, "I have a feeling she'll come around."

"After what I witnessed today, I don't know if I ever want to see her again. Today, I didn't recognize the girl who made me want to save this world."

Josh says, "Time will tell… If you need me, uncle, just call me, okay?"

Allen does the warrior's salute lightly against his chest. Josh doesn't know the Atlantean salute. He smiles and then leaves.

Meanwhile, Jake and Francisco have gone home to change clothes for their spy mission. Jake whispers to himself, "I have to look like a million bucks if I'm going to blend in at the Casa Blanca Hotel." He chooses a white designer suit, pink shirt, his gold presidential watch, and white sneakers with no socks. He admires himself in the mirror and says to himself, "Today, I'll be Sonny Crocket spying on this guy."

He calls the Star Island Twins. "Hey, Samantha. Can you and your sister meet me and Francisco at the Casa Blanca Hotel?"

"That sounds like a great idea. The Casa Blanca is one of the hottest hotels in South Beach," exclaims Samantha.

Athena has already checked into the hotel without letting Max Coastal know she's there. She doesn't want him to think he has complete control over her, however, if he wants to woo her that night, she knows she'll happily oblige. She's so in love with him. She can't resist him any longer.

While Jake makes his way to the hotel, Francisco rents a Jet Ski, rides it to Star Island and parks it where the twins' yacht is docked three houses away from the mysterious man's house. Francisco walks to the back of the man's house in his trendy plaid shorts, white shirt, and boat shoes. He easily looks like he belongs on Star Island.

As Francisco jumps into Max's yard, he says telepathically to Jake, *I'm here on the mystery man's property.*

Jake replies telepathically, *Be careful, Fran! I want you back in one piece.*

Francisco transmits, *There's nothing to worry about, bro. It looks like a normal house to me.*

He walks to the back door and tries the handle. It's locked. He takes a few steps back, looks up and notices that a second-story window is slightly open. He scratches his head, then spies a trampoline in the backyard. He grins to himself, pops his collar, and proclaims, "I'll jump up to the second-story window." He pats himself on the back. "Genius."

Francisco gets on the trampoline and jumps. A finger touches the windowsill. He jumps up again, and this time a few fingers touch it. On the fifth jump, Francisco is finally able to grab onto the ledge and hoist himself inside. He stands up, brushes himself off and telepathically says to Jake, *I'm inside, bro. In the master bedroom!*

He opens a large closet and looks around. *Jake, this guy has about 50 white suits… it reminds me of—*

Jake telepathically blurts out, *The red-headed albino brothers.*

Exactly, says Francisco as he moves a couple of suits to the side. He notices one with red hairs on the collar. He transmits, *This guy has red hair on one of his suits.*

Jake telepathically yells, *No way! Search the pockets and see if you find anything in there.*

Francisco searches the breast and pants pocket but finds nothing. Then, in one jacket pocket, he finds a business card. Francisco transmits, *Bingo! I see a business card with his name, Drogan Reptilly! I'm going to check the bathroom now.*

In the bathroom, he sees a box of dark hair dye sitting next to a tiny bottle of cologne labeled "Spy Cologne." Francisco looks in the trash can and sees a box with a note attached to it that reads:

Boss,

Here's the second batch of love potion. Be extra careful with this one. It's super strong and can produce side effects like migraine headaches and moodiness.

Sincerely,

Evil Scientist Barrington.

Francisco telepathically says out loud, *I hit the motherload! Jake, I found the cologne that put a spell on Athena and a note from the scientist who made it to Drogan saying to be extra careful with it because it can produce bad side effects!*

Francisco then notices a magazine page tacked on the wall with a photo of Drogan's head in his albino form pasted on top of a bridegroom's head, and a picture of Athena's head pasted over the bride's head.

Francisco telepathically shouts, *Jake, we have to save Athena. This guy is Drogan Reptilly! And he's using this love cologne to get her to fall for him!*

Jake shouts telepathically, *No way*! Suddenly, he sees Athena exiting the elevator and walking toward the front desk. Jake transmits, *Here's my chance.*

Be careful, transmits Francisco.

Jake excuses himself from the twins for a moment and walks up to Athena. "Hi, Athena, I need to talk to you, please."

Athena looks surprised. "What is it, Jake? I have a slight headache... I'm not in the mood to talk to you right now. I have a meeting soon." Jake notices that her pupils are dilated and that she seems unsteady on her feet.

Jake says, "Allen's in the hospital… he's seriously injured. He has a broken arm and a few cracked ribs."

"Oh no, it's my fault… but I have a meeting in a half hour with someone." Athena turns pale and looks like she might vomit and pass out.

Jake takes her arm and says gently, "Let me take you to see Allen."

Jake asks the twins to bring the limo around and get some water for Athena.

They help Athena into the limo just as Drogan walks into the lobby. He glances at Jake just as Jake closes the limousine window.

Drogan doesn't see Athena. He asks the concierge, "Has my friend Athena checked in with you?"

The concierge replies, "I think I saw your friend leave with a blond-haired teenage boy and his friends." Drogan ponders. *This can't be happening. It must be the blond-haired boy that was in the limo and the same boy who is a part of Allen's gang.*

Drogan dashes to his boat docked behind the hotel and drives it back to his house in Star Island. He says to himself, "My recently improved Reptilian/Gargoyle senses tell me that there was an intruder earlier, and from the smell of the intruder, it was the cocky Latino teen I faced on my yacht last summer."

Dorgan clenched his fists and says to himself, "Now, I'm angry. I wonder how the teens could have possibly known about my home in Miami?"

Drogan follows Francisco's scent out to where the Jet Ski was parked by the Star Islands Twin's yacht. Drogan instantly knows there has to be a connection. He runs back to his mansion and goes upstairs, where he sees that the spy cologne was taken with the note in the trash can. The super strong Drogan, the Invincible, slams his fist on the counter of his bathroom sink, breaking it into huge chunks. He becomes angrier and lets out monstrous screams between high-pitched Reptilian shrieks

Drogan thinks to himself, *I have no choice but to leave Miami. Allen will soon find out who I am.* He races out his front door, leaps thirty yards into his convertible Porsche and speeds off to the airport. He flies his private jet back to Sydney and on the plane he says to himself, "I have to patiently wait for the Atlantean's next move, which will be during the summer in Hawaii, where I intend to steal the King's Crown from him and make Athena my bride."

CHAPTER SIX

THE ATLANTEAN PRINCE AND GREEK GODDESS REUNITE

The limo rushes to the hospital entrance. Jake jumps out of the vehicle screaming, "Help! Please help! My sister is burning up with a fever, and she's slipping in and out of consciousness."

An orderly brings a wheelchair to the limo, pushes Athena into the emergency room and checks her vitals. Jake contacts Uncle Zadok telepathically. *I've found Athena and we're at the hospital. Athena is in bad shape, but she asked me to ask you to please bring Allen's golden ring and crystal necklace, and Athena's crystal necklace. She thinks the crystals might heal them.*

Zadok replies, *Thank you, Jake. I will grab the crystals for them.*

Zadok asks Aoki to look for Athena's necklace, while he goes to their bedroom to grab Allen's jewelry, which is safely ensconced in Cordelia's golden jewelry box.

Aoki yells, "I found it, Z Bear!"

Zadok gasps with relief. "Perfect, sweetheart, let's get to the hospital pronto."

In the emergency room, a nurse runs blood tests on Athena, which reveals a toxic compound in her bloodstream.

Athena screams out for Allen as she's being strapped down to a hospital bed. "Where is my prince? Allen! Where are you, my love!?"

Aluna works in the ER; she goes to Athena's side. "Calm down, child… everything's going to be all right."

Several hours later, Athena is slowly recovering in her hospital bed, while Allen rests in his hospital bed. Zadok is with him and he says, "Nephew, I have to explain everything to you about what happened to Athena. Drogan disguised himself to trick Athena and he drugged her with a toxic fragrance to make her fall in love with him."

Allen sheds a single blue teardrop of happiness and says, "I realized that my Goddess was tricked and not responsible for her hurtful comments and actions toward me."

Zadok smiles. "She was not the Athena we know and love."

He sighs with joy. "I knew my love wasn't herself. I… I just knew it from the bottom of my heart."

Zadok gives Allen his crystal necklace and emerald ring. Allen puts them on, but can't telepathically contact Athena. Distressed, he says to Zadok, "I can't reach her."

Aluna enters Allen's room, smiling with good news. "Don't worry, young man, now you can."

She pulls his curtains back, revealing Athena lying in bed on the other side of the hospital room. Athena turns her head and looks lovingly at Allen. She smiles with immense relief and whispers, "Please forgive me, my love, I don't know what came over me. I couldn't control myself… my anger. I don't know why I acted that way."

Allen is overwhelmed with joy. "Everything will be okay."

The entire family is now there, including Josh. He locks eyes with Zadok and approaches him. Aluna intuitively feels that Josh is somehow related.

Zadok extends his hand out to Josh. "It's a pleasure to meet you, son."

Uncle Zadok turns his attention to Aluna. "Thank you for helping out my niece."

"I'm a nurse, it's my job," says Aluna.

Aluna indicates Allen and Athena and whispers, "They need to rest… they should check out in the morning."

Everyone walks out of the room except Zadok and Aoki.

Zadok says with love, "You two get some sleep."

Allen looks at Zadok and says, "Please forgive me for what I said earlier."

Zadok says, "I understand. That wasn't you, neph. That was you missing your other half keeping you whole, that's all."

Athena smiles and smooches her lips toward Allen.

"There's only one thing missing to make you two complete," says Aoki. She hands Athena her crystal necklace. Athena sheds a tear and lifts her head off the pillow. Aoki lays the necklace around her neck. Athena kisses it and says, "Aunt Aoki, thank you."

Aoki hugs her. "You're welcome, my beautiful niece." Aoki and Zadok leave the room.

Allen gets out of his bed with the IV still in his arm. The crystals are slowly healing his wounds. He kisses Athena.

She says to him telepathically, *Are you hurt, my handsome prince?*

He telepathically replies, *Not anymore, my love.*

Athena moves a couple of his dreads away from her face as they continue kissing. Allen whispers, "I know you well. You were partially right about the crystals healing us. It was our love for each other that instantly healed our wounds." Allen feels like he was never in an accident and Athena feels like the evil Hybrid's love potion has never poisoned her. Allen's eyes glow an alluring blue-green color, while Athena's glow a striking golden-brown. The couple removes their IVs and talk telepathically until they fall asleep cuddling together in Athena's hospital bed.

The next day when Athena and Allen arrive back home, Francisco and Jake declare simultaneously, "Today's a joyous day. Our family is back together again."

Athena and Allen laugh and hug everyone.

Zadok says, "We decided the family should go on another cruise, like the one we went on in Australia."

Athena says with glee, "That sounds like a splendid idea!"

Allen happily says, "That's a great idea, Uncle Zadok."

Smiling, Zadok replies, "Well then, let's go!" He and Aoki lead the way to their new yacht, docked in a private harbor nearby. He has another surprise. The Star Island Twins, Josh, Mercedes, and Aluna are on board. Allen, Athena, Josh, and Francisco are thrilled.

Zadok says, "Since my father King Leon refuses to accept Josh, I figure I'll get to know Josh and then speak to my father… try to change his mind."

Allen kisses Uncle Zadok on his bald head and shouts with delight, "You're the best, Unc!"

Uncle Zadok says, "Alright! Alright! Now what I tell you about me and my sexy cue ball head. Only Aoki can kiss that." Zadok lowers his head and says to Aoki, "Go ahead, baby and kiss that lollipop." The family laughs.

Josh extends his hand out to everyone as they board the vessel. Josh says to Athena, "Hi Audrey, I mean, Athena."

Athena politely replies, "Thank you, Josh."

He grabs Allen's hand, smiles and says, "Mr. King."

Allen smiles and says, "Mr. Stone…"

A crewmember unties the dock lines, and the captain leaves out of the harbor.

Josh whispers to Allen, "Don't worry, Allen… Mercedes doesn't know anything about us. But my mother does of course."

Allen gives Josh a pat on the shoulder. "Thank you for keeping our secrets in the family."

Everyone sits down to eat lunch in the dining room on the second level. Zadok has outdone himself. He's even installed a cowbell inside the boat! He rings it: "*Ding! Ding! Ding!*" and laughs uproariously at his little joke.

Allen says to Josh, who is sitting next to him, "Josh, you'll get used to Uncle Zadok before you know it."

Zadok says, "I want to celebrate all of us hanging out together… I'm thankful that our new friends, Aluna, Josh and Mercedes have been able to join us. I see nothing wrong with playing hooky from school when you're with the ones you love. Don't make it a habit because if you do." Zadok takes off his belt and makes a popping sound. "I will tear your young asses up." Everyone laughs. Zadok says with love, "All jokes aside. I'm truly thankful that Allen King and his future Queen are healthy and safe. Now let's eat!"

Allen stands and clinks on the side of his tea jar with his knife. "Before we eat Uncle Zadok's incredible meal, I just want to say to everyone from the bottom of my heart, thank you for showing me what a real true loving family is. I'm forever indebted to all of you." He looks at Francisco and Jake and proclaims, "To my brothers, thank you for doing what you had to do to keep our family intact. We'll never break the bond we have together." Allen looks at Zadok. "To Uncle Zadok, you're the best uncle a nephew could ever have, and I thank you for continuing to believe in me when I didn't believe in myself. Aunt Aoki, thank you for being the beacon of light for Uncle Zadok. He's a very happy man thanks to you. To the Star Island Twins, thank you for hanging in there with this crazy family. To Josh and Mercedes, may you two continue to grow together, and live a happy life together. And, to Aluna, sincerely from the bottom of my heart, thank you for raising such a great young man. I know his father would be proud of him. And I especially thank you, Aluna, for helping bring my queen back to her beautiful, radiant self. I can't see another sun or moon without her."

Aluna gives Allen a warm embrace. "You are an extraordinary, young man. Thank you for the kind words you said about my son and his father."

Allen replies, "I said it from the heart."

Josh intervenes. "Hey, mom, let's eat."

Everyone enjoys the meal as they continue talking amongst themselves. Zadok smiles and says, "Aluna, it's amazing to hear you talk about the soulful music you grew up on. I also love listening to the greats like Lionel Richie, the Commodores, Zapp, and the Gap Band."

Aluna replies, "Zadok, you have a broad catalog of music in your head."

Zadok brags. "I know everything from "Candy…" He sings a little bit of Cameo's hit song, and then switches to, "Tutti Frutti." Everyone snaps their fingers as Zadok sings Little Richard's lyrics: "A-wop-bop-a-loo-bop-a-wop-bam-boom!"

After lunch, Zadok, Allen, and Josh talk in the dining room, while Aoki and Aluna clear the table and do the dishes in the galley. Athena hangs out on the deck with Mercedes, Jake, Francisco, and the Star Island Twins. They're dancing to a Party Boys mix.

Francisco asks the twins, "Now you hear what the Party Boys sound like… How do you like it?"

Samantha and Suzy say at the same time, "They're really gnarly!" Samantha gives the guys a thumbs up!

Mercedes says to Athena, "This whole time at school you've been pretending to be just a normal student, but you're a socialite, fashion designer, and an author?"

Athena says shyly, "I want to keep it low-key. I don't want to spook the school board. If they discover I'm writing a book about the American public-school system, they'll probably kick me out."

"Girlfriend, I understand," says Mercedes with a smile. Athena's relieved and thinks. *Thankfully, Mercedes still doesn't know that I am a Greek Goddess and I'm also known as Glam Girl Warrior Princess to my adoring fans.*

Back in the dining room, Zadok says to Josh, "Son, I was wrong about you. I figured that since the Gargoyle spirit came through you and you have Reptilian blood, you might be a threat to my nephew and his friends."

Josh explains to Zadok, "My mother doesn't know that Allen's the Teen Warrior who saved her from the Hybrids, and I think it's better we keep it that way."

Zadok says, "Are you sure, son? We're family now you know. I think Aluna knows that we may be related. Eventually, she'll figure it out."

Josh replies, "Let's give it some time. Please tell me some things about my father, Leroy."

Zadok beams and says, "Well, Leroy loved being a longshoreman working on the docks. He completely forgot he came from royalty. Leroy didn't want to believe it since he wasn't born in Atlantis, and he didn't know anything about the city, about the beating of the African Zulu warrior drums, or the beautiful Atlantean women who would perform Mediterranean and Zulu dances. Atlanteans were strong warriors and built like you and Allen. Anyway, Leroy cared for his family, even though Allen wasn't his son. He felt that it was his responsibility to give Allen a comfortable life, teach him morals, and how to be a hardworking man. That's the way Leroy was. I understand you met him from time to time?"

Josh nods with pride. "Yes, sir, I did. He was always happy to see me, and he took me to a few football games. He knew I wanted to be a football player. We would go to Dolphins games together. He would take me out for ice cream and come to my football games whenever he could. I was always pleasantly surprised when he showed up."

"I'm pleased to hear that. Leroy was headstrong. His wife, Alicia, was like me. She couldn't have any children… Now I understand why Leroy stayed with her, I guess. He had you, and he wanted Alicia to feel like a mother to Allen. Leroy was a little strict with him… That's probably because every moment I had, I let Allen know who he really was, and Leroy rejected that part of his heritage. I guess I can't blame him for that."

Josh says a little shyly, "You know, Uncle Zadok… do you mind if I call you that?"

Zadok smiles. "Not at all, nephew."

Josh confesses, "I was always jealous of Allen for some reason. I guess maybe it's the Nomadic Indian and Reptilian blood in me that sensed he was Atlantean… The crazy thing, which is wild to me. I'm also part Atlantean! Isn't that strange?"

Zadok nods in agreement. "I thought the same thing when I first found out, nephew. I've told Allen this many times… things come across your path when you're ready. Circumstances may present itself to you a few times, but only when you're truly ready… wham!" Zadok slaps his hand on the table. "It hits you like a sledgehammer, and there's nothing that can change or remove that unstoppable force in front of you. That's why you and Allen have always had your little beef. He wasn't ready for you for a long time, and when he was—"

"Yeah, I know what you mean, Uncle Zadok," says Josh. "I felt Allen's unstoppable force." He, Allen, and Zadok laugh out loud.

Allen says from the heart, "I felt yours as well. You've truly made me more resilient… That inhaler was a security blanket. I didn't have asthma; it was just in my head. Leroy loved making me feel as if I were weak. His death made me strong, along with you, Uncle Zadok, my brothers Francisco and Jake, and especially Athena. Without her, I wouldn't be where I am right now. She's my true love until I breathe my last breath on this Earth."

Josh declares with admiration, "I can see that she truly loves you also."

"We're all truly blessed men to have the women we have in our lives," states Zadok.

He raises his sweet tea as they cheer. "Here, here!" Zadok pounds his fist on his chest, as do Allen and Josh. Uncle Zadok says, "Hail Atlantis," and his nephews repeat. "Hail Atlantis."

As Aluna puts the dirty dishes in the washing machine, she says to Aoki, "You have a good man."

Aoki smiles and says, "Thank you, Aluna. Zadok's a beautiful spirit inside and out—"

"I know Zadok is related to Leroy, and that Zadok is an Atlantean," says Aluna, coming straight to the point.

Aoki is taken aback. "You do?"

Aluna nods and smiles. "Yes, and I'll keep quiet until he feels comfortable talking about it. I also have a feeling that handsome young man sitting next to Zadok is extraordinary beyond this world."

Aoki pauses for a moment and replies, "Yes, Allen's something else all right."

Aluna looks at Aoki seriously. "You know what I mean. He brought us together as a family."

Aoki agrees. "He sure did, didn't he?"

Aluna blurts out, "He saved Josh's and my life! I can't prove it, but I just know. Okay, enough about teenage superheroes, which sounds so crazy."

Aoki is at a loss for words. "It sure does. You caught me by surprise, Aluna. I really don't know what to say. You're very intuitive."

Aluna smiles and says, "Thank you, Aoki, let's change the subject and talk to Zadok and see what the kids are doing."

Aluna replies, "Sounds good to me."

Allen and Josh go upstairs to the top deck as Aoki opens the galley door. Zadok glances over his shoulder at his wife and Aluna as they walk in. Aoki gives her husband a kiss on the cheek. He teases. "I was beginning to think you two ate the rest of the sweet potato pie."

Aluna grins and says, "No, not yet, but we enjoyed our little chat. You know, Zadok, you're one of a kind and so is your nephew, Allen."

Zadok displays a chivalrous smile. "Yes, ma'am, I guess we all are. So, who's good at playing gin rummy… or dominoes?"

Aluna brags, "I know everything there is to know about dominoes, okay."

Zadok widens his eyes and arches his brows, "Well, I'm scared now. Look at you?"

Aoki giggles. "It sounds like we have a challenger who knows how to play."

Zadok pulls something out from the pouch in the back of his wheelchair. "I just happen to have some dominoes." Boisterously, he yells, "Let's play! When I was a child chess was the game of choice, but through the years, I've become a fan of dominoes. It's more exciting… It gets your brain going when you look across the table and see the numbers as you're waiting and planning for the monster hit. I think if I'd had dominoes when I was growing up, that would have gotten the city going."

Aoki stares at Zadok. "Honey, you're about to give away too much information."

Zadok thinks Aluna is the one playing dumb with them. He assumes she already knows about Atlantis and their family. He figures she's just waiting to see if he's going to spill the beans.

Up on deck, the teens are dancing and listening to the Star Island Twins do a live performance, lip-synching one of the songs they think will be a hit. Francisco and Jake are in awe of their fine-looking starlets.

Jake picks Francisco up and yells, "We have hot superstar girlfriends in the making!"

Francisco nods. "Yeah, bro. They're not ditzy when they sing. They're totally hot!"

Allen and Athena yell out together, "Woo hoo! Yeah, sing it, twins!"

Athena turns around to face Allen, "I never want to yell at you or lose you again, Allen King."

Allen says with passion, "And you won't, soon-to-be Athena Dranias-King."

They kiss, and Athena smiles big. "I love the sound of that."

Allen grins with delight. "When we find the crown, and when I'm king, you'll still be a socialite who needs to protect your name and keep your legacy going in regard to your books and foundations."

Athena whispers, "Babe…"

Allen replies, "I sense something is wrong. What's going on?"

Athena stammers, and then cautiously says, "I must confess. I think… I… uh, told that Hybrid swine in disguise that we'll be looking for the crown in Hawaii this summer."

Allen ponders for a moment and says, "He can't stop us, between you and me, Jake, and Francisco, and hopefully with the aid of Josh. Drogan and whatever henchmen or beast he unites with can't stop us."

Athena feels guilty. "I hope not, my love. I wouldn't know what to do if something terrible happened."

Allen looks at their friends singing and dancing. "Josh is working on meeting the Gargoyle in a middle playing field, and if there's a full moon around the time, we look for the crown, Josh told me he may be able to help once he learns the ancient Nomadic Indian way to conquer the demon."

Athena asks, "You admire him, don't you?"

Allen replies, "How could you not? Josh carries the blood of all races- Atlantean, Reptilian, and Nomadic Indian, and he became a Gargoyle. Josh is a true warrior."

Athena smiles and telepathically says, *I am happy for your newfound love and respect for your former bully.* Allen nods. "Thank you."

Athena telepathically declares, *You must still keep your guard up and protect yourself at all times, my handsome prince.*

Allen replies telepathically, *I will never risk losing you ever again.*

Below deck, Zadok yells, "Dominoes!" He comes back to his senses. "Sorry, ladies… dominoes takes me to another zone." He laughs. "We could play spades if you like, or twenty-one."

Aoki replies with a wink, "Z Bear, you know I love twenty-one."

Zadok laughs as he nods. "Yes, you do, don't you? We need to practice before we go back to Vegas. Remember when we were there last time. It was magical… Our room overlooked the strip from the balcony. Your good friend Karina stopped by to visit us, and she happened to be in town. She was in awe of the incredible sight."

Aoki sighs and smiles. "Yes, we enjoyed ourselves, sipping champagne while we gazed at the beautiful skyline."

Zadok smiles. "I remember you won about thirteen thousand dollars, didn't you, honey?"

Aoki blows a kiss to Zadok. "Sure did, baby!"

Zadok says, "That's my girl…Twenty-one it is."

He shuffles the cards and gives the deck to Aluna as she says, "I used to love playing cards with Josh's father. He also loved playing twenty-one and dominoes. However, twenty-one was his game of choice."

Zadok listens intently. "Really now?" he asks.

Aluna nods. "Hmm-mmm… Yes. He would take me to a casino over in Atlantic City. Josh's father loved smoking his cigar and drinking his cognac. He would sit down at a table for about two hours straight. One time, he won twenty thousand dollars, and he gave me fifteen thousand. He kept the five grand to take care of bills for his family. That money put Josh in football clinics, which probably helped make him the star quarterback he is now."

Zadok's so happy he blurts out, "I didn't know Leroy had that in him. All he ever talked about was work. If he was gone for a few days on the weekend, he said he was working offshore in New Orleans or something. The whole time that sneaky devil was with you?"

"Yes, he was," answers Aluna with a smile.

Zadok laughs. "I'll be damned! I guess he did have some fun. He always seemed so serious." Zadok suddenly says, "Oops! I just realized I told you that Leroy's my nephew. "I'm sorry, Aluna."

She winks and says, "I figured that out earlier today. Don't worry, Zadok. Your family's secret is safe with me."

Zadok chuckles. "I just got my engine under my tongue running."

CHAPTER SEVEN

THE ATLANTEAN WEDDING NIGHTMARE

The yacht excursion comes to an end. As the boat docks, and everyone is saying their good-byes, Athena telepathically says to Allen, *My sweet prince, let's go to my compound in Australia and spend the night. I want some alone time with you.*

Allen blushes and nods. As they say their goodbyes, Allen takes Athena's hand, summons the most stunning rainbow cloud, which includes all the usual colors as well as black and white, and they disappear into the ethers.

News reporters are baffled, and on live TV, a meteorologist exclaims, "I have no explanation for this! I don't know how a rainbow can include black and white within its spectrum. It's out of this world."

The couple teleports directly to the botanical garden, where they're greeted by thousands of multi-colored butterflies, fluttering happily at their presence. Above the garden, hundreds of golden butterflies flap together and slowly spell out the words: *Allen and Athena Forever in Love,* while the red butterflies form a heart shape around the words. Allen and Athena are astonished by what the butterflies are doing and are inspired to dance a romantic waltz in the moonlit sky through the garden toward the pool overlooking the cliff where they first fell in love.

Before they reach the pool area, Allen dips Athena elegantly, which makes them giggle like children. They kiss, throw off their clothes and jump into the pool and gaze at the panoramic views of the ocean below the cliff, in the distance.

Allen says, "My love, this is exactly what we needed... It feels like we've been married for a hundred years and coming back here, to where we first fell in love, feels like I'm renewing my vows with you." Allen pulls off his Atlantean ring, offers it to Athena and says, "Athena, I thee wed, through sickness and health, forevermore."

Athena gazes lovingly at Allen. "I, Athena Dranias, take you, Allen King, to be my lawful wedded husband until death do us part."

Allen laughs. "I think we're messing up the sacred vows," Athena says, giggling. "This is so magical, but I can't wait until we get married with our family by our side."

Allen whispers, "I think we should have two weddings. We should get married here after we're officially married as King and Queen in Atlantis."

Athena squeezes Allen tight and says, "I love that idea. I'll have the Athena Dranias socialite wedding here. My closest friends will come, and my dog Lesbos will be the ring bearer."

Allen laughs. "That sounds like a reality show of a fairytale wedding."

Athena immediately acts like a bridezilla in the making. "Of course, darling, I'm Athena Dranias. I wouldn't have it any other way." She giggles. "You know I'm joking. I only want my supporters, the people who've supported my charities, and our family and friends. It'll be our decoy wedding. The superhero royals will be privately married in Atlantis, and the debonair socialite couple will be married here, with the world watching us. I love it! I should be my own publicist."

"You're my everything, Athena. I can't wait to marry you and finally make love... you'll be a great mother one day," replies Allen, beaming with joy.

Athena smiles. "I agree, we promised not to have sex until we're married... and once we graduate from college, we'll have a little Allen King Prince Charming running around playing with Princess Athena King. We'll go on sunset strolls, ride the dolphins, and take them to the Underwater Tree of Life and the Waterball Games. It'll be so perfect my Prince!"

"It will happen, my Princess."

The star-crossed lovers relax in the grotto, gazing at the stars above.

"I wonder how far planet Zion West is from here. Is it a billion or maybe a trillion light-years away?" asks Allen.

Athena replies with reassurance. "One day, you'll have the honor of meeting your Alien ancestors. I'm sure they're looking forward to seeing you and having contact once again with the people they created to make this world a better place."

"After I ate the fruit from the Underwater Tree of Life, I could see and feel the harmony the Aliens experienced in the creation of the Atlantean race. And now the Atlantean race will be mixed with Greek blood through you."

Athena teases. "The children will have their intellect from me and their brawn from you."

Allen snickers. "Hey now, we Atlanteans are pretty smart. My alien ancestors left immense knowledge for mortals to learn from in Africa, especially in South Africa and Egypt. I know where the sacred Atlantean tablets are in a hidden chamber beneath the Great Pyramid of Giza." Allen suddenly becomes serious and says, "I hope when summer comes, we'll be able to defeat the Hybrid Reptilian and the Gargoyles."

Athena places Allen's ring back on his finger. "You, Allen King, were built for this. You are the most sensitive strong man I've ever met. You have the perfect balance in your heart. You would make a perfect president for the whole world if every person on this Earth knew what I know. You, Allen King, are all love."

Allen kisses Athena and says, "Thank you, sweetheart. When you were under that Hybrid's spell, the thought of losing you made me feel like I didn't want to live. I never asked you… how did he disguise himself?"

Athena feels nauseated. "I don't want to think about him. You didn't see him at Tyrone's memorial?"

Allen shakes his head. "No."

Athena explains, "He looked like a normal human being. His skin was the same color as mine, not that eerie pale color. He had crystal blue eyes, close to the speck of blue color in your gorgeous eyes. He had dark hair and smiled like a Hollywood hunk. I don't ever want to think about it. Our foe makes me so angry… he almost killed me and you at the same time."

Allen grinds his teeth and says, "I will have my revenge when the time is right. I wish I could track him down right now and feed him to Bucky.

His day will come... maybe Destroyer will come through him instead of Josh. I would love to see the Gargoyle turn into a cannibal and eat himself."

Athena smiles menacingly. "We can only wish... Hey, changing the subject... When we were on the yacht earlier, I noticed Josh had a tattoo of an Indian and that Gargoyle beast on his arm. I vaguely remember seeing it in the school's parking lot when you first mentioned he had a new tattoo, but I didn't realize it was the beast that killed Tyrone."

Allen replies with uncertainty, "He sort of explained it as a way for him to conquer his demons through ancient Nomadic Indian traditions, by helping him get rid of the monster."

"I hope whatever Josh does, it will help him," says Athena. "Let's go inside... It's getting a little chilly out here..."

They take a shower and lie in Allen's bed wearing matching T-shirts and boxers. They gaze at the stars through the open ceiling, and quickly fall asleep.

Allen dreams of his royal wedding to Athena in Atlantis. Athena is dressed in a white Greek Goddess silk dress with a long train. She approaches two infantrymen who open the tall golden doors into the King's Chamber. Two Atlantean generals facing each other on either side of the doorway salute the soon to be Queen by holding their golden spears high and touching the tips to reflect the Atlantean pyramid symbolically. As Athena walks through the door, the generals lower their weapons and perform the warrior's salute, pounding their fists against their chests three times. The generals proudly announce, "Hail Atlantis! Hail Athena! The soon-to-be Queen of Atlantis!" The two infantry warriors blow golden seashell horns.

After Athena's introduction, she continues walking along the royal red carpet into the King's Chamber toward the throne, where her King awaits her arrival. The royal court and guests inside the chamber are listening to the beating of African Zulu drums, the strumming of Spanish harps, and the singing of Mediterranean flutes as Athena walks gracefully through the crowd of people who will soon be her devoted subjects.

Plato and Zadok I catch up on old times while watching from a cloud above. Zeus and the Elders from Zion West City watch from inside the chamber. The Gods and Alien Elders have come together for the grand occasion to celebrate the most splendid royal wedding in the history of the universe. Athena's white butterflies sprinkle magical rose petals on the red carpet in front of her, which makes her appear to be floating toward the throne. Allen stands on the steps below the throne in his warrior's uniform without the golden headgear, spear, or shield. He wears his loincloth, golden shin guards, red robe, and all his imperial jewelry-golden ring, crystal necklace, crown, and bracelets. Allen is Adonis to Athena's Aphrodite.

Jumper, Dance II, and Checkers play in the water before the ceremony begins, while the spirits of Atlantean women dance and yell ancient Mediterranean and Zulu chants. The rhythmic beating of African tribal drums puts the beautiful Atlantean women in a trance.

Perseus Jr. escorts Athena up the golden stairs next to Allen. He kisses her Greek style on the cheeks, and says, "My beautiful daughter, I am proud of you. You look lovely wearing the Atlantean crystal necklace you inherited from Plato."

Athena smiles and says, "Thank you, father." She looks up at Plato beaming down at her from the cloud with delight. He winks proudly at her.

For the first time, Athena sheds a blue teardrop. The enchanting Greek Goddess stands next to Allen and the Atlantean ghost who is the spiritual advisor to King Zadok III and King Leon.

The advisor says, "Do you, Allen King, take Athena Dranias to love and cherish for all eternity through sickness, health, and prosperity until death do you part?"

Allen happily says, "I do."

The advisor looks at Athena and says, "Do you, Athena Dranias, take Allen King to love and cherish for all eternity through sickness, health, and prosperity until death do you part?"

"I do," replies Athena with love.

The advisor smiles at Allen and asks, "Do you have the ring?"

Uncle Zadok, standing upright on his new legs, wearing a warrior's uniform with his big potbelly sticking out. He hands Allen a stunning ring with a ten-carat diamond surrounded by blue, green, and yellow crystals, which create the illusion of a rainbow arch.

The advisor says to Allen, "Put the ring on Athena's finger and repeat after me: I, Allen King, take Athena Dranias to be my lawfully wedded wife here in Atlantis." Allen repeats the vows.

The advisor looks at Athena and says, "I, Athena Dranias, take Allen King to be my lawfully wedded husband here in Atlantis." Athena repeats the vows.

The spiritual advisor looks around and says, "Should anyone here present know of any reason that this couple should not be joined in holy matrimony, speak now or forever hold your peace."

Suddenly, Allen starts sweating and becomes tense. He's not in Atlantis. He's on the hot volcanic rock of planet Zion West and Drogan is the spiritual advisor. He grabs Athena and then turns into the Gargoyle Destroyer. The Gargoyle laughs as he stretches out his wings, and flies away with Athena. Allen screams from the fiery hell below yelling up to Athena as the royal court is being devoured by Destroyer's Gargoyle brothers.

Athena shakes Allen furiously trying to wake him up. He opens his eyes, gazes upon his girlfriend, and says, "My love, I shared a part of your dream… we were connected. I dreamt about our magical wedding in Atlantis, but after the vows were said, I woke up."

Allen jumps out of bed and walks to the window. He proclaims, "I'm going to kill Drogan, that Hybrid scumbag!"

Athena whispers, "Allen, don't think about it. It was only a dream… I wonder why I didn't see that part. I'm so happy I didn't… I can't stand that monster."

Allen nods. "I know. When summer comes, I'll be ready for him. This time he won't escape me. I'll personally take him to the island of Lesbos and watch the bull sharks and the great whites feed off his flesh."

"Please, for now, let it go. We'll return to Miami tomorrow. Let's rest today."

Allen nods. "Okay… Hey? I wonder if I was suspended from school. I never went to the principal's office."

Athena giggles. "Allen King, you say the funniest things when you get mad. One minute you want to kill Drogan, and the next you're worried about being suspended from high school. You're one of a kind." She kisses him on the cheek.

Allen blushes. "I guess I'm all over the place sometimes, aren't I?"

Athena whispers, "I love you just the way you are."

They fall back asleep with Athena lying in Allen's arms.

CHAPTER EIGHT

JOSH DISCOVERS THE PURPLE CRYSTAL

Josh checks his cell phone and sees an email from Detective Wringer with a photo of a cave painting. The email explains that the image was recently discovered in one of the caves in Detective Wringer's tribal village by a man who was searching for gold. The old-timer didn't find gold; he saw the painting of a gargoyle-like creature with a human face that resembles Josh's face, painted in blood.

The Detective wants Josh to meet him after school to investigate the painting together. Josh is completely freaked out and writes back. *I want to meet you NOW!*

Detective Wringer replies, *Okay, the reservation is south of Miami, near the Everglades.*

When Josh drives up to the entrance of the reservation, he sees the Detective leaning against his car with his arms crossed. His massive biceps are on display, and he has a toothpick dangling from his mouth.

The Detective greets Josh with a stern look. "I never thought I'd see anything like that painting. Even the Elders were surprised."

Josh says, "The photo looked pretty bizarre."

"It sure does, son," replies Detective Wringer.

Josh asks, "Why do you think there's a painting of a Gargoyle with a head that looks like me?"

Detective Wringer shrugs. "I'm baffled, Josh. I hate to bother you with this. You're only a teenager, and you deserve to live like one. But we both know that you have other things you have to live with and face."

The Detective shows Josh where to park. They get in the Detective's car and drive into the reservation. After a few miles driving in silence, Detective Wringer says, "I promise you. I'm going to help you figure this out. How do you feel after practicing the ancient Indian chants I taught you? And, has the tattoo helped at all?"

"It felt weird at first to have a gargoyle tattooed on my arm. But if it's going to be one of the ways for me to defeat this monster, then I'm fine with it."

Detective Wringer says, "To get to where the cave is located, we'll have to take an airboat."

Josh mumbles with a shaky voice, "Are airboats safe?"

Detective Wringer nods with assurance. "Sure, they are. A big strong football player like you has nothing to worry about. Just stay in it. Don't worry, none of the gators are going to grab you from the water and pull you in."

Startled, Josh says, "Okay. I'm going to play for The Gators. I don't want to get eaten by one."

Detective Wringer laughs out loud. "Now that's funny."

They finally come to a stop at the edge of the marshlands where the old-timer who found the painting meets them. Detective Wringer talks to him in their native tongue. The old-timer smiles displaying his brown teeth. Three are missing on top and one on the bottom. He gestures for them to hop onto the boat. Josh gets on and straps himself in the chair. He sees a snake swimming by.

Detective Wringer smirks like it's not a big deal. "Cottonmouth… they're all around these parts, but hey, no gators yet."

Josh whispers to himself, "What did I get myself into?"

The airboat flies over grass, water, and some land. The old-timer drives them to an open area where Josh notices an island with a cave at the base of a small mountain.

Detective Wringer says, with his toothpick hanging out of his mouth, "There it is, Josh."

A stalactite hanging in the cave's entrance makes the cave look like a gargoyle's colossal open mouth waiting to devour unsuspecting passers-by. The old-timer flies the hovercraft onto the edge of the island.

Detective Wringer says to him in their native tongue, "We will be back as soon as we possibly can."

The old-timer replies, "No worries, young shaman. I'll be here."

Detective Wringer has a couple of miner's helmets with flashlights on them; he puts one on his head and one on Josh's head and gives Josh a handheld flashlight. They slowly and cautiously enter the cave. Josh observes cave paintings on the walls drawn in white chalk of Indians hunting deer and buffalo with bows and arrows. They make their way to a rickety open elevator and get in. It lowers them into an old mining shaft, where they must crawl through a narrow tunnel.

A few moments later, Detective Wringer yells with excitement, "We're almost there!"

They continue crawling until they enter a huge open area inside the cave. Detective Wringer grabs two flares in his back pocket and lights them up. The whitish glare illuminates the space. Josh aims his flashlight at the walls and suddenly freezes. He stares at the huge mural of his face attached to the body of a Gargoyle. He trembles, not knowing what to make of it.

The Detective says, "You see the Gargoyle's clawed hands pointing over there?" He throws a flare to the other side of the cave. A small hole glows with a purple light. They walk toward the light, which begins to grow brighter.

Josh says, "I know what it is." His eyes turn purple.

Detective Wringer says, "It's the crystal that'll take you to the Gargoyle World, isn't it?"

Josh nods. "Yes."

Detective Wringer sighs. "I'm feeling a little apprehensive. It might not be such a good idea for you to put it on. You have to learn the Nomadic Indian chants so you can fight the Gargoyle in the spiritual plane as a warrior. If you go to his world, there's no telling what this thing will do to you or what he'll do if he attempts to come here."

"You're right, Detective. I don't want it. You keep it in your possession until the time is right this summer. Maybe this purple crystal necklace will give me the strength to beat the Gargoyle when the next full moon comes and brings out the rage in me."

Detective Wringer says encouragingly, "Josh, you're a star quarterback who has to make precise decisions in a split second when you're in the pocket. I have no doubt you will do the same when you learn the chants. You will beat this monster. I don't want to see your mother and girlfriend bowing down to this beast. He would have to kill me first before I see him harm your mother… or anyone for that matter."

Josh replies, "I agree. I wonder why there's an image of my face on the Gargoyle."

Detective Wringer says with pride, "You know I'm a shaman. I believe you were reincarnated. At one time, centuries ago, you had this beast inside of you. I wonder who drew the picture back then."

They search around and discover behind the crystal necklace a golden box covered with rocks.

"Well look at that," exclaims Detective Wringer.

The lid of the golden box has an etching of a blue dolphin on top of a pyramid that looks similar to the all-seeing eye on the American dollar bill. Under the image, inscribed in gold letters, is the name Navian. An ancient scroll written in the Nomadic Indian language sits inside the box.

Josh is ecstatic. "I'm related to this man. He lived among the Atlanteans, and he was half-Reptilian and half-Nomadic Indian!"

Baffled, Detective Wringer says, "Let me read this, I can interpret the writings on this tiny papyrus scroll. The diary is well preserved. Navian talks about how he longed for his love Ahana, the daughter of the Nomadic Indian Chief. He can't wait to see her once he can get away from the city in Atlantis. "The Atlanteans are good people and loyal friends to me, but I belong here with the Nomadic Indians and Ahana. I must stay close to the city. I sense something dreadful may happen with the evil Damius, the Hybrid Reptilian who despises the Atlanteans.

He has tried several times to start a revolt against them. Each time, I talked the other Hybrid Reptilians down who were afraid of Damius. I'm not afraid of him. I want harmony between all of us, Hybrids, Reptilians, Nomadic Indians, and Atlanteans. The only thing that keeps me strong is my love for Ahana. I'm forever grateful for the officer who risked his life to take me on his whale to visit Ahana anytime he could before the rage of the Indians unites through the Gargoyles. I guess when I saved his wife who was choking on a grape, he felt indebted to me. It wouldn't have mattered even if I were not in love with Ahana. I am happy for the officer's love. Ever since I came to visit Ahana. I've seen many visions of a Gargoyle coming centuries from now, one who is more powerful than anything the Atlanteans or Nomadic Indians have ever had to deal with. I hope this Gargoyle doesn't come from my loins. I've had visions telling me that this could happen. I used my own blood through the visions. This is what I've drawn on the cave wall.

The greatest Gargoyle and potential threat the Atlanteans and possibly the Earth will ever know… I hope I'm wrong. I also have visions… If this Gargoyle does come through my blood, he'll have the good in me so he may conquer the beast before he devours his soul and destroy the Earth. I've taken the purple crystal shaped like lava from Damius's living quarters in the Atlantean kingdom. The precious stone comes from the volcanic mountain where the Gargoyles live on planet Zion West. I overheard Damius talking to the Gargoyles through the crystal. They have been manipulating Damius to control the Hybrids and Reptilians living in Pyramid City. They have been plotting to take over the kingdom. If the plan doesn't work. Damius was given instructions to destroy the empire by any means necessary. I hope whoever's worthy of holding the lava crystal has the strength to fight the rage that boils in your blood. I hope it will save your soul and the Earth's if the Nomadic Indian who turns into the Gargoyle on the wall is from my loins. You'll be a true hero by helping other brave men and women fight to keep the world safe from destruction. If anyone reads this before I die, please give my love and regards to Ahana. I must do whatever it takes to keep Atlantis safe from Damius. I wish there will never be another evil Hybrid Reptilian on Earth like this one. If he possesses the Gargoyle spirit in him, we will indeed be doomed. These are the words of Navian, loyal servant of King Zadok III.'" Detective Wringer rolls up the scroll, and says, "That's it."

Josh says with awe, "Wow! That was one of my great-grandfathers."

Detective Wringer replies, "He was part of a great civilization… right here it talks about Atlantis! This isn't like some science fiction movie. This is the real thing! Now everyone will believe me. I have all the proof I need right here to show the world that there is a lost city called Atlantis. I'm sorry, Josh… It's not up to me to share this knowledge."

Detective Wringer hands the scroll to Josh with the purple crystal. "As much as I would like to be a star on the evening news, something like this is best to keep secret. This is yours, Josh. Your forefather saw you as the savior or destroyer of this world. Whatever you do, it's your decision."

"Detective Wringer, I'll practice the chants and get it right, and I will fight the monster, as you did."

Detective Wringer says with pride, "That's mighty brave of you, but you have the key right here - the crystal necklace. With it, you can demolish the Gargoyle who took over your body. He almost killed your girlfriend."

"That's why I want to try it your way, and if it doesn't work, I'll try this way," says Josh.

Detective Wringer replies, "I still feel a little uncertain. We don't know if you'll get another shot at it if you try it both ways."

Josh nods. "I understand what must be done. I'll do whatever it takes to keep Destroyer from entering me or anyone else. I have to kill him or myself along with him."

Detective Wringer looks at Josh with awe. "You're a courageous young man. I'm proud to call you one of our own. I just want to see you make it through this summer and go back to your life as a soon to be college football star." The Detective asks modestly, "Do you think I could have season seats to your Gator games? Even though I'm a Miami Hurricane alum, I would be proud to see you play in our great state of Florida."

"Detective Wringer, you'll have VIP sideline passes… for the Dolphin games as well," says Josh with love.

Detective Wringer smiles happily. "I would feel so proud yelling, 'Josh Stone is a part of my tribe.' I'm just kidding, but I would love to see you play."

They crawl back into the elevator and pull themselves up. The old-timer is waiting for them. He caught two baby gators to pass the time. The gators' mouths and feet are bound; Josh is no longer afraid of them.

Detective Wringer cheerfully says, "I think this is a lucky sign for you."

Josh displays a courageous smile. "I hope so, I really do."

An hour later, they're back at the front entrance of the reservation. The two shake hands and part ways. Detective Wringer yells at Josh before Josh drives away. "Remember your Nomadic Indian chants before summertime!"

Josh nods his head and throws a thumbs-up as he peels out onto the road.

CHAPTER NINE

JAKE'S THE BABY DADDY?

Allen and Athena teleport to the backyard of the mansion in Miami. Zadok shouts from the balcony of his bedroom, "I see the soon-to-be royal couple is back. How's everyone feeling today!?"

Allen looks up at Zadok. "We're great, Unc. How are you?"

Zadok does the warrior's salute and replies, "I'm fine, my warrior nephew. I'm happy to see you two together."

Zadok looks at Athena and says, "I have something for you." He throws down a little cardboard box containing an antidote he created from Athena's blood sample at the hospital, courtesy of Nurse Aluna. Zadok says, getting straight to the point, "I'm not taking any chances with you, my niece. You're like a daughter to me. I will not see that repulsive Hybrid beast take control of you again."

Athena blushes and says, "Thank you."

Zadok becomes serious. "There's an alcohol swab and bandage in the box. I want Allen to inject it into you right now."

Allen protests, "Uncle Zadok, we just returned home from Australia."

"I don't care. Athena, please take the antidote now. There aren't any side effects, I promise you. I can't bear to think about what happened to you and Allen ever again… If it does, there will be no Atlantis. So please do it for me."

Allen and Athena both say, "Okay, Uncle Zadok."

Allen looks at Athena and whispers, "Are you sure you're all right with this?"

Athena sighs and says in a soft voice, "I have to take the antidote. Uncle Zadok's right. We can't take any chances with Drogan. His evil ways almost destroyed us."

"I understand," Allen says as he wipes Athena's arm with the alcohol swab and injects the antidote. He puts a Band-Aid over the puncture and kisses it. "You'll be fine, sweetheart."

Athena blushes and whispers, "I will as long as I'm with you."

They walk into the mansion and see Francisco and Jake hanging out with Becky Honeycomb.

Jake nods at them and escorts Becky to his bedroom.

Allen looks quizzically at Francisco, who says, "She's helping him with his algebra. So… how're you two feeling today after your little trip to Australia?"

Allen smirks and says, "We're feeling great, thank you. How was school today?"

Francisco replies, "It was fine. I don't think you were in trouble with Mrs. Ramirez."

"How do you know?"

"Because I ran into Josh and Mercedes at lunch, and Josh told me to tell you that he spoke to Mrs. Ramirez about you two fighting and that she didn't say anything to the principal. She knew there had to be something awful going on for you to act that way. She said she'd never seen you so angry, and that she was happy to know that Josh was willing to stick up for you and apologize for the disruptive behavior. Everything's fine, but she did ask Josh why you weren't in school today, and Josh told her that you were sick."

Allen sighs. "That's a relief. It's very cool of Josh to vouch for me. I owe him one."

Athena smiles and says, "I'm happy to know that Josh has your back."

Francisco nods enthusiastically. "So am I. It's crazy how we all get along now! Last year, I wanted to smash Josh's head into the lockers, and now we all act like we've been friends for years. Crazy how life changes in the blink of an eye."

"You're right about that," says Allen.

Upstairs in Jake's bedroom, Jake and Becky are sitting on his bed surrounded by backpacks and schoolbooks. Jake points to a page in his algebra book and asks, "You're going to show me how this formula works?"

Becky winks and nods. "Yeah, it's easy." She grabs a pencil and a piece of paper out of her backpack and writes out the answer to the algebraic equation as he gazes at her legs.

As Becky explains the formula for Jake, she notices him looking her up and down. She stops, smiles at Jake with her attractive straight teeth and seductive green eyes. "Jake, I'm here to help you with your homework, and you're staring at me as if I were an ice cream sandwich. You have a girlfriend."

Jake displays a devilish grin. "I know, but we aren't married, and I really like you." He moves her backpack and scoots closer to her. He puckers up and moves in for a kiss.

Becky suddenly slams Jake on the bed and climbs on top of him. She whispers, "You like it rough, bad boy?" She slaps him hard in the face.

Jake's in shock and gives Becky a befuddled glance as she kisses him passionately. He surrenders, letting Becky take control.

She whispers in his ear, causing Jake to shiver. She laughs and coos, "Jakey, you have a condom?"

Jake's eyes instantly bulge. He stutters, "Uh... no... I... I don't, Becky."

She replies sounding naughty, "It's okay... we'll pretend that you have one." She takes off her top as Jake quickly takes off his clothes.

After they make love, Jake mumbles, "I'm sorry, Becky. We shouldn't have done this. I'll get an Uber to take you home."

Becky smiles and says, "It's okay, Jake. We'll just pretend nothing ever happened... Okay?"

Upset with himself, Jake nods and mutters, "Okay."

Jake walks Becky outside and sees the Uber driver waiting in front of the gate. The guards open the gate, Becky gets in the car and waves goodbye. Jake cringes a little, hoping she really won't say anything to anyone. He realizes that he really likes Samantha.

When Jake was an orphan, he never thought twice about being with a girl if he had the chance. In the past, he never thought about the consequences, but this time he feels angry at himself for having unprotected sex.

Jake thinks. *How can I fight Gargoyles with my superhero pals if I'm receiving phone calls in the middle of the battle from Becky yelling at me over the sounds of a screaming baby, 'You need to go to the store right now and get some diapers and a bottle of milk! Little Jake needs his daddy!' I'm not ready to be a daddy yet. I love fighting monsters and going on cruises with my family. I want to graduate college and open the new Your Last Resort restaurant bar.*

Jake runs back upstairs to his bedroom, looks in the mirror and says to himself, "I can't screw my life up. Becky's a great girl, but friends are all we're ever going to be. No one saw us… I'm not even telling the guys what I did."

Jake jumps in the shower and washes away his lies and guilt. He looks at his penis and says, "Why do you want to get me in trouble, dude?" He gets out of the shower and puts on the shorts and shirt Samantha bought him. He looks at himself in the mirror again and says, "You have a wonderful thing going, Jake, don't screw it up."

Zadok's voice blasts through the intercom: "It's dinnertime… let's eat ya'll!"

Jake forgets about the incident with Becky, runs to the staircase and slides down the banister, feeling gigolo cool. He bops into the dining room smiling and whistling a made-up tune.

Francisco is already sitting at the dining room table, calmly observes Jake and asks, "How did your study go with Becky?"

Jake replies with a grin, "It went rather well."

Francisco stares at him suspiciously.

Allen and Athena walk downstairs to the dining room, and Zadok asks, "How is my beautiful family doing today?"

Jake replies, "We're good, Uncle Zadok. I'm happy to see my brother and sis are happy again."

"Aren't we all," replies Zadok.

He looks at Athena and asks, "How is your arm feeling, honey?"

She touches it gently. "I'll be fine, Uncle Zadok. Thank you again for the antidote."

Francisco heaps creamed corn on his plate with his steak and baked potato and asks, "Uncle Zadok made an antidote for Athena, so that she won't be susceptible to that devil's love potion anymore?"

Allen winks and says with delight, "He sure did." Allen gazes into Athena's alluring eyes and kisses her.

Francisco grinds his teeth and says, "I swear I hope to see that swine before anyone else at this table does so that I can—"

"Alright, alright, family!" yells Uncle Zadok, interrupting Francisco in the middle of his thought, "It's my fault for mentioning that thing. We need to relax and enjoy this wonderful meal of steak, lobster, and chicken kebabs."

Jake says with passion, "I love the surf and turf, Uncle Zadok."

Francisco laughs, takes a big bite of steak, and with a full mouth sputters, "You love it as much as Becky Honeycomb?"

Everyone at the table says, "Oooo!"

Feeling embarrassed, Jake yells, "Shut up! We're just friends!"

Aoki looks at Jake. "You're not two-timing Samantha, are you?"

Jake scratches his neck and opens his shirt collar like he needs air. The room is getting too hot for him. Jake stammers, "Of course… of course not, Aunt Aoki. I really like Samantha." Jake turns red.

The family continues looking at Jake while he tries as hard as he can to keep a poker face. They say, one after another, "Jake, we all know you, and you can't bluff us."

Aoki says in a joking manner, "We're together every day. I even know if you lie about not putting the downstairs toilet seat back down after you use it."

Jake caves in and says, "Okay, we just kissed, and that's it! I feel bad for even doing that."

Aoki says with love, "All right, Jake, we're not going to gang up on you, honey. Please, for your sake, be faithful to one of these girls. You don't want to break any hearts, including your own."

Jake says with a smile, "Got it, Aunt Aoki."

Zadok says, as he takes a bite of lobster, "I have to confess, this is by far one of the best dinners I've ever created. I marinated the lobster in my special butter sauce, herbs and spices."

"It sure is, Uncle," says Allen, after taking a bite of lobster.

Francisco can't keep his eyes off his plate. He eats and talks with his face down in his meal. "Unc, you're going to have the best restaurant ever created."

Zadok replies with enthusiasm, "Speaking of restaurant, I have some great ideas, Athena - Zadok's Soul Kitchen in Australia..."

"Okay, whenever you're ready, Uncle Zadok. I'll have my publicist and architects help you start your restaurant whenever your heart desires," says Athena.

Zadok bows his head. "Arigato, niece." Out of nowhere, he produces a papyrus scroll.

With a flourish, Zadok unrolls the scroll the length of the table, revealing his recipes and drawings of plans for the interior of his restaurant.

Athena is ecstatic. "Wow, Uncle Zadok, I see you put some work into this."

"If you're going to do something, you do it with pride all the way," replies Zadok.

Athena picks it up. "You have really great ideas. I don't think you need anyone telling you how to design your restaurant."

Zadok graciously replies, "Once you have the time, I would like to talk to your publicist and architect, so that we can get started."

Athena winks. "Right after dinner, I'll call my publicist, Nicole. She'll have everything started for you in no time."

"Yeah baby! Uncle Zadok's soul food is coming to a restaurant near you!" shouts Francisco.

The family applauds, and Francisco says, "I want to help you out, Uncle Zadok... when you're ready to open."

Jake chimes in: "And the same goes for me. When I buy out the Your Last Resort bar after I graduate college, we could serve some of your popular recipes there!"

Zadok grins gaily. "I like your idea, Jake. That sounds great to me, nephew."

Allen's happy and proud. "You see, great things come about in this family when we put our minds together."

The next morning, the teens drive to school together in Allen's repaired Range Rover. Allen pulls into the parking lot and notices several Goth girls and guys wearing T-shirts with "Glam Girl Warrior Princess" printed on them.

Allen telepathically says to the ASB as they stroll to their lockers, *They love us, don't they?*

They hear one of the Goth girls say to her friends, "We really miss the Teen Warriors. We don't know anything about them. No one has ever interviewed them."

Allen telepathically says, *You know, she's right.*

Athena replies telepathically, *I don't think we should. We're here to help save the world from destruction. We don't want to inadvertently encourage anyone to hurt innocent people to trick us into revealing ourselves. We have to concentrate on the real task at hand... preparing for Destroyer.*

You know, as much I would love to, you're right, Athena. We have to be safe and only show ourselves when needed, transmits Francisco.

Allen nods and says out loud, "I agree, it was just a thought."

The teens approach their lockers. As Jake opens his, Becky Honeycomb appears out of nowhere. She greets him with a friendly smile. "Hi, Jakey, how are you?"

Jake is startled by Becky's boldness. He stutters, "Uh... hi... uh... Hell-hi, Becky." Then he lowers his voice and says, "I thought we were going to be cool and not let anyone know about us."

Becky smiles naughtily and says, "What are you talking about, handsome? I just wanted to say hi to you, that's all."

Jake says abruptly, "Okay, I heard you already. So, hi. I'm going to be late to my class."

"All right, Jakey. Bye," says Becky with a smirk as she walks away.

Francisco looks at Jake, and says telepathically, *You had sex with her, didn't you?*

Jake responds telepathically, *Leave it alone.*

Francisco says out loud, "You're my brother, but I don't want to be mixed up in this. You know how much I care about Suzy."

Jake replies in a cool manner. "Don't worry, Fran. I'll make sure Becky doesn't mess anything up. I apologize for my screw-up."

Francisco says, "Good. I know we say Wonder Twins and all, but I really like Suzy, and she could be the one. Even though I didn't do anything, I don't want to be involved with your shenanigans... and I don't want to be caught up in your web of lies."

"Okay Francisco, agreed. Just chill and everything will continue like always with us."

Francisco mutters, "Fine, just as long as you know."

They walk to their separate classes.

Allen walks into his history class and Mrs. Ramirez says, "Good morning, Mr. King. I'm happy to see you back in class."

"Thank you, ma'am," says Allen.

As he sits down, he catches Josh's eye. They smile and nod at each other.

Athena telepathically says, *It's good to see everything is back to normal.*

Allen replies telepathically, *I feel so relieved. I'm happy Mrs. Ramirez didn't say anything to Principal Jenkins. I don't want to blemish my academic record. You never know, I might become valedictorian by the time I graduate.*

Athena smiles and says telepathically, *I agree, you most definitely could be, my prince.*

Allen transmits, *Thank you for the support. You'll be a sophomore in college and a queen when I graduate.*

Athena laughs telepathically and transmits, *And don't forget, socialite extraordinaire.*

How could I ever forget that? chuckles Allen.

During class, Josh sends Allen a note that says, *I need to talk to you briefly after class.* Allen nods his head, letting Josh know that it's okay.

Allen telepathically tells Athena, *I'm becoming more connected to Josh. He wants to talk to me after class.*

Athena transmits, *Your relationship with Josh is becoming very interesting. Please be cautious.*

Allen says, *Don't worry I will.*

CHAPTER TEN

FRANCISCO LOSES FAITH IN JAKE

After class, Allen and Josh hide in the bathroom to talk. Josh checks under the stalls to make sure they're alone, and when he's satisfied knowing that they are, he whispers, "I went to the Indian reservation yesterday with the detective who's a friend of my mother's. He found this." He shows Allen his cell phone photo of the Gargoyle with his face on it.

Allen is taken aback by the photo. "That's creepy. Did you find anything else?"

Josh shakes his head. "Yes, and there was an ancient scroll in another section of the cave with this." He shows Allen the purple crystal that can summon Destroyer. Allen tenses up when he sees the stone and thinks. *This isn't good if Josh attempts to bring the Gargoyle back to Earth.*

Josh says with confidence, "I'm going to defeat this monster as I prepare for my final battle. I hope to destroy the Gargoyle Destroyer. The Hybrid Reptilian that drew this Gargoyle with my face is one of my great-grandfathers who served under one of your great-grandfathers, Zadok III. His name was—"

"Navian," answers Allen. "I remember seeing him in one of my dreams. He was a great and loyal man to my family. He hated Damius, the grandfather of Drogan."

Josh nods and says, "Yes. It was all written in the scroll. It's so strange that I'm a part of your royal blood and a part of the royal servants' blood."

Allen puts his hands on Josh's shoulders as he declares, "You're here, for the same reasons as I am. I'm happy you've shared what you discovered regarding your other half. You're the perfect specimen. I hope when the time comes to retrieve the crown, we'll together bring Atlantis back."

Josh replies, "With all due respect, I'm happy right here being a football player, and I want to have a life playing professional football. I will still love it if I'm able to... maybe visit you from time to time if that's okay."

Allen says, "Yes, of course... Have you told your mother what you discovered in the cave?"

"No, not yet. I'll tell her later today, but I won't mention the mural. I'll tell her about the scroll Navian left. I'm not sure if I'll show her the crystal necklace. All my mother wants is for me to live a normal life. This crystal necklace will give me an upper hand on Destroyer. I'll be ready for the Gargoyle and Drogan."

"I thank you again for being at my side. We're family, and I pray we'll be victorious for Mother Earth."

The guys hear the bell and rush to their next class.

Later at lunch, Allen is talking to Athena when Francisco joins them. In a slightly irritated tone, he asks, "Hey, you two, either one of you seen Jake?"

"No," they both say.

A little worried, Athena asks, "Is everything all right?"

Francisco's anger rushes out as he explains, "No, it's not! I can't lie to you two... you're my brother and sister. Jake slept with Becky Honeycomb."

"He did what!?" shrieks Athena.

Francisco shushes her and then whispers, "Yes, and I have a feeling he got her pregnant. It's going to mess up everything with Suzy and me. I'm so disappointed in him. Everything he does affects me, especially when the twins are concerned."

Athena says calmly, "Maybe you're just overreacting. Maybe she's not pregnant. They were only together once from what we know."

Francisco grinds his teeth and says, "I know, sis. Nevertheless, girls like Becky Honeycomb, accidents happen. I bet she has super fertile eggs.

I was researching online about the percentage of teenage girls who get pregnant after the first time they have sex or even the second time for that matter."

Allen says in a soothing voice, "Francisco, just cool it for now. Jake's actions are not going to affect yours, okay."

Francisco sighs, still a little heated. "Yeah, maybe you're right. I'm just concerned that if this girl is pregnant, his mind may not be focused for this summer. If Jake's going to be a dad, it'll just be the three of us fighting the Gargoyle and who knows what kind of snake-headed monster Drogan may have crawling around in the grass."

"Don't worry, bro, we'll be fine. We also have Josh and Uncle Zadok even if he's in his wheelchair. The ASB is here to stay."

Francisco replies, "I hope so, Allen."

On the other side of the quad, they notice Jake talking to Becky Honeycomb, who is smiling and acting flirtatious.

Allen listens in on their conversation with his acute hearing.

He hears Becky say, "I'm sorry, Jake. I don't mean to bug you, but I can't wait to see you again."

Infatuated, Jake replies, "Neither can I."

Allen gasps and says, "Uh-oh!"

"Uh-oh what!?" asks Athena and Francisco out loud at the same time.

Allen says, "It appears that Jake is playing the field."

Francisco becomes upset. "That's it! I'm going over there, and I'm kicking his ass!"

Allen quickly grabs Francisco. "You have to calm down, dude, there's nothing we can do. Jake made his bed. He has to lie in it."

Francisco yells, "I'm going to bury him in it if he ruins it for Suzy and me! He's really pissing me off. If Jake wants to be that way, I will never forgive him for putting me in the middle of his predicament."

At that moment, Jake struts over to them and smiles, displaying his pearly whites. "How ya'll doing?" he asks with his Southern drawl.

Francisco replies with anger in his voice, "How are we doing!? You're playing with fire my friend, and I'm not going to join you by getting burned."

Jake shrugs. "Chill out, Fran. I'm just buttering her up to keep her cool so she won't stalk me all day, that's all, nothing more."

Francisco replies with sarcasm, "Well from where I stand, it looks like you've already done buttered her up, dude."

Jake says quietly, "Okay, Francisco, everything's going to be fine." He looks at Athena pleading for her acceptance. "Athena?"

The socialite looks at Jake. "Neither Allen nor I want to be involved in your love triangle. Jake, it would help if you stay focused on school, and this summer, help us search for the crown. And... what about your future goals for your restaurant? If you get involved with two girls, you're going to be working your whole life to pay child support, saying I could have done this and I could have done that."

Jake mumbles, "Okay... okay, sis. I get it. Everything's fine."

"I love you, bro, but please don't throw us under the bus with you," says Francisco.

"We're all here to help each other if you want it," says Allen. "We're teenage superheroes, not teenage superheroes and a father. That doesn't even sound cool. Jake the Teen Warrior, Superfather. You see that doesn't even belong in the same sentence."

"Alright, now cut it out! I'll see ya'll in PE," replies Jake.

Francisco spits out more insults as Jake runs to his locker. "Yeah, we'll see you with your *Teenage Baby Mama* doing jumping jacks!"

Allen whispers to Francisco, "Okay, Fran, please let it go."

Francisco replies, "I'm sorry, guys. I can't lie to Suzy if her sister suspects something's going on with Jake. Then I'm going to be screwed. This is one of the times I wish I weren't so close to him."

Later in the afternoon, Francisco walks into PE class, dreading another encounter with Jake. He sees Becky exercising next to Jake, who is smiling and looking back at his warrior family. Francisco can't bear to see Jake's face anymore. He jumps behind one of the big guys in their class, to block his view of Jake and Becky.

Allen telepathically says to Athena, "Maybe Francisco is right. Jake's acting like an ass."

"It's sickening to see a guy play with a girl's heart. I never thought Jake would act like that," agrees Athena.

Allen nods in reply.

After PE, in the locker room, Athena notices Becky grinning from ear to ear as she's getting dressed.

Audrey/Athena says, "Hi, Becky, I see things are heating up between you and Jake."

Becky replies with a smirk. "Hi, Audrey, I guess you can say that. Jake is the coolest guy ever."

"Ever, huh? You've been dating other guys as well?"

Becky shrugs and says, "Well… not really. You know, just a movie here and there. Audrey, may I ask you something?"

"Sure, anything."

Becky asks in a soft voice, "Does Jake like me?"

"I don't know. We never talked about you."

"Thanks for being honest with me. I was just wondering."

Audrey/Athena blurts out, "Becky, to be quite honest with you, it's none of my business what Jake does with his life. We all try to support each other, but I try not to pry into his affairs."

Becky nods. "Thanks, Audrey. I was just wondering."

Audrey/Athena says, "No problem." She exits the locker room and meets the ASB at Allen's Range Rover.

Jake telepathically tells the group that Becky is going to give him a ride home. Francisco wants to say something obnoxious, but Allen blocks him. Athena shakes her head in disbelief. "I'm beginning to think Becky used the same love spell potion on Jake as Drogan did on me."

Allen says to his team, "There's nothing we can do. If Jake likes this girl, we have to accept it."

Francisco feels defeated. "Okay, bro. I don't like it, but it is what it is."

Minutes later, Francisco receives a text from Suzy asking what he's doing then. He cheers up, and texts back: *I'm going to be at home doing homework for a bit.*

Suzy replies: *Do you mind if Samantha and I stop by to see you and Jake?*

Francisco texts back: *Let me find out what Jake's doing. He didn't drive back with us.*

Francisco texts back several minutes later: *Jake had to go to the dentist, I'll text you back when he's home, ok beautiful?*

Suzy replies: *Ok,* with a smiley face.

Francisco becomes angry. "You see, guys! I'm already lying for this jerk! I just told Suzy that Jake's going to the dentist! She wants to come over later with Samantha… Now what am I going to do? I have to reach Jake telepathically please, Allen."

"All right, but be reasonable with him. I'm not going to eavesdrop on your conversation," replies Allen.

Francisco says, "Thanks, Allen."

Francisco immediately reaches out to Jake. *Jake, can you hear me? It's Francisco.*

Breathing heavily, Jake answers telepathically, *Hey… Fran.* Francisco hears moaning.

C'mon, bro, you're going to blow this good thing you have with Samantha.

Jake blurts out, *No I'm not.*

Becky asks with confusion, "Huh? You're not what, sexy?"

He whispers, "Never mind, I was in the moment."

Jake telepathically brags, *As you can hear, Fran, I'm a little… busy.* Jake screams like he is about to erupt in a volcanic explosion of ecstasy, *Oh my gah!*

Francisco cuts the conversation off. *Oh well, there's nothing I can do. I'll work out whatever I can with Suzy.*

Minutes later, Jake telepathically responds to Francisco, *I'm sorry, Francisco, I think you heard… I was a little busy.*

Jake, the twins want to come to the mansion, and you're hanging out with the girl who just had her grill removed!

I'm down, bro. I'm going to be home in twenty minutes.

Francisco transmits, *I'm not covering for you anymore. I told Suzy you had to go to the dentist.*

Jake says, *Good work, Fran. I received a text from Samantha. I haven't replied yet, so that's what I'll tell her, that I went to the dentist.*

Francisco snarls, *I'm serious, bro. You put me in a bad position. I'll never forgive you if I lose Suzy covering for you.*

I understand… I'll behave, I promise, says Jake.

Francisco replies with bitterness, *Your promises aren't looking so good right now.*

CHAPTER ELEVEN

SPRING BREAK IN GREECE

Allen pulls into the driveway, parks and runs to the passenger side to open the door for Athena. He bows and says, "Milady."

Athena giggles. "Chivalry is not dead with you, babe."

Francisco mumbles, "It's going to be more than dead if Jake makes me look bad."

"Hey, Fran, we have your back. We'll hang out with you and the twins to keep the tension down," says Allen.

Francisco smiles. "Thanks, you guys. I owe you two."

Allen replies from the heart, "Don't worry about it, brother. That's what family is all about, right?"

They walk inside and find a note Zadok left for them on the fridge: *Aoki and I decided to visit her brother and mother for a couple of days in Japan. We'll see ya'll over the weekend. I made enough food to last all of you for a few days. If you run out, then go to the store or a restaurant.*

Love,

Aoki and Zadok.

Allen puts the note on the kitchen counter and says with pride, "I want to have the energy of that legless man when I'm his age."

Athena nods. "What will you do when I die of old age, and you're still looking as sexy as you are now? You'll be all alone..."

Allen gives Athena a big hug and a kiss. "I doubt you will ever die. You're a Greek Goddess… but if you die, I die." They both laugh.

Uncle Zadok cooked Kobe burgers, turkey hotdogs and an assortment of delicious side dishes labeled in ceramic food storage containers.

Jake walks in happily whistling, "Hello, beautiful family."

"Hey, how was your day, Mr. Jake? Was it peachy?" asks Allen.

Francisco rolls his eyes, takes a bite of the burger, and mutters, "Sour peach, I bet."

Athena gives Francisco a look that says, be nice.

Jake washes his hands in the kitchen sink, and Francisco says cynically, "Thank you for washing those hands. After hearing you through the crystals, I don't want any cooties on any food."

Jake teases, "Aw, Fran. Are you jealous?" He tries to kiss him on the cheeks.

"Come on, bro! Cut it out!" shouts Francisco.

Jake shouts, "Okay, Fran, just chill! I'm fine… see, my hands are clean… no cooties."

Francisco says, "Dude! The twins are coming by in a few hours."

Jake smiles and brags, "Alrighty then. I'll take a quick shower and be ready for round two."

Athena and Allen glare at Francisco ready to punch Jake.

"I was only joking guys, geez. I'm not talking to Becky anymore. We're done," says Jake as he smirks. He grabs a burger and bites half of it as he winks at Francisco.

Allen quickly intervenes. "Hey, cut it out, you guys!" Allen looks at Jake. "Bro, what are you doing? You have one of the hottest ladies in Miami… next to my girl, of course."

He winks at Athena. She flashes back and says, "Thank you, babe."

Allen says, "Jake, you're going to blow it with Samantha."

Jake shoots back, "No I'm not! I'm sorry, Becky is also a very hot-looking girl. She loves my pearly whites and my long, beautiful blond hair." He whips his hair around, boasting, "I'll give those male models on the romance novel covers a run for their money."

Athena wonders what kind of monster is being created before them. Allen covers his face with his hands feeling speechless.

He pleads. “Jake, please keep your focus on school… I need you this summer with the rest of us.”

Jake reacts nonchalantly. “Don’t worry; I’m still an Atlantean Superhero Baller. I’m all in and ready to fight.”

After they finish their meals, the teens go to their bedrooms to do homework. Athena finishes her studies easily. She’s totally focused, which makes studying very easy for her. She decides to flip through the journal she keeps regarding the many changes that need to be made at South Beach High. Athena sighs, pondering the improvements she could make. *They could have Wi-Fi in the cafeteria like they do in coffee shops. They need more organic foods instead of the processed corn dogs and soggy fries with all that salt.*

She thinks about having a taco stand designed as the cafeteria kitchen and different rows of conveyor belts showing what type of food, fruit and salads the teens could choose from during lunch. *The students could order lunch from their cell phones. This would make the long lines move faster, eventually giving the teens more lunchtime to socialize.*

Athena screams to herself. *That’s brilliant!* The socialite pats herself on the back. *You go, Aussie Greek girl. It may be a little cheeky for these Americans, but I love it!*

Athena hears a knock on her bedroom door.

“Hi, babe… are you busy?” asks Allen in a soft voice.

Athena shrugs and closes her journal. “No, just brainstorming ways to make our school cafeteria better. Next, I’ll think about what we can do to remodel those dreadful classrooms we sit in every day.”

Allen says with confidence, “I bet you could whip that place into shape.”

Athena brags, “And you know I will, bro.”

Allen grins and says, “Athena, you’re so silly.”

She happily replies, “I learned it from you... Allen, I’m a little worried about Jake and Francisco. They seem to have so much tension lately. Even more than when I was under the Hybrid’s spell.”

Allen sighs as he nods. “I know, they sometimes need some parental control. But I do love our independence and being able to do anything we want without an adult hovering over us every second. Don’t get me wrong, Uncle Zadok and Aunt Aoki have done a great job with us so far. The guys will eventually get it together.”

"You're right, but you forget, I've been emancipated for quite some time now," says Athena.

Allen acts dumbfounded, "Oh yeah, I forgot. I know I can count on you. It wouldn't be the same without Jake and Francisco living here though. I feel in my heart that we can depend on Josh."

Athena replies, "There's still a few months away before we go to Hawaii. I wish I never told you-know-who about going to Hawaii this summer."

Allen strokes Athena's hair. "I know, and there's nothing either one of us can do about that now. All we can do is what Uncle Zadok said, kick some Reptilian butt. We'll get through this, like we always have. I want to see our achievements with the guys."

Athena winks with a kiss. "And we will don't worry."

A few hours pass by, and Jake yells from the top of the stairs after hearing the doorbell ring, "I'll get it!" He dashes downstairs in his fruit-print swim trunks and orange tank top with fruit-print sneakers.

Samantha and Suzy say, "Hi." The stunning sisters walk in wearing matching pink bikinis.

Samantha jumps in Jake's arms. "Baby, I missed you!" she says in a high-pitched voice.

He replies with affection, "I missed you too, darling."

Francisco slides down the banister with his arms folded, looking like captain cool to impress Suzy.

She yells, "Ay, papacito!"

Francisco grins and says, "Look at my mamacita… learning Spanish. It's more like Spanglish, but hey, I love it!" Suzy leans in and gives Francisco a big kiss on her pink lips.

Allen and Athena join them. Athena is wearing a yellow and white striped bathing suit with matching shoes.

Suzy and Samantha gasp at Athena's outfit, and simultaneously ask, "Where did you get that outfit? I love it."

Athena models it for them, showing her attractive legs and flat tanned stomach. She brags, "Oh, this old thing, I got it at a fashion show in Milan last spring. It's one-of-a-kind."

The girls giggle like little kids as they skip out to the pool.

Francisco has forgotten about the tension with Jake. "I love you, guys. Don't worry, we'll be fine."

Jake smiles and says, "Yes, we will, my brother."

The guys lock arms together, and skip toward the pool, imitating their girlfriends.

"Okay, that's it," says Allen, snickering. He breaks out of the arm lock and grabs the guys in each arm like a football. He runs to the pool passing the girls, and shouts, "Excuse us! I have a few bros I need to cool off." He dives in the pool with his brothers.

Suzy gasps and says to Athena, "Wow, Allen's strong… and handsome!"

"Yeah, Athena, you're a lucky girl," seconds Samantha.

Athena says admiringly, "Aren't we all." She grabs the girls and shouts, "Come on!" They all scream and jump into the pool.

A few hours pass and everyone gets out of the pool, to grab water and sodas to drink.

The twins change into different clothes.

Athena looks at their outfits. "I'm getting inspiration from you ladies. Let's come up with some ideas and start a new line of swimsuits and accessories for next summer. The summer is almost upon us, and designers are already doing fashion shows. Next year, those designers aren't going to know what hit them. We'll knock their knickers off."

The girls laugh and drink their beverages. Allen whispers joyfully as he eats his food and drinks his soda, "You see that, guys? These are incredible, beautiful girls. We're not going to get any better than this, I tell you."

"I know you're right, bro. Samantha makes me feel like a million bucks. It's more like a billion. Hell, a trillion," replies Jake.

Allen says to Jake in an Australian accent, "Now that's the spirit, mate."

Francisco tries to up the ante and teases Jake. "You're a cheeky bloke sometimes, aye… but we still love you."

Jake replies, "Thanks, guys. I know I haven't been the easiest brother to get along with the last few weeks, but I'm back. No more Becky Honeycomb."

The impromptu pool party ends. Francisco and Jake escort the twins to their black Maserati. The girls kiss their guys good-bye.

A few weeks pass, and Jake has kept his word. He hasn't spoken to Becky Honeycomb since the last time he had sex with her.

Becky walks up to Jake at his locker and says, "Jake, may I talk to you for a moment?"

He feels annoyed. "It's finals, Becky, and I can't be late for my algebra test."

She whispers with urgency, "It'll only take a minute I promise."

Jake rolls his eyes and closes his locker. "What's going on? I really—"

"I'm pregnant!" Becky blurts out.

Jake yells, "What!?"

Becky whispers as she looked around to see if anyone else heard her spew out the dreaded word, "I'm sorry, Jake, but you're the only guy I've been with."

He stutters, "Uh… let's talk about it after school, okay?" Jake is devastated. Francisco and the rest of the family tried to warn him about the repercussions of his actions.

He didn't want to listen, and now this is the consequence. Jake goes through his day like a zombie. He takes his last final exam and tries to stay focused by not thinking about anything but his test. Spring break starts after his last class. Jake and the Teen Warriors are going to Greece. They'll stay at Athena's château in Santorini with the Star Island Twins.

Jake puts on his best poker face. He meets the ASB before they drive off in his jeep for home. Allen taps Jake on the shoulders, getting him pumped up for the big trip to Greece.

Jake fakes it by announcing, "You know it, amigo. I'm ready to fly in the Heavens with my senorita."

Athena stands up in the topless Jeep and screams, "You and Ms. Star Island Samantha are going to have the time of your lives, yeah!" They arrive home in a matter of minutes.

Uncle Zadok and Aoki plan on spending quality time together at home without any loud, noisy teens. He's prepared their picnic basket which is sitting on the dining room table for them.

He speaks to the teens on the Intercom while receiving a deep tissue back massage from Aoki. "Hey… ughh… kids… " Aoki digs her elbows deep into Zadok's lower back. "…have a good… ughh… time."

They yell back, "Thanks, we will." Their bags are already packed at the front door. All the teens have to do is put their duffle bags in the limo's trunk.

The Star Island Twins drive up to the mansion in Samantha's black Maserati.

Francisco and Jake grab the girls' bags and kiss them on the cheeks before hopping into the limo.

Francisco roars with excitement, "I can't wait to swim in the warm water."

Athena says, "The water is a little warmer now. The changing of the seasons has just begun. If we were there two weeks ago, you would have frozen your little ass off. I can't wait to take all of you to the hot springs in Santorni. It's invigorating. You'll feel like newborns, full of energy afterwards."

Francisco and Suzy say at once, "We can't wait."

Francisco looks at Suzy. "We're talking at the same time. I love you, mami."

She kisses him on the lips, whispering with passion, "Mi amor…"

They drive through the private entrance of the Miami International Airport. The limo parks by a red carpet that leads into Athena's G5. The teens step out and strut down the carpet into the plane.

They celebrate by opening a few bottles of specially made nonalcoholic champagne the twins created; they call it the Star Island Twins NA Champagne. The twins brought enough to last them throughout their vacation in Greece.

They joyously shout, "Cheers!" Everyone taps their champagne flutes before downing the expensive liquid.

Allen makes a toast, "To new memories and continued fun in the Greek sun."

Everyone screams, "Woohoo!"

Francisco says, "I have great music for the occasion. A cool group called The Party Boys remixed your song. Check this out." The twins gasp in amazement, as they listen to new music The Party Boys created.

The twins scream excitedly, "*Oh my gosh!* We love it!"

Samantha jumps in Jake's lap and kisses him.

"I think you have a hit," says Jake with a happy smile.

Samantha happily nods. "Yes, I believe so as well, handsome."

Suzy and Francisco dance in the aisle, jumping up and down with their hands in the air. Athena grabs Allen to dance while Samantha catches Jake who has two left feet. He dances, feeling cool anyway. Everyone's having a great time.

Suzy giggles and shrieks in delight - she's on top of the world flying on a G5 in pure bliss. "This is so incredible! I need to make these Party Boys our producers. The world will know all about them when we come back from Greece."

Athena nods in agreement. "They're outstanding."

Jake brags, "Just remember who put you on to them."

Francisco jumps next to Jake laughing and pointing at himself. He boasts, "Me."

Jake puts his arm around Francisco and proudly says, "Us."

They continue dancing until they work up a hunger. Everyone sits down as the stewardess prepares the meal Uncle Zadok made for them.

The stewardess announces, "Here's your meal, and I must say, whoever prepared it for you did an excellent job."

Athena nods with a friendly smile. "Thank you. Our Uncle Zadok made it for us. You're welcome to have some… and so are the pilots."

The stewardess replies gratefully, "Thank you very much. I can't wait to taste the lobster and delicious crab."

The teens start to eat their meal. Francisco acts sophisticated, putting his napkin under his chin. He raises his left eyebrow and asks, "Does anyone have any Grey Poupon?"

Everyone laughs at Francisco's earnestness.

Jake says, "Fran, cut it out before you make one of us choke on our food."

Francisco replies, "Seriously, bro. I want some mustard."

The stewardess hands Francisco the mustard. They finish eating, then watch one of Athena's all-time favorite movies starring Marilyn Monroe, *Some Like It Hot.*

Delighted, the Star Island Twins say at the same time, "I love this movie. Wasn't Marilyn so divine?"

Jake smiles and nods. "Yes, and she was fine as wine."

"Okay, guys. Let's watch this chick flick with the girls," says Allen making lighthearted fun of his girlfriend.

Athena hits him in the chest and whispers as the movie starts, "This is one of the best classic films ever made, Mr. Novice. I have a feeling you're going to love it"

"We shall see," says Allen as he sighs.

"I love Jack Lemon and Tony Curtis in drag. They were so funny and they pulled it off looking like women," says Francisco.

Jake teases. "You like the men dressed as girls?"

Francisco gives Jake a stern look and says, "Only in the movie."

Allen whispers loudly, "Hmm… it's not a boring movie after all."

Athena barks sarcastically, "Shhh! You're going to miss the best part."

Everyone watches quietly until the movie ends. The teens applaud and compliment Athena, "Great movie choice." Athena graciously takes a bow. "Thank you."

The couples sleep snuggling next to each other until the jet finally lands in Santorini, Greece. Athena's driver, Gianni meets them. Everyone smells the fresh spring air as Francisco asks, "Athena, will the weather get warmer?"

Athena replies, "Yes, we're in Thira at the beginning of spring… Around August and September, the weather is scorching hot and humid."

Jake asks, "Why did you say we're in Thira?"

Athena smiles and replies, "There's much history on this island. Thira was the original name until the Venetians conquered it and renamed the island Santorini. Later, I'll take you to Emporio village, where time seems to have stood still. We can also explore the castle on top of the hill there."

Allen hugs Athena and says, "That sounds really cool. I've never been in a castle before."

Athena kisses him and says, "Then we will explore it. I had an opportunity to buy the castle awhile back, but I decided to stay in the mansion my family left me. They lived in it for centuries… It's in the Caldera area."

Gianni grabs the bags as the group prepares to leave for Athena's villa. They all pile into the vintage white Rolls Royce limo.

Samantha gushes, "Athena, you exude style and grace."

"Yes, I agree… you're our favorite socialite," says Suzy.

Athena blushes. "Thanks, girls."

Francisco and Jake gaze out the window and see an old man leading a convoy of donkeys carrying loads of supplies on the narrow two-lane road. Cars, trucks and people on ATVs quickly drive around the old man and his asses.

Francisco whispers in awe, "This is a whole new world I never knew existed. It's a history book in real life."

Allen smiles and takes Athena's hand. "You said it, Francisco, there's nothing like this in Miami."

Jake nods his head. "I agree with all of you… and, as far as I know, there's nothing like this in Australia."

Gianni drives up a secluded narrow cobblestone road.

The teens ooh and ahh at the incredible views as they drive up the mountain in Oia. They marvel at the white caldera villas, hotels, and shops built into the cliffs next to and on top of each other. Samantha exclaims, "Santorini is out of this world. The cave villas standing out against the blue Aegean Sea appears magical, and the white churches with blue domes add to the scene."

Jake says, "You're right, what an amazing sight. I feel like we're in a living postcard."

Gianni replies with delight, "You have the best views in all of Greece. It's as if you're related to the Gods, who have given you the gift to see the islands on this beautiful clear day."

"Yes, it is. I need to come back more often to visit. I love my heritage and everything Greek," replies Athena.

Allen gently rubs Athena's hand. "I had no idea your homeland is just as beautiful as you are," he says in a soft voice.

She blushes and says, "Babe, stop being so sweet to me… you make me melt every time."

Allen says from the heart, "I can't help it. You are."

Gianni drives up to a massive white cast iron gate with a golden butterfly engraved in the middle. The butterfly wings appear to flicker, opening the gate.

The twins stare in awe, and Samantha says, "I love your gate with the enchanting golden butterfly. It's unique and gorgeous."

Athena smiles. "Thank you. I wanted it to feel magical when you approached the entrance. It makes me feel like I'm at home and in the presence of the Gods, embracing everything that's Greek."

Suzy yells, "Viva la Greece!"

The teens yell together, "Viva la Greece!"

Gianni parks at the front entrance. Athena and her guests are greeted by two male servants who bow as they say, "Kalimera,"

Athena replies to the servants. She explains to everyone, "Kalimera means good morning or good day."

The teens try to pronounce it the best they can, but Francisco says, "Good-day, sirs."

They enter the gorgeous ten-bedroom villa. The villa is similar to Athena's mansion in Sydney, but it's an older estate with more character to it, and the interior is distinct from any other home in Santorini. Painted on one wall of the foyer is a huge gold circle with Athena's initials inscribed in Greek letters in the center and a white dove holding an olive branch in its mouth under the initials, just like the one in Athena's mansion in Australia.

Jake and Samantha are amazed by the antique decor that dates back to ancient Greece. Athena leads them through a botanical garden similar to her compound in Sydney, and like the botanical garden in Sydney, butterflies are flying around. The butterflies land on Athena's arms and hair and flutter around her as if they're saying to her that they've missed her.

Suzy spontaneously shrieks, "I love this place!" and the startled butterflies fly away.

Athena whispers, "It's okay… but if you keep your energy down just a little, they'll fly back and land on your arms."

Suzy giggles, and whispers, "Okay. I'm sorry, Athena… I couldn't contain myself." Minutes later, the butterflies return and land on the girls' arms and hair. A few lands on the guys' shoulders and feet as they all continue strolling through the garden. They fly around Allen as if they know that he and Athena were made to be together. "The butterflies are giving us their blessings," says Athena in a soft voice.

The butterflies gather together and spell out with their bodies: *Welcome Home Athena and Friends.*

The twins are amazed, they gasp and ask at the same time, "How on Earth did the butterflies do that?"

Athena is surprised to see the butterflies write out a message; she knows it's from one of the Gods on Mount Olympus.

She telepathically says to Allen, *The Gods on Mount Olympus know that we are in Greece.*

She can feel and hear a butterfly's wings close to her ear, speaking through its wings as it starts to move unusually fast, creating a sound wave through vibration that transmits my voice: *Welcome home, my granddaughter. I cannot speak for the other Gods. I am excited to see you and your Atlantean boyfriend in Greece. Your Aunt Athena may have a few things to say about the young man you chose as a companion. Pay her no attention whenever she comes to visit you in your dreams.*

Athena smiles at the butterfly and then moves her lips without saying a word. I read what Athena is saying: *Thank you, grandmother. I am not afraid of my Aunt Athena anymore. I am no longer a child. I welcome her to speak to me anytime she likes.*

I reply cheerfully, *I'm happy to hear that you're not as stubborn as the last time I visited you in Australia. You are turning into a remarkable woman, and you are of course a Greek Goddess, thanks to Zeus. I will not show any more signs of my supernatural powers to your mortal friends. Welcome home.*

Athena mouths, "*Thank you,*" and gives a slight bow to her grandmother.

No one seems to notice that Athena is speaking to her grandmother through the butterfly and Allen isn't using his acute hearing.

Athena whispers in Allen's ear, "My grandmother, Andromeda, says it's a pleasure to have you visiting our sacred land."

Allen politely bows and says to me disguised as the purple-and-red butterfly, "Thank you."

I fly away as I lead the other butterflies back into the botanical garden. I transform into my body as I return quickly to Zeus' apartment in Athens, and I continue to watch on TV what happens to my granddaughter, the Atlantean and their friends.

Everyone strolls to the back of the mansion to gaze at the spectacular view. The young teens are high above sea level and can almost touch the clouds above their heads.

Jake says in awe, "This is so amazing. It feels like I'm in heaven."

The view down below appears as an optical illusion. They can still see the people sailing on boats and driving cars.

Athena announces, "Welcome to Plato's villa. There's a dining room table set up for us on the lawn. We'll sit, relax, and eat the traditional Greek dishes - Lentil soup, horiatiki salata, fasolada, lamb and bread." The teens applaud Athena's hospitality and compliment her chef for preparing the wonderful meal.

After lunch, Athena says, "Everyone should bring an overnight bag in case we stay on my yacht, which is docked at Ammoundi Port in Oia. Make sure you have a few other things to wear so we can be stylish for this evening... For now, we can chill and relax."

Everyone goes upstairs to their separate bedrooms to shower and change. After everyone is fashionably dressed, they are transported down to where everything is happening. Gianni drops them off on the docks in front of Athena's yacht, *Gods of Olympus*.

The captain will take them to the famous Red Beach. This particular weekend, a prominent European artist, who is Athena's good friend, has rented the entire beach for a festival. It's a trendy tourist spot where people go to sunbathe and party to hip-hop, electronica, and dance trance music.

The teens layout on trampoline nets to observe the beautiful people who are dressed like they're in Miami. The girls wear bikinis and the guys are shirtless and wearing swim shorts.

The twins yell at the same time, "I love it!"

"I feel like we are dressed too conservatively," declares Suzy.

Athena is between them with her arms around their waists as they bounce on the trampoline net. She says, "That's why we have our bags... so we can change into something more stunning for the world to see."

The twins giggle and shout at once, "I want to change now!"

The girls quickly go down below to change while Jake and Francisco dance at the stern of the two-hundred-foot yacht. Francisco proclaims while listening to the music playing on the boat's sound system, "This is heaven, bro! We can't get any better than this. We're the rock stars of Santorini Island."

The girls rush back on deck in their new outfits. The guys say at the same time, "We're going to be your bodyguards all day, beautiful ladies."

"We're fine, silly boys," says Athena, giggling. She points to her bodyguards on jet skis next to the boat. She's hired a new guard to take the place of the guard Destroyer killed in Josh's house. The bodyguards wear their beach uniforms - white tank tops, shorts, and boat shoes.

Allen smiles wide and says, "I love your surprises. You plan things well in advance."

Athena's golden-brown eyes gaze into Allen's blue-green eyes. "Thank you. I always have. Wait until you see the biggest surprise." The vessel anchors offshore in the Aegean Sea and Athena's bodyguards transport everyone to shore on their jet skis.

The teens hear people pointing and cheering, "Athena! Athena!" The socialite is well known around the world especially in Greece.

CHAPTER TWELVE

THE STAR ISLAND TWINS BECOME POPSTARS

The teens walk to the massive stage on Red Beach. They're in awe of the multitudes of gorgeous teenage girls and boys dancing and having fun. They notice the lounge chairs and cabanas with generators blowing AC to keep the partygoers cool and relaxed.

The Emcee says over the microphone, "Ladies and gentlemen, welcome Athena Dranias!"

Francisco remarks, "That voice sounds familiar."

The Emcee continues speaking: "And her guests: Allen, Jake, Francisco and the beautiful Star Island Twins, singers from South Beach Miami!"

The twins jump up and down screaming, "They're talking about us!"

Euphoric, Jake yells, "Look, Fran! It's The Party Boys!" Athena proudly says, "I flew the guys in for the weekend to DJ the festival."

The Party Boys play the Star Island Twins' song, "I'm All Yours Baby." Only they've created a mash-up by throwing in a bit of electronica dance trance and hip-hop. The twins rush on stage feeling the electricity of the crowd. They grab microphones and start singing their song. The spectators go wild. Francisco and Jake go crazy, jumping up and down while they watch the girls perform.

Francisco screams to Jake over the roar of the crowd, "Can you believe it, bro?! They're our girlfriends! We hit the lottery, baby!"

Jake screams back, "I know. I can't believe these girls picked us out of all the guys in the world... They love us!" Jake has forgotten all about Becky Honeycomb.

The girls finish their first song and give The Party Boys a wink as they dance off the stage and into the adoring arms of their boyfriends.

Two of the four Party Boys stop dancing and sneak behind the DJ booth, and then they pop up from behind the booth with water guns filled with liquid gold glitter which they spray out into the hot, sweaty crowd. The crowd begins chanting: "Star Island Twins, Star Island Twins, encore, encore!!!" The gang stares in astonishment at the crowd begging for more of the twin's music. The twins are happy and ready to oblige their new fans.

Suzy and Samantha hop back up on stage and grab the microphones again.

Teasing the crowd, Suzy asks, "Should we give them more, Samantha?"

The crowd chants, "We want more! We want more!"

Samantha replies, "Sure, why not."

They sing "Socialites in Miami," a rap song about the South Beach socialite lifestyle.

Francisco and Jake look at each other and yell together, "They can rap? Cool!"

Allen and Athena can't believe what they're seeing. Their jaws drop in astonishment. "Wow! The twins are going to be big stars when we return home to Miami," says Athena.

Allen kisses Athena and says, "Babe, I love you. Every time I think something you do is great; it only gets better."

Athena whispers, "Only for you, handsome. You have extraordinary powers and spend your time-saving people... and your athletic abilities are out of this world. This is the one thing I'm really good at. Planning things and making events memorable."

"Yes, you do. I know our wedding in Atlantis will be unforgettable!"

Beaming, Athena replies, "And the wedding we put on in Australia for the mortals will make Prince Harry and Meghan's wedding look boring and lackluster by comparison!"

Allen grins. "I can only imagine."

Athena grabs Allen by the waist and looks up at him. "Let's enjoy the moment we have right now, darling." They kiss and dance as the crowd goes crazy over the Star Island Twins. Suzy and Samantha bow graciously after they finish their setlists and bounce off the stage strutting back to their friends who are now sitting in the VIP section behind the DJ booth.

The twins never make it to the VIP section. Every step they take a new fan stops them for a selfie.

"This is unbelievable, guys. We're lucky we met these girls before the whole world knows about them," says Francisco.

Allen smiles. "I love what we are witnessing. This is the distraction we need to take our attention off being the Atlantean Superhero Ballers and having to save the world. We first need to get through high school."

Francisco says with a grand smile, "I think we have the most attractive girlfriends who ever walked the face of the Earth. I have to pinch myself sometimes to prove to myself that this dream is real." Jake pinches Francisco's butt.

"Ouch!" yells Francisco.

Jake laughs devilishly. "Is that pinch real enough for you, Fran? This is real all right. Nothing can get better than this."

The girls are done signing autographs and taking pictures. The bodyguards stop the line of people trying to see them. The teens have enjoyed themselves but are ready to go back to Athena's yacht for a little privacy.

Back on the boat, they notice a school of dolphins playing. The twins point and exclaim simultaneously, "Look at the dolphins, they are incredible."

Allen smiles and says, "They're one of the most majestic and loving creatures in this world."

Athena replies, "Let's swim with them." She takes off her sandals and dives into the crystal-clear blue water. Allen and the group follow Athena's lead. The dolphins play fondly with Allen, knowing that the Atlantean is one of their greatest friends. He swims with the largest dolphin, holding onto its fin as they swim together around the boat. Athena rides a dolphin for a moment before she slips off. She eventually manages to hold onto its fin and swim with Allen and his new friend. The others try to ride the dolphins but keep falling off.

Allen says, "This is how you ride." He jumps on his new friend's back and the dolphin dives underwater with Allen. Just moments later, they fly out of the water. Allen yells, "Yeehaw!" as if he were a rodeo cowboy.

The twins scream in awe and exclaim, "Look at Allen! He's riding on the dolphin. He's amazing!"

Athena rides by on her new dolphin friend and shouts, "My man is one of a kind!"

"Does anyone feel like racing?" Allen asks.

Everyone screams, "Yes!"

Allen says as he points, "Does everyone see that sailboat over there?" They all look at the sailboat.

"Let's do it," says Athena.

The dolphins with their riders line up six in a row.

Allen says, "On the count of three we race. Okay… one, two—"

"Three!" yells Athena laughing as she takes off on her dolphin. She jets ahead of everyone else following close behind.

"Okay, that's how you want to play it?" asks Allen, bumping his knees gently against his dolphin's side.

The sailboat they're racing to is two hundred yards away. Allen comes close to Francisco and Samantha who are a few feet ahead. Jake and Suzy catch up to Athena.

"Whee!" Athena shouts as she steers her dolphin to the right, blocking Jake and Suzy. Allen draws near Samantha and Francisco and waves hi and bye as he passes them grinning. Jake closes in on Athena who is still a few feet ahead. Allen passes Suzy as she gains on Jake.

Jake doesn't see Allen until Allen taps him on the shoulder. Allen gesturing with his hands. *"How you doin'?"*

Allen's dolphin is fast, like a missile in the water. The Atlantean and his dolphin approach their target: Athena. They're only a few inches away when Athena sees Allen gaining on her. The Greek Goddess smirks and splashes water on her boyfriend's face. "Not today, my love." She raises her hands up in victory as she flies past the boat.

Allen comes in second, Jake third, Suzy fourth, Samantha fifth and Francisco sixth. Everyone but Francisco shouts with glee. Francisco is a sore loser and mutters, "Yay, yippee! Fun for all of you, but I lost."

Suzy rides her dolphin up to Francisco and kisses him. "Feel better now, handsome?"

Francisco suddenly develops amnesia. "Yeah, that works for me, mamacita. What race?" Everyone laughs at Francisco's short tantrum.

The dolphins take the teens back to their boat. Athena and Allen hold each other's hands as they glide through the water. Athena confesses, "This is the best vacation ever. I don't want it to end."

Allen nods. "I agree, being in Santorini and riding on the dolphins is a dream within a dream of a dream."

Suzy and Samantha shout at once, "What can top this!"

Francisco and Jake proclaim, "This is the life, dude!" They cheer and laugh as they climb back on the yacht.

The dolphins sing and smile at their new friends one last time before swimming away.

Suzy says to Allen, "That was so cool. The dolphin's seemed to be talking to you."

"It's surreal," says Allen.

Athena declares, "This is something we will never forget… sharing this moment with the people we love."

The yacht takes the gang back to their limo. Athena's bodyguards ride on scooters, following them back to the villa. "What an eventful day, I am tired," says Samantha.

Jake nods. "Same here."

Francisco yawns, "Yeah, bro. I'll see everyone in the morning."

Everyone goes to their bedrooms.

Allen and Athena lie down on her bed, and she opens the ceiling.

"Wow, Athena… we can gaze at the stars in the bedroom just like your home in Australia. Thank you again for another wonderful time, my love."

Athena smiles. "You're welcome, handsome Prince. I'll never stop calling you that. I love how it rolls off my tongue, handsome Prince."

"What about handsome, battered and bruised King, after this summer?"

Athena cuddles next to Allen and whispers, "I doubt I'll ever see your well-built armor of a body damaged. You're as strong as steel."

Allen says from the heart, "I'm only as strong as the woman I love. Also, we as a group – the ASB… if one link of the chain is broken, we all fall apart."

"Allen, don't ever think like that. Are you having any doubts about this summer? Have your friends or I ever let you down?"

Allen kisses Athena's forehead. "Of course not. I don't have any doubt about any of us. We're a unique group of teenagers. We were made to be together, to fight monsters and keep the world safe from destruction and disorder… I'm a little worried about Josh. I hope he can conquer his inner demons before he has to fight real demons like Destroyer and his kind."

"We can't worry about Josh. He's a big boy. He can take care of himself. You're the only one I have to worry about… Francisco and Jake have strong wills, and they truly love you."

Allen nods. "I know, sweetheart."

"I don't know what would have happened if they weren't there to save me when Drogan tried to seduce me with his toxic poison… Allen, you stay strong for all of us, okay. We're here for you."

Allen smiles a little. "Thank you, Athena. I trust you with all my heart and soul. You know me better than I know myself."

Athena gazes into his alluring eyes. "I will always be here by your side, my future King. We will triumph in our quest. Nothing will ever split us apart."

Allen kisses Athena. "We'll never be apart, my love," he says in a soft voice. They fall asleep in each other's arms.

CHAPTER THIRTEEN

DROGAN CRASHES THE PARTY

The next morning everyone wakes up happy and ready for another exciting day, but the Star Island Twins wake up feeling like rock royalty. As they gather downstairs to go out for breakfast, Samantha exclaims, "We have over one million hits on YouTube. So many people love the video of our performance last night!"

Athena says, "This is awesome, ladies. You're going to be superstars."

Samantha checks an email from their publicist that says a famous producer from Miami wants to collaborate with them. She screams hysterically and says, "Suzy, we have a huge producer who wants to meet with us when we return to Miami."

Suzy yells excitedly, "That's awesome! We can't thank all of you enough… especially our debonair guys for believing in us." Jake and Francisco give their girlfriends congratulatory hugs.

The fashion-conscious teens (the twins are in purple and pink, and Athena wears an all-white ensemble from her clothing line) walk outside to the limo which is ready to take them to breakfast at a local place called Emporio Village Cafe. The restaurant is located not too far from the 17th century Emporio castle and the Perissa Black Sand Beach. The bodyguards accompany them on scooters, two in front and two behind.

They arrive at the café and at Athena's direction, wend their way through the long line of regulars and tourists to her reserved table on the patio. A few locals ask to take selfies with Athena and her friends.

She happily obliges before donning her shades, to avoid eye contact with onlookers so they can eat breakfast in peace.

"Athena, I have to thank you again for the lovely time in your wonderful country," says Francisco, beaming with joy.

Athena smiles and says, "It's my pleasure to show you my native land." Everyone says cheers and clinks their orange juice glasses and espresso cups.

Jake stands up to express his admiration for his family and girlfriend. "I want to thank all of you again for a wonderful time. Samantha, you're the love of my life. I never thought I would meet such a beautiful, sweet, loving, and down-to-earth girl like you. You have many talents, and you're going to be mega stars in the future. I'm fortunate to be in your presence with Suzy and my family. May we have another incredible day and night in beautiful Santorini."

Everyone shouts, "Cheers!"

After breakfast, Athena asks, "Are we ready for the tour of the castle? We will have to change shoes to walk up the narrow cobblestone street."

The twins' reply at once, "We are ready!" The girls change their heels into flats that match their outfits.

The bodyguards escort the teens up the narrow street. The locals, who have gathered along the street, feel proud to have Athena tour their village. As they stroll up the road, they pass kids riding down on bicycles. Everyone smiles at the group when they recognize Athena, and a little girl says to Athena as she walks by, "You are so beautiful, even more than the pictures in the magazines and on TV."

Athena smiles and bends down to the little girl. "Thank you, you're adorable, and you're a little Princess yourself."

The little girl blushes. "I am?"

Athena nods. "You sure are."

They continue to walk until they come to a fork, at which point the bodyguards lead the way. As they approach the castle, Francisco stares in awe at the narrow stone steps leading up to the castle. He says, "This is amazing, Athena! It's a good thing that we're all in great shape. Climbing those steep stairs looks like a killer workout!"

Jake pats Francisco on the shoulder and says, "You said it, amigo. This is a workout, indeed."

A church bell rings and Allen remarks while watching the man ringing the bell, "What an amazing sound that man is creating."

Athena says proudly, "There's a lot of history in this village. The Venetians built the medieval castle and village. This rural community and citadel was also a place the treasures were stored and protected against pirate invasions. You're in a real history book just standing here."

The teens say at different times, "Wow, this is amazing."

Athena says as they walk inside in single file, "Some areas in the castle have been converted into apartments for tourists who want to experience what it's like to stay in an authentic castle in Greece."

The bodyguards escort the teens back to the limo and lead them to Fira, the capital of Santorini to do a little shopping. They buy souvenirs and take pictures. During the afternoon, Athena takes everyone back to her catamaran to tour the volcano and swim in the famous hot springs next to the volcano. After swimming and everyone's back on the yacht, they are sprayed down with fresh water to rinse the salty seawater off their skin. The guys and girls change in separate staterooms before enjoying the sunset as they're taken back to Ammoudi port and to Athena's villa in the limo.

Francisco stretches his arms out in the back seat and remarks, "I feel rejuvenated like a newborn baby. Look at my skin, it feels silky smooth."

Touching Francisco's skin, Suzy says, "Franny, your skin is silky smooth like a baby. I should sprinkle some baby powder on your behind and then diaper you." She laughs out loud and says, "Would you like a pacifier as well?"

"Very funny, chica," replies Francisco. He throws Suzy on his lap and says, "I'm going to spank you."

Suzy screams as she laughs out loud, "Franny, don't do it!"

Francisco replies in his tough-guy voice, "Oh yeah, baby! I'm going to do it!" He raises his hand up and gently taps his girlfriend's butt. "How do you like that girl?"

Suzy blushes and teases, "Francisco, don't you *ever* pretend that you're going to spank my ass unless you're going to do it for real."

Samantha and Athena yell playfully, "*Oooo*, Suzy *loves spankings!*"

They return to Athena's villa, and everyone goes to their separate bedrooms to get ready for the evening. Athena and Allen put on matching outfits. Athena wears a tight black designer dress and shoes influenced by Audrey Hepburn, and Allen wears a black designer suit, shoes and the watch Athena bought him when they went on the shopping spree in Miami.

The twins are matching, and so are Francisco and Jake. Suzy and Samantha wear white strapless dresses, and Francisco and Jake wear presidential watches with matching off-white suits and shoes. The teens look like they should be in GQ magazine. The gorgeous couples are ready to hit the local hot spot in Fira.

They arrive at the trendy club called Club Olympus accompanied by Athena's bodyguards. The narrow backstreet entrance of the club features tall bronze Greek Goddess statues standing in fashion poses and wearing designer outfits like mannequins. The front entrance also has two large marble Greek warrior statues pointing swords toward each other as if they were saluting the patrons as they walk into the club. Allen notices that the statues' salutes with their right fist on their chest are similar to how the Atlantean warriors salute their King and Queen. He smiles and salutes the statues as he passes by the long line of the hottest teens patiently waiting to enter the club.

Athena is the guest of honor and Princes and Princesses from other countries must wait until the Greek Goddess enters her temple of musical worship. The nightclub doorman lifts the red velvet rope letting the teens enter. Athena's bodyguards watch from nearby.

The Star Island Twins' nonalcoholic champagne and sparkling water are chilled on ice in Athena's private area on the second level of the club. They sit and toast to the good life as The Party Boys begin playing music for the exclusive event.

Exotic teenagers and young adults from around the world dance on the dance floor without a care in the world. Athena bounces her head to the music as she gazes down at the crowd having a great time.

Allen hugs Athena and says, "Another epic night. I'm beginning to sound like Uncle Zadok repeating myself… nothing can get better than this."

It suddenly goes from blissful to nightmarish. Athena freezes and starts trembling. Downstairs she sees Drogan walk in the club with ten bodyguards.

Allen looks concerned and asks, "What is it, Athena? What's wrong?"

Francisco and Jake notice the Hybrid Reptilian masquerading as the man who almost succeeded in seducing Athena.

Suzy and Samantha say at the same time, "Look, it's our neighbor. The gorgeous hunk." They point at him.

Allen looks at Drogan, engulfs Athena in his strong arms and reassures her, "Don't worry, you're safe, my love."

Calming down a bit, Athena whispers, "I'm fine, I was taken aback for a moment. I know I'm safe. That monster no longer has power over me."

Drogan smirks as he looks up at Athena.

Enraged, Allen double flips over the rail and lands on the dance floor below. He walks through the crowd as a few girls touch his chest and hair saying flirtatiously, "Hello, handsome," in their different accents.

Allen doesn't notice them. His eyes are fixated on Drogan Reptilly. Francisco and Jake suddenly see the confrontation below. Allen approaches Drogan in the middle of his bodyguards who are surrounding him.

Allen's blue-green eyes glow as they change to a fierce red color. He yells, "You Hybrid swine, you have the nerve to show your half-Reptilian chameleon hide in Greece!"

Drogan replies snidely, "It's still a free country until I have control of your crown… you will bow down before me, Atlantean." Allen takes a step forward as a large bodyguard stands between him and Drogan.

The bodyguard folds his arms, and says menacingly, "Be careful, my friend. We don't want to hurt you."

Allen snarls, "Hurt? Man, get your punk-ass out of my face!"

The bodyguard puts his hand on Allen's chest. "That's right little man. I'm going to hur… *arrrghhh!*" He falls to his knees screaming as he stares in shock at his crushed hand.

Allen yells, "Who's the little man now, bitch!? You need to shut the hell up and learn respect when the future King of Atlantis is talking!"

The loud music drowns out the bodyguard's cry.

Allen looks at the other guards as he makes his knuckles crack. "Who's next in line? I'm kicking-ass and taking names, believe me. It will be much worse than your pathetic friend."

Looking Allen up and down, Drogan sneers, "I see that you're still strong as ever. I'm looking forward to the summer in Hawaii, right? A while back on my lunch date with the Greek Goddess.

She accidentally gave me a couple of clues, and I read your girlfriend's mind for a moment without using fear. I figured out you will be searching for the crown off the coast of Maui, which is not too far from the Molokini Crater. There is an undiscovered island close by with an active volcano. The powerful alien crystal embedded in the King's Crown hid the island from the human eye like the pyramid in the Bermuda Triangle. It is a perfect location for the hidden crown. I cannot find it until this summer, and neither can you. Even though you are half-Alien and you can see the pyramid in the Bermuda Triangle. There are rules you must follow to become king. You will have to wait for the King's Crown to reveal the island to the mortal eye, and once the volcano is ready to erupt this summer. The crown will connect with your necklace and ring, and the pitchfork you use for mining will make it easier for you to find the crown. I will have to beat you to it first."

Allen smirks. "You think you're clever?"

Drogan grins menacingly. "I'll take that as a compliment. I also know that the deadly red crystals were found in the ocean near that area. Damius used them to destroy your people. I will make my grandfather proud...I will find the crown before you, and I will be your king."

"You're lucky there're hundreds of people in this club. I'd make mincemeat out of you if there weren't," replies Allen with rage.

Drogan yawns and says, "You don't scare me anymore, Atlantean. You killed my brother. Remember the Gargoyle head you cut off on my yacht? Damon lives on. His powerful blood flows through my veins." Drogan hisses and boasts, "I also have a portion of your blood. You tried to wash it away, but science still prevailed. How do you like my eyes?" The Hybrid's blue eyes are the same color as the speck of blue in Allen's blue-green eyes.

Drogan's eyes glow slightly next to the Atlantean's crystal necklace. He remarks, "I can feel a bit of the power from your crystal necklace. If only I had just a little more of your blood. I'd probably feel more of your powers to use against you."

Allen roars as thunder erupts, "You will never have the blood of an Atlantean flowing through your veins! During our final battle, I will drain every last drop of your evil Reptilian blood and feed your carcass to sea crabs!"

Drogan doesn't budge, trying to provoke Allen to lose control in front of the crowd dancing around them. "I'm looking forward to it, before that happens…let's see if you can stay alive longer than your brother and sister-in-law did."

Francisco and Jake rush down to the dance floor. Drogan smiles as he sees them approaching. "You still have the orphans clinging to your side as usual. Are they better servants than my ancestors were in your kingdom?" Jake grabs Francisco before he punches Drogan.

Francisco loudly exclaims, "We're not servants. We're something you don't have, you snake. We're friends! And so were the Hybrids in Atlantis until your ancestor, Damius killed them." The wind howls as the nightclub doors rattle like they're about to fly off their hinges.

Drogan smirks. "I'm impressed. I see your power is stronger. I will go for now. I'll be seeing you in a few months. Please send my regards to your girlfriend."

"I've had it with you!" says Allen. He teleports a camouflaged tornado cloud inside the nightclub, which sucks Drogan and his henchmen up and deposits them miles away. It happens so fast no one in the club notices the supernatural event.

Jake and Francisco yell, "How do you like that, you billionaire punk bitch!"

Allen says, "Drogan is fortunate I can't do anything to him."

Jake replies in an angry voice, "Don't worry, Allen. You know what to do like the game of chess you play. You have to be patient so you can finish him off for good."

Francisco says, "You're right about that, Jake. We'll be ready this summer in Hawaii."

Allen nods gravely and thinks. *I need to kill Destroyer and it has to be Drogan's body and not Josh's body. The next time I face the monster, I will have no choice. Destroyer must die before he kills another innocent victim like Tyrone and before he makes climate change on Earth worse than it already is.*

CHAPTER FOURTEEN

A FAMILY SURPRISE

The twins haven't noticed anything out of the ordinary happening on the dance floor below. They've only seen people having a great time dancing.

As Allen climbs the stairs to return to the VIP section, Athena rushes to meet him and whispers, "Allen, are you okay?"

"Yeah, I'm fine. He won't be intruding on our vacation again. I promise you that."

Athena hugs and kisses him. "Do you want to go?"

Allen shakes his head. "No, let's stay and forget about that clown. You're my girl, and there's nothing on this Earth that will ever take you away from me."

Are you sure everything is all right? Athena asks telepathically.

Allen answers, *Yes. My powers are stronger than before. The Hybrid knows it... he'll have to think smarter if he wants to hurt you or me.*

Athena blurts out loud, "I wish you could kill that asshole right now."

Allen says softly, "I understand how you feel, Athena... I can't, believe me I want to. The game is still being played out. I wouldn't be surprised if Drogan ends up killing himself. We shall see."

Suzy asks Jake and Francisco, "How do you know that guy who lives by us?"

Jake gasps in anger and snarls, "It's a long story. I want you two to do Francisco and me a favor. Keep away from that guy if he ever comes near you when you're at home or hanging out near your boat. He's a very dangerous man. You do not want to be involved with a guy like that, believe me."

"I believe you, Jake. Don't worry, we'll stay away," says Samantha.

Jake gently grabs his girlfriend by the arm and implores, "Please, Samantha, I'm serious. You call me whenever you see that guy even stares at you."

Samantha nods. "Okay, I will, handsome."

They kiss and dance until the wee hours. When they finally leave, they notice a line of people waiting to get in.

Francisco says in a surprised voice, "This is crazy. The club is still going, and people still want to go inside. It's almost four in the morning!"

Athena smiles and says with delight, "That's how we do it in Greece. The clubs usually don't close until six A.M."

Allen smiles a little and says, "I remember you wanted to take me to a club in Sydney when we first met, but I was so intrigued with my family history, I just wanted to stay at your home and listen to you talk about my ancestors." Allen doesn't want to say too much since the twins are with them.

Athena cuddles in Allen's arms and says as her bodyguards escort them to the limo, "That would have been fun when you first came to Sydney. There was a raging party at an outdoor pool club on George Street. We'll go next summer."

Allen is quiet as they hop into the limo. Athena whispers telepathically, *Babe, sorry if I'm repeating myself, but are you sure you're okay?*

Yes, I'm fine. I'm not afraid of anyone or anything. I will never lose you to my enemy again, answers Allen telepathically.

Athena kisses him. *You know nothing can tear us apart... I don't know how your powers are stronger than before. It's like the Greek Gods have blessed you.*

Allen smiles a little as he thinks. *I want to tell you, Athena that I drank the water of the Gods and that Zeus granted me permission to marry you, but I can't tell you. Not until I find the right moment.*

The gang walks into the villa to find that breakfast is prepared for them. They have an American breakfast - scrambled eggs, turkey bacon, sausage, toast and hash browns.

Francisco says, "Geez, Athena. I thought you'd surprise us with another great Greek breakfast and here we are being all-American."

"That's what surprises are all about... the unexpected," replies Athena with a smirk.

Exhausted after eating breakfast, everyone goes upstairs to bed. Francisco falls asleep in his suit. Suzy takes his shoes and suit off and tucks him in.

Allen and Athena sleep in boxers and T-shirts. Athena coos, "Your boxers are so soft and comfortable. I love wearing them."

Allen kisses Athena, and says, "Good night, even though it's daytime."

The teens sleep over nine hours except for Francisco, who has a nightmare about his biological mother being beaten up by one of her boyfriends. "Leave her alone! I'll kill you! Leave my mommy alone you troll!" Francisco screams in his sleep.

Suzy shakes him and whispers, "Francisco! Francisco, wake up!"

"Huh... wha... what happened?" Francisco stammers.

Suzy massages his neck and whispers, "You had a bad dream. You were calling out to your mother. Do you remember anything about your dream?"

Francisco gets up and sits at the foot of the bed. "No, I don't remember any of it. I guess I looked pretty scared?"

Suzy replies in a loving voice, "No, not at all. I admire that about you... deep down in your subconscious, you have love for your mother. Maybe you should search for her one day."

Francisco snaps. "No! I'm sorry, Suzy... I don't want to sound mean. I remember my dream now. My mother's boyfriend molested me. He used to beat her. How fucked up is that? I'm just not ready to find my mother. My family is with Allen, Jake, Athena, Uncle Zadok and Aoki. They've never let me down. I'm too young to think about my mom. I have so much more to gain in my life. Maybe after I graduate college, I might be ready to search for her, but not now."

Suzy kisses Francisco on the cheek. "I understand. I'm here for you no matter what, okay?"

Francisco smiles a little and says, "Okay. You know I was ashamed of telling anyone my last name is Gomez. It would remind me of my mother."

Suzy replies, "There's nothing to be ashamed of. My last name is Stevenson. My sister and I are so used to being called the Star Island Twins, than our actual names."

She hugs him.

He smiles a little. "Thank you, chica. You're the best. I feel like I can act like myself around you, without pretending to be macho. I'm very fortunate to have you as my girl."

Suzy whispers adoringly, "I feel the same about you. I am fortunate to have you in my life."

Athena eagerly waits for everyone downstairs. When the whole crew has gathered, she says, "This is our last day in Santorini. I thought we should all go parasailing."

The twins scream excitedly, "We can't wait, Athena!"

Allen chimes in, "Now that sounds like fun. Something I've never done before."

Jake thinks. *The training I had climbing the lasso in Pyramid City has prepared me for this.* He says, "I was afraid of heights. I'm not anymore. Let's go for it, dude."

Francisco adds, "Yeah, this will be the best thing we've ever done so far." He hugs Athena and says, "You're the best sis a bro could have."

"Thank you, Fran. Shall we go?" asks Athena, blushing from the compliment.

They hop into the limo, and the driver drives down the island with Athena's bodyguards escorting them. They arrive at the Ammoundi Port in Oia and get in three speedboats that take them parasailing.

After a few hours, the teens are finished.

"Is anyone hungry for dinner?" asks Athena. Everyone agrees to eat on the yacht. She says gaily, "Let's have a ball and the time of our lives since this is our last night in Greece."

The twins scream at the same time in their high-pitched voices, "Hell yeah! We are so thrilled." Francisco and Jake cover their ears.

Francisco looks at Jake and says, "I have to say, this is a once-in-a-lifetime experience."

Jake nods and with a smile. "Yes, it is, amigo!"

Allen slaps the guys on their backs and says, "What a time, huh?" Jake and Francisco stumble forward and almost fall from the force of Allen's backslaps.

Allen laughs and says, "Oops! I'm sorry about that, guys. I keep forgetting my strength."

"I'll say, bro. You're a freaking freight train. I'm just happy to be on your team. I wouldn't want to be on team Reptilian," says Francisco.

The twins hear Francisco and ask at the same time, "What do you mean Reptilian?"

Francisco plays it off. "It's nothing, ladies. It's just a saying a couple of the football jocks at school say about a player who can't play. They're always on the bench or something."

Suzy winks and smiles. "Okay, I get it, it's a jock thing."

The teens sit at the dining table ready to eat the mouth-watering chicken, steak, ribs, corn on the cob, sweet potato, pecan and apple pies. The table also has jars filled with sweet tea.

Perplexed, Allen asks, "What is this, Athena? This looks like something Uncle Zad—"

"Dok would make. Well, here I am, nephew. Surprise! Why don't you take a seat and enjoy your meal," says Zadok with a big grin. He even has a portable golden cowbell in his hand. He rings it three times: *Ding! Ding! Ding!*

The teenagers are happily surprised. Uncle Zadok says in his loud laughing voice, "Now, you know that I'm the only one who can prepare a good old-fashioned throwdown soul food meal for my favorite family."

Allen replies proudly, "Nobody does it like you, Unc." He looks at Athena and asks, "Athena, how long have you planned this surprise?"

Athena replies, "Uncle Zadok and I had this last dinner in Santorini planned for a few days."

Zadok winks and nods. "Yes, we did my wonderful niece." He looks at everyone and says, "I think you knew Aoki and I were coming, but you didn't know I had this special meal planned for everyone. Aoki and I have never been to Greece before. It was nice of Gianni to show us around. We enjoyed the sights and having romantic dinners at night."

Gianni says, "It was a pleasure for me to show your Uncle Zadok Santorini."

Zadok crows, "We can't thank Athena enough for her hospitality." Zadok and Aoki grab their jars of sweet tea and shout, "Cheers!" Everyone raises their glasses, and they shout, "Cheers!"

"Did we have a hell of a time here? I know none of you didn't do anything crazy?" booms Zadok.

Allen thinks. *Uncle Zadok would lose it if he found out Drogan was here.* He clears his throat and says, "We had an incredible time, Unc. This is supposed to be our last night hanging out on vacation. Don't tell me we need a chaperone?"

Zadok laughs and says, "Of course not. Aoki and I have plans of our own, don't we, honey?"

"Yes, we do, we're going to take the yacht out and cruise around and gaze at the stars above," replies Aoki.

Uncle Zadok grins with a wink at Aoki. "You see we grown folks have a few fun things planned for ourselves. We're staying right here on the yacht tonight. After we're finished with dinner, we'll sail you back to the port and Gianni will take you back to Athena's villa so you can go out and have a great time this evening."

The teens applaud and shout, "Yeah, Uncle Zadok! All Hail Zadok!" They clink their sweet tea jars again.

After dinner, the teens leave the boat waving at Uncle Zadok and Aoki. "Thank you for the wonderful surprise and the great food like always."

Zadok and Aoki wave back. "You're welcome."

"Now wasn't that a great dinner with great company?" asks Athena with a grand smile.

Everyone agrees as Francisco and Allen lift Athena up and bellow, "Hail Athena! Hail Athena, Princess of surprise parties and events!"

They hop into the limo and Allen holds Athena's hand and whispers, "I don't know what you could do to top what you've already done."

Athena replies with a wink and a smirk. "We shall see."

When they return to the villa, Athena says gaily, "I know we'll all look good… but still… look your best for tonight. This is our last night to remember in Greece."

The twins rush upstairs with their usual excitement. "I know what I'm going to wear tonight," says Suzy.

Samantha adds, "Let's look epic and cool."

"Agreed," they say at once.

Jake and Francisco dap each other on the fist. Francisco declares, "We're going to have to kill it tonight, bro!"

Jake says, "I'm right behind you, amigo."

Allen and Athena walk up to their bedroom, and Allen says, "I don't know what to wear. I feel like we outdid ourselves last night."

Athena replies with a hint, "Don't worry, handsome. You already know I love having surprises."

Allen walks into the master bedroom and sees hanging on the bathroom door a one-of-a-kind white tuxedo with black trim on the lapels. The suit is custom-made by one of Allen's favorite designers. Athena is wearing a matching white, one-of-a-kind dress with a train that almost resembles a wedding gown.

After Allen gets dressed, he walks out onto the balcony and spies a white watch bezel sitting on a marble table. "Wow, Athena… Is this for me?" he asks with adoration.

"Yes, my Prince."

Allen gives his girlfriend a warm embrace. "I feel like Cinderella in this story… but I'm Cinderfella, aren't I?"

"You've always been Cinderfella, but you never knew it until last summer. This summer you will be King. You should continue to enjoy nice things. You will have it all, including me," Athena says with joy.

Allen kisses his girlfriend again. "I want to be with you now, but we both know everything will be more magical after we're married… so no sex until we're married."

She looks at him and smiles. "I can't wait for that special day."

Allen replies with confidence, "I think August is good. I'll have my crown in July so the following month should work out perfectly."

Athena gazes into her boyfriend's eyes. "And after we're married in Atlantis, we'll have a wedding that no one else has seen on Earth since the days of the Great Kings of Egypt and Greece." Athena hugs Allen and says with elation, "I can't wait!"

He gently strokes her hair, whispering, "Neither can I."

Athena slaps him on the butt. "Let's rock this town tonight."

Jake and Samantha are dressed to the nines. Jake wears a black suit and boasts, "I'm going all black tonight, baby. After everyone sees us, they'll know we're killing the fashion scene." He smiles his million-dollar smile at himself in the mirror.

Samantha wears a white strapless dress cut high up the thigh, showing her tanned legs with white high heels. She says, "I'm wearing all white… It's like we're getting married and you're my handsome blond knight in shining armor."

Jake's taken off guard. He stammers, "Married?"

Samantha giggles. "I'm just pretending, silly. Girls love to do that you know… pretend to be married, and pretend to have a baby…"

Jake's eyes grow wider; the word *baby* hits him again like a sledgehammer. He laughs a little nervously. "Yeah, that sounds awesome, sweetie."

Francisco wears a white dinner jacket, a pink silk shirt, matching pink slacks and white sneakers. Suzy wears a one-of-a-kind pink gown with white lace at the hem and pink heels.

The teens look like they've stepped off the runway in Paris.

Athena walks down the staircase escorted by her Atlantean Prince. When everyone is assembled, she asks, "Are we ready to have the time of our lives tonight?"

Jake asks, "So where are we heading to?"

Athena says, "Before we leave, let's take a stroll out back."

The couples walk through the botanical garden and out onto the lawn where they're greeted by servers who offer them the Star Island Twins' nonalcoholic champagne.

The couples sip their drinks and continue to stroll toward the cliff. At the cliff's edge, Athena lights an ancient Greek oil lamp, and swings it back and forth, signaling to the yacht below. The teens stare down and see Athena's boat with Uncle Zadok and Aoki waving and smiling.

Zadok nods at a gentleman holding a torch on deck. He lights it, and suddenly fireworks shoot toward Athena's villa bursting overhead. A school of blue dolphins appears and looks like they're swimming in the star-filled sky. The dolphins are accompanied by a great white shark who morphs into a giant orca. The killer whale looks like it's swimming straight toward the teens.

Francisco ducks with his hands covering his head as if he were trying to keep from being eaten by the whale. The fireworks fizzle out after the killer whale opens its mouth.

The teens cheer and jump up and down laughing and screaming, "Yeah! That was incredible!"

Uncle Zadok and Aoki look through binoculars and laugh at the Teen Warriors and their twin friends. Zadok teases through a loudspeaker, "Francisco, you thought that firework of an orca was going to eat you."

Francisco shouts back, "Ha, very funny, Uncle Zadok. I wasn't scared. That was fun, Unc! We want more."

The teens chant, "We want more!" And more fireworks explode a dozen red, white, and blue butterflies appear and look like they're flying toward the group in single file. The butterflies continue to grow larger each time their wings flap in the moonlit sky. The butterflies one after another looked like they're smiling at Athena before flying away and exploding in a rainbow arch of red, blue, green, and yellow. The signs of an Atlantean Prince controlling a rainbow wormhole cloud.

The girls jump around in hysterics.

Francisco and Jake say together as if they were twins, "That was totally amazing!"

Allen is in awe. He holds Athena's hand. The super couple watch the rainbow-colored fireworks disappear in the night sky. "That was the most amazing thing I've ever seen with my eyes."

Athena puts her head on Allen's chest. "I'm so happy you liked it."

"Liked it, I loved it!" shouts Allen as he joyously lifts Athena up and spins her around in his arms.

The teens hear Uncle Zadok down below screaming, "Woo! hoo! Now, that was a show folks!"

Athena asks everyone, "Are we ready to go out?"

The teens happily scream, "Yeah! Let's do it! Athena! Athena! Athena!"

Allen says in awe, "I don't know what you can do to top that."

Athena replies, "I have nothing left in my bag of tricks at the moment. I'm just happy that everyone has enjoyed the evening so far."

Suzy and Samantha say in unison, "Enjoyed it? We loved it!"

Jake yells, "Fran and I second what they just said."

"Sis, that is… that was… incredible. I've never seen a fireworks display like that in my life!" gasps Francisco.

CHAPTER FIFTEEN

The Battle Of The Athenas

The gentlemen escort their dates to the vintage limo. The driver takes them to their final outing in Greece.

Athena says, "Let's hang out at Club Olympus again. What do you say? I want us to enjoy ourselves and forget about the drama that happened last night." She nudges Allen playfully in the ribs with her elbow.

"Don't worry, I'm fine," says Allen with a suppressed laugh.

The limo pulls up to the club, and Athena's bodyguards lead the couples up the cobblestone street to the club's entrance.

Francisco is thrilled. He enthuses, "This looks better than last night."

The twins look at each other and say, "We're about to have the time of our lives again."

The crowd is standing outside waiting to go in chants, "Athena! Athena!" The Greek Goddess smiles at her adoring fans, and she and her entourage walk into the club.

The Party Boys are performing again, and the DJ says over the microphone, "Let's hear it again ya'll for the Princess of Greece, Athena Dranias… and the Star Island Twins from Miami! Let's not forget their dates: Allen, Jake, and Franciscooo!"

Francisco shouts with delight, "I love it! They said my name last like I was a soccer player who just scored a goal."

"Calm down, dude and enjoy the night," says Jake grinning.

Like the night before, their reserved table overlooks the DJ booth and the crowd below.

The nightclub owners have dancers perform for Athena and her guests, and the owners have huge posters of The Star Island Twins plastered on the walls of the club. The DJ plays the songs the girls sung the night before mixed with hip-hop beats and electronica music. The girls and Athena go berserk, screaming and jumping up and down with glee.

In awe, Francisco remarks to Jake, "Bro, I'm saying it again. We have huge stars right in front of us."

Jake smirks and asks, "Can you feel this?"

Francisco yells, "Ouch! Why'd you pinch me?"

Jake laughs. "I want to make sure this is real."

"Oh, okay," says Francisco with a sly grin. He slaps Jake in the face. "Are you awake now? Is that real enough for you?"

Jake nods and winks. "Yes, it is, amigo. This is the real deal. I don't want this to end. I could live in Greece forever." They hug each other and Allen smiles at them and ponders. *I'm happy my brothers are enjoying this special night. When we return home, we'll be back in school and counting down the days until July. Then we search for the King's Crown.*

The Party Boys continue mixing music as one of their dancers joins Athena and crew to say hello. He says to Athena and Allen, "The Party Boys and I would like to thank the both of you for the love you've shown us. We will keep everything quiet about who you really are, Athena. You're still, Audrey Monroe at South Beach High."

"Thanks, I appreciate that. We'll see if anyone figures anything out… especially after they watch the twins' performance on social media and see all of us dancing and cheering in the audience," replies Athena.

The Party Boys dancer says, "We shall see." He walks back downstairs.

Allen whispers, "Of course half the school is going to figure out you're not, Audrey Monroe."

Athena laughs and says, "I don't care anymore. There's no harm in a socialite going to a public school. This will be my last year in high school anyway."

"I know! I still have two years left," says Allen.

Jake jumps on Allen's back and says, "You still have me."

Francisco grins and jumps into his arms. "And you have me, brother."

Athena giggles. "I can see that you will be fine in high school without me."

Allen whispers, "I hope so." He drops Francisco on the sofa and falls back like he's doing a body slam on Jake to get him off his back.

Jake crows, "C'mon, dude. You know you're going to be all right with the two of us. You'll be king and also a junior in high school with us. It'll be fun!"

Before the group exits the club, Athena gets on the microphone and yells, "I enjoyed my time here in Greece!"

The crowd chants, "Athena! Athena!"

She smiles and says, "I promise I'll be back soon! Enjoy your night!"

The crowd cheers louder as foam begins flowing onto the dance floor. The twins shout at the same time, "It's a foam party on the dance floor… that's so cool!" The dancers spray the crowd with their foam guns.

The group files out the door and are met by Athena's bodyguards who lead them back to their limo.

Out of nowhere, lightning flashes in the night sky. Athena sees a silhouette of her Aunt Athena dressed in battle attire holding a bronze shield and spear. No one in the limo notices it.

Athena says to everyone a little nervously, "I have one last thing planned for everyone. I will have my driver take you to the speedboat since Uncle Zadok has the yacht. You have to see the glowing fish that swim near the Perissa Black Sand Beach. I can't go with you… there's something I must do."

Allen asks, "Is everything okay?"

Athena smiles a little awkwardly. "It will be after I visit a family member."

Allen kisses Athena and says, "Whatever it is, will I see you soon?"

Athena hides her anxiety and says, "Yes, you will, my love."

Everyone but Athena gets out of the limo to board the speedboat to Perissa. Alone finally, Athena closes her eyes and meditates. She sees her Aunt Athena.

"Niece, I think it's time to teach you some manners. You have the gall to come to Greece and not acknowledge me. Grab your battle armor and meet me at my temple in the Acropolis. I want to see what you've learned from the Atlanteans. You'd rather learn how to fight from Hybrid Aliens than your own kind."

Athena replies, "I'm ready to meet you, Aunt Athena. I'm not a ten-year-old child anymore."

Aunt Athena smirks and says, "We shall see little girl."

Athena teleports to Miami and suits up for battle. Within minutes, she teleports back to Greece and flies in a cloaked wormhole cloud to the temple, which is illuminated by the lights that surround the Parthenon. Athena exits the wormhole in the middle of the ancient arena. The buildings of the citadel are severely damaged, but the large marble stone bricks that make up the arena are still mostly intact.

Athena yells, "I am here, Aunt Athena!" Her voice echoes in the empty stadium.

Aunt Athena stands on top of the arena smiling down. "Niece... how brave of you to come meet me in person."

She floats down with her shield poised and her spear transforms into a double-edged sword. Her gold and bronze breastplate shines in the light, and her ancient golden helmet displays sword scratches and dents from battles she has won. Her gladiator sandals have golden kneecaps to protect her knees, which are exposed beneath her white and gold skirt. She looks to be around thirty and has thick dark hair and light golden-brown eyes like her niece's. Her bronze and golden armor complement her smooth olive skin.

Aunt Athena walks up to her niece and stares down at her. "Niece, how attractive you are. You are practically a woman now. You're only a few inches shorter than I am and your muscle tone almost matches mine. Let's see if your strength matches mine?"

Athena replies, "Yes, let's see... I'm ready to prove that I'm worthy of my Greek blood. Do you have blood? Just wondering... since you were born from my Godfather's forehead, a fully-grown woman."

Aunt Athena snarls, "If you can cut me, you will know." She strikes her sword angrily at her niece's head. Athena blocks the blow with her shield and kicks her Aunt in the chest. She flies backward and lands with a thump on her rear. Aunt Athena nimbly jumps up and charges her niece. She shakes the ground with a thunderous roar.

Athena takes a firm stance and waits for her aunt to come within inches of her. She quickly moves to the side and kicks her aunt in the back. Aunt Athena stumbles forward. She catches her balance and says, "You are very surprising, niece. Your training with the Atlantean spirits has made you a strong warrior… but there's one thing you should know about battling in a war."

"And what is that?" asks Athena.

Aunt Athena kicks dirt in her niece's eyes temporarily blinding her. She hits her in the chin with the butt of her sword. Athena falls hard on her side and drops her shield.

"War is not fair, and there will always be a dirty scoundrel in the fight to the death." Aunt Athena leaps in the air and comes down with a blow that is blocked by Athena's sword.

Athena executes a sweep kick and knocks her aunt on the ground. "You hate me because I make my own decisions without receiving permission from you and the other Greek Gods. You made up rules that prevented my great-grandfather Zeus from allowing me to see my family unless you train me! You are not my parent. You were merely added to my family's history because of my great-grandfather who is my Godfather. My Godfather created you to be the hero of mortals. That does not make you my hero."

Aunt Athena lunges her sword at her niece's chest.

Athena hits her aunt's wrist with her golden shield, knocking the sword out of her hand. She quickly strikes her aunt in the mouth with her elbow, drawing a little blood.

Athena says with humility, "I guess you do have blood. You are a great warrior."

Aunt Athena spits the blood out of her mouth and smiles a little. "I cannot hide behind arrogance. You have shown me wisdom. You are very wise, my niece. I was wrong about you. You have proved yourself, and you now have my blessing to choose the life you want in this mortal world. You may see your family anytime you want."

Suddenly, Athena's parents appear in the arena. Athena feels pride as tears flow down her cheeks. "Mother and father. It's so good to see you finally after you left me with my grandmother, Andromeda."

Hugging Athena, Perseus replies, "My beautiful, daughter, what a woman you have become. I can't believe my eyes. My mother tells me everything I need to know about how you're doing on Earth. Life seems cruel, but I knew we would see each other again."

"Thank you, father, for never giving up on me." Athena turns and hugs her mother. "I'm so happy to see you, mum. You're as beautiful as ever. I hope I've made you proud."

Gorgophone replies with a grand smile, "You have, Athena… my lovely daughter. Your father and I are very proud of you. You have made your decision to be with the Atlantean boy you love?"

Athena nods her head. "I have… I'm sorry that Allen is not Greek. I love him. I know the course of Greek history could change with my decision. But it won't. I will continue to teach and lecture about our times past. Even through the children, I may have with Allen once he is King and we are married."

Gorgophone smiles and says, "Then it will be what you and the soon-to-be King decide for your future. I want you to be happy and come see us on Mount Olympus whenever you have time. Don't worry about the other Greek Gods. You have given your father and me the strength to talk to the other family members about your decision."

Aunt Athena approaches her niece and says, "Don't worry about the other Gods. Once they hear from me, they'll understand. And Zeus has approved of your decision. No one will argue with my father. Now go and continue your life and training with the Atlanteans. Once your boyfriend is King of Atlantis, you may return to Mount Olympus and train with me and spend time with your family."

Athena hugs her aunt. "Thank you, Aunt Athena. It means a lot that you've given me your blessing to live my life on Earth however I want."

"I may learn a thing or two from your training with the Hybrid Aliens when you come to train with me," says Aunt Athena with a wink.

Aunt Athena embraces everyone before a lightning bolt takes her family back to Mount Olympus.

Athena quickly teleports to Miami, puts her gear away and returns to Santorini. She speaks to Allen telepathically, *My love, I have completed what I had to do. Have the bodyguards take you and everyone to the airport. It's time to go home to Miami.*

Allen transmits in an upbeat tone, *Will do, beautiful! Thank you for allowing us the opportunity to see the glowing fish. It was amazing.*

The teens drive straight to the airport to meet Athena. Their bags are already packed and waiting on the G5.

Zadok had texted Athena earlier: *Aoki and I love it here. We're going to stay on the yacht for a few extra days.*

No problem. The jet will be ready for you whenever you're ready, Athena texted back.

Uncle Zadok happily replied, *Thank you, Athena. You're very special to us… I'm grateful you're giving Allen something to live for.*

Athena texted back a smiley face.

The teens jump on the plane. Everyone's tired. They fall asleep and arrive in Miami twelve hours later. Their limousine waits for them on the tarmac in the private VIP section of Miami International Airport. The twins also have their limo waiting to take them home.

The twins hug Allen and Athena, and Samantha says, "I want to thank you both for showing my sis and me a great time in Greece."

Allen smiles and nods as Athena says with affection, "We will always be friends, and I'm here if you ever need me."

"I feel now we are more like sisters than friends," Samantha says.

"I feel the same way," Suzy chimes in.

The girls kiss their guys and jump into their limo. Jake watches the twins leave with tears in his eyes.

He sighs deeply and thinks. *The dream vacation is over now and the next day is school, I will have to talk to Becky Honeycomb and deal with my impending fatherhood.*

In the limo, Allen looks at Jake and telepathically says through the crystal, *Jake, I can sense that you are sad. No one else can hear us talk, are you okay, bro?*

Jake replies telepathically, *I don't know, man. It's nothing I can talk about at the moment.*

Okay, I understand… you know you can talk to me anytime you have something on your mind. Anyone of us… we're family, you know that, says Allen.

Jake nods. *Yeah, I know, bro. I'll be fine.*

They drive into the compound followed by the bodyguards in a black SUV. The warriors grab their bags and head to their bedrooms to unpack.

While Francisco unpacks his bag, he looks at the framed photo on his dresser of himself with his mother, taken at a carnival when he was two-years-old. "I'm trying to forget you momma, but I can't. When I have the courage, I'll search for you. Right now, I'm just not ready. I'm sorry." He puts the photo in his drawer.

As Allen puts away his things, he sees in his mind's eye the play-by-play of Drogan and his thuggish bodyguards barging into the nightclub in Greece. "Sooner or later Hybrid… I'm gonna get you."

In her bedroom, Athena whispers to herself, "Drogan, I used to be afraid of you. I will never look weak around Allen or my warrior brothers again. You don't frighten me anymore. Your evil ways will not ruin my life with the future King. I will kill you myself if I have to. Nothing will keep me from being Queen."

The next morning Athena wakes up feeling energetic. She gets dressed for school and runs downstairs for breakfast, but no one else is out of bed yet. She transmits telepathically through her crystal necklace: "C'mon, guys, it's time to get up! We have to be at school in forty-five minutes!"

CHAPTER SIXTEEN

GOOD TIMES FOR FRANCISCO AND BAD TIMES FOR JAKE

Francisco whines telepathically, *Just twenty more minutes of sleep.*

No! Get up now! Athena yells back telepathically, *We're not going to be late for school!*

Francisco snarks, *Okay, den mother, I'm up. You sound like the administrator back in the orphanage.*

Athena laughs. *Then administrate your ass up and out of that bed!*

Francisco rolls out of bed, saunters to the bathroom, and splashes water on his face.

Jake's been awake for the last two hours staring hopelessly at his ceiling. He knows he has to face the responsibility of being a father to Becky's unborn child.

Allen steps out of the shower and says to Athena telepathically, *I'm awake, sweetheart. Would you like to go to school together? I'll let you drive.*

Are you sure you can handle my driving? asks Athena.

Allen snickers. *Sure, I can. I'm wide-awake now, so bring it on. I'm not afraid of your leadfoot.*

The boys meet Athena in the hall by the stairs and walk down together.

Allen says to the guys, "I'm going to school with Athena."

Jake replies, "I think I'll drive Samantha's car to school and go see her afterwards."

Francisco snickers and says, "Oooo! Jake's big pimping in the Maserati today, showboating at school."

Jake turns red as he retorts, "No, it's nothing like that, Fran. I want to see Samantha after school, that's all."

"I understand. I'll drive solo. Tell Suzy I said hi when you're there." says Francisco.

Jake nods. "No problem. You don't feel like going with me?"

Francisco shakes his head. "Not today. I don't know what kind of homework I'm going to have in my new classes. I'll probably see Suzy tomorrow."

They grab a quick breakfast snack that was prepared by a temporary chef. Allen sulks a little and whispers to Athena, "I miss Uncle Zadok's breakfast."

Athena hugs him and murmurs, "He'll be back soon. I'm happy Uncle Zadok is enjoying himself with Aoki."

Allen nods. "Yeah, I agree. He deserves all the rest and relaxation. He's spoiled us too much."

The second semester, no one has a class together. They only see each other during lunch or at their lockers.

After a few classes, Allen sees Josh in the hallway. He walks up to him and asks, "Hey, how was your spring break?"

Josh looks at Allen and smiles. "It was good. I still feel normal. Nothing's trying to interfere with me at the moment… But it's only a matter of time until summer."

Allen says, "Well, that's good news so far."

"Yes, and I'm learning a lot about my Nomadic Indian heritage… I much prefer the Nomadic Indian side. I know I have Atlantean blood in me, and I know my father never embraced it. No offense. I'm proud of my mother's heritage, and I'm going to keep the traditions alive even though my mother wasn't a part of it that much after she left the reservation. I think that side of me is what has made me braver and stronger on the football field. I'm a Nomadic Indian warrior."

Allen says with admiration, "I'm happy for you, Josh, and no offense taken. I appreciate you helping me get rid of the Gargoyle this summer."

Josh thinks about his dead friend. "I owe it to Tyrone. I hope to fight the demonic Gargoyle in the middle plane. His spirit against my spirit. I won't allow him to inhabit my body again."

Allen says encouragingly, "I know you will prevail."

The bell rings, and the guys take off to their classes.

Josh yells, "I'll see you around, Allen." The Atlantean throws up a peace sign as he runs to his next class.

Jake is about to have a bad day. He has a science class with Becky. He walks into class and pretends not to notice her. To avoid her, he takes a seat in the front row for the first time in his life. The teacher, an African American woman, named Mrs. Jones, enters the class and begins roll call. She calls Jake's name, and he raises his hand. "Here."

She calls Becky Honeycomb next.

When she says, "Present," she sounds like she might be sick.

Mrs. Jones stops and asks, "Are you okay?"

Becky replies, "I'm sorry, Mrs. Jones. I feel like I'm going to lose my breakfast."

Mrs. Jones grabs the trashcan and gives it to Becky, who springs out of her seat and runs out of the classroom. Jake feels like he's two feet tall. His palms start to sweat, and he's afraid he's going to have an anxiety attack.

Mrs. Jones says, "All right class, it's time to pick a partner for the project."

Jake can't hear anything but his pounding heart. He ponders. *I should run out of the classroom and go home right now. I wonder how many people Becky has told about us having a baby together.*

Becky rolls back into class and says to Mrs. Jones, "I'm feeling better."

The students have partnered up except for Becky and Jake. Mrs. Jones says, "Jake, you and Becky are partners for this assignment."

Jake protests. "How can that be? I don't want to work with her!"

Becky looks shy and says nothing.

Mrs. Jones glares at Jake and says in a commanding voice, "There will be no yelling in my class, young man. You will respect me, your classmates, and Becky. She's your partner. I won't hear anything else. Period! Do you understand me?"

Jake lowers his head in defeat and whispers, "Yes, ma'am."

She turns away from him and says to the students, "Before class ends, I want you to sit next to your partner and tomorrow you'll sit in the same seats. You will start working on your experiment… right here in the biology lab as soon as class starts. Everyone knows who their partner is?"

The students reply, "Yes, Mrs. Jones."

She gestures. "Okay then, sit next to your partner."

The students grab their backpacks and move to their new seats.

Becky sits in the empty seat next to Jake and whispers, "I guess we're going to be working on this together? I'm sorry if you're upset, Jake."

He mumbles, "It's not all your fault. It's mine too."

The bell rings, and the students grab their things and rush to lunch to see their friends.

On the way out of the classroom, Jake gets odd looks from some of the girls. He walks a few feet ahead of Becky and hears them consoling her. "Becky, how are you? Are you going to be okay?"

Becky smiles cheerfully and says, "Yes, I will be fine, thanks for asking."

Jake overhears someone say, "That jerk is a disgusting pig. He ruined an innocent girl's life."

Jake stops at his locker to put his backpack away before going to lunch. He hears a few girls talking behind his back. One of the girls, says cynically, "I hope Becky knows that guy is a freeloader. I don't know how he got all those expensive clothes, and I saw him on a website with the Star Island Twins living it up while she's here getting sick from being prego with his baby. He needs to be spayed and neutered. What a dog!"

Jake storms off to lunch while telepathically calling out to Francisco through the crystal necklace. *Fran, are you there? Where are you?*

Francisco answers telepathically, *I'm hanging out in the quad having lunch with Suzy. She left school to spend lunch with me. Can you believe it! How cool is that! I already have dudes giving me props with the head nod. Even some of these stuck-up South Beach Miami High chicas are flirting. I know we're popular now. I see a few hating on a playboy's status. I love it.*

Jake snarks, *That's fine… just fine, Fran!*

You sound irritated. What's gotten into you, bro? Are you going to hang out with us for lunch? asks Francisco.

Jake answers, *Nah. I'm not hungry. I'm feeling a little sick. I'm heading home.*

Francisco says, *Okay, feel better. I thought you were going to see Samantha later. That's why you drove her car to school today, wasn't it?*

Jake mumbles, *That was a bad idea. I'll see her tomorrow.*

All right, replies Francisco. *I'll just pretend to Suzy that I received a text from you saying that you're sick and you're going home to get some rest.*

Thanks, Fran. I appreciate that. I'll probably see Samantha tomorrow.

Jake can hear Francisco and Suzy cheerfully yelling as The Party Boys play the song, they mixed for the Star Island Twins when they were in Greece. The students go crazy when they see Suzy. A crowd flocks around her and Francisco have to pull her into the DJ booth to escape being mobbed by the overexcited teens. The group of star-struck teens chant, "Star Island Twin! Star Island Twin!"

Athena and Allen see the commotion, and Athena says, "Luckily they haven't noticed us yet. I didn't think it would be pandemonium like this."

Principal Jenkins walks through the crowd with his loudspeaker. "Move away from the DJ booth at once!" He tells The Party Boys to turn the music off. "You kids are acting like you're at a Justin Bieber concert or something. You need to back away from the area at once."

Suzy calls her publicist to have someone come get her. Suzy's publicist is in a helicopter coming from the Casa Blanca Hotel and offers to swing by the school to pick Suzy up.

Suzy shrieks, "My publicist has a chopper coming to pick me up. I have to go to the football field."

Francisco stammers crazily, "Wha-wha-what a chopper! Wow, that's the coolest thing this school will ever see."

They tell Principal Jenkins who wants the socialite off the school's campus as safely as possible. He lets the coaches know that for the next hour, no students are allowed around the football field. He has the janitor bring him his golf cart, and he drives Suzy and Francisco to the football field. As the Principal drives away with Francisco and Suzy, a hundred students go crazy trying to touch Suzy and taking pictures of her on their cell phones.

A group of girls scream, "Francisco you're the coolest ever! You're dating one of the Star Island Twins!"

Athena says to Allen, "For now, we'll keep our distance from Francisco since no one has recognized me yet."

Allen replies, grinning, "Maybe it has something to do with Suzy. She is actually a part of the social scene in Miami. You just started a year ago doing your appearances in South Beach. I'm sorry, babe, but the Star Island Twins have you beat in this town. You're known around the world, but in Miami, there are celebrities everywhere."

Athena replies, "You think so? I'm happy to know that. I couldn't bear going through what I've just witnessed. I think, for now, we'll stay apart at school. There are only a few months left of school anyways."

"Are you sure, Athena?" asks Allen a little stunned.

She nods. "Yes, we had a great time in Greece, and there were over a million likes on several social media sites of people checking us out, and now it's over twenty million views of us being together on YouTube. If these students figure out, they saw us with the Star Island Twins… and they now see Francisco's dating Suzy… they already know you and Jake are friends with Francisco. And when they see Jake walking with you and Fran, they'll put the puzzle together."

"You may be right," says Allen sounding a little sad.

Athena teases him as they walk away. "Are you jealous of your brothers getting all the attention?"

Allen smirks in reply. "C'mon. I'm happy for Francisco and Jake. They're having their fifteen minutes of fame. They can suck it all up this way. They can't when they're dressed as the Atlantean Superhero Ballers."

"Let's hope nothing goes to their heads especially now. The world knows us as the Teen Warriors and Glam Girl Warrior Princess," says Athena with a wink.

Allen laughs and says, "There you go, Athena. The warrior thing isn't killing your ego, or is it?"

Athena boasts, "Hmm… just a tiny bit. No, not really. I think America is more crazed about our superhero persona than the rest of the world."

Allen replies, "Well, the rest of the world hasn't seen us in action yet. One day they might… you never know."

The couple walks to their next class. Meanwhile, Principal Jenkins takes Suzy and Francisco to the football field in his golf cart. He starts to act like a fan. "I'm sorry about that, miss. These teens are really star-struck."

Suzy smiles politely. "No problem. It comes with the territory."

Principal Jenkins acts extra friendly like he is a star-struck teen. "Ms. Suzy, would you sign this for me? It's for my daughter, Natalie."

Suzy beams. "Sure, my pleasure,"

Francisco mumbles, "And who's the groupie here? Trying to mack on my lady, bro?"

Principal Jenkins pretends he doesn't hear Francisco and says a little sarcastically, "Your boyfriend is such a fine young man."

Francisco thinks. *Now this guy is really kissing my ass.*

He begins to brag out loud, "You know, I got it like that, bro."

Principal Jenkins gives Francisco a stern look as if he were saying: "No matter what, you're still a student here, and you will act appropriately." He lets Francisco slide since he's dating one of the most prominent socialites in the United States.

The helicopter patiently waits.

"I'm taking you to the helicopter," says Francisco with pride.

"Thank you, chico, my handsome Latino boy," says Suzy with a grand smile.

Francisco grins confidently. "I'm a man, baby. Well, in two years when I'm eighteen."

Suzy says while wiggling her nose on Francisco's nose, "That's why I'm crazy for you."

She gets into the helicopter with her publicist, and the aircraft takes off blowing pieces of grass and dust all over Francisco's expensive white linen shorts and green shirt. He runs back to the golf cart, and Principal Jenkins says with a smirk, "What do you think you're doing, son? Your girlfriend's a socialite… not you. Get your ass to class. I won't give you a tardy this time, but next time I will, bro." Principal Jenkins smiles and takes off in his golf cart.

Francisco mutters, "What an ass! I hooked him up with a picture and an autograph, and he can't give a player a ride to class. What a punk!" Francisco brushes the debris off his pants and shoes and walks to his last class.

CHAPTER SEVENTEEN

JAKE ATTEMPTS SUICIDE

Jake feels like his world has ended. Standing in the foyer looking up at the railing on the second level he thinks. *If I tied a rope and jumped, I would end all my worries. I won't have to worry about having a kid or facing Samantha, who has been so sweet to me. I can't bear being ridiculed by those jerks at school.*

Jake walks into the kitchen and searches through the cabinets to see if he can find a rope or an extension cord. He finds a long brown extension cord in one of the closets. He grabs it and writes a note: *Dear Francisco and Allen,*

You two are the best brothers a guy could ever ask for. I wish I could be around when you save the world. I'll truly miss you both. And, Athena, thank you for giving my brothers and me a wonderful home to live in. You're the best big sister a guy could ever have. You're so mature and responsible, almost like a mother, which is weird to say. Allen's so lucky to have you in his life. I will also really miss Uncle Zadok and Aunt Aoki. You two are so amazing together. I know, Uncle Zadok that your soul food down under will be the best thing Australia will ever experience. And to the love of my life, Samantha, you're very special to me. I am sorry for what I've done to betray you. I hope you will have it in your heart to forgive me. I'll always love you.

Love,

Jake.

Jake tapes the note on the white designer T-shirt Samantha bought him. He grabs a bottle of Jack Um he'd hidden in a cabinet and downs half of it while crying and thinking about how he's destroyed his relationship with Samantha and let his family down. He knows he shouldn't have gotten involved with Becky Honeycomb who was a sweet innocent girl he took advantage of.

Jake ties the extension cord around the railing on top of the stairs, and he ties the other end of the cord around his neck after finishing the bottle of Jack Um. He steps over the railing and jumps, but the extension cord breaks, and he falls onto the marble floor of the foyer. He lands on his right foot and breaks his ankle. He rolls into a ball and screams in agony.

Allen sits in the back of his astronomy class hearing Jake scream through the crystal, which vibrates and thumps like a beating heart. Allen telepathically tells Athena and Francisco, *Jake sounds like he's in trouble. I'm teleporting to the mansion.*

Francisco yells telepathically, *No, Allen! We all go together.*

Allen sneaks out of class and telepathically says, *Meet me by our lockers now.*

Athena transmits, *I'm on my way.* Allen sees Athena and Francisco as he creates a rainbow cloud and teleports them inside the mansion. They are by Jake's side in a matter of seconds.

Francisco looks at the broken extension cord around Jake's neck and sees the note taped to his T-shirt. In a panic, Francisco shouts, "Jake, what the hell happened, bro! What were you trying to do!?" He grabs the note off Jake's shirt and reads it.

Crying, Athena whispers through her tears, "Jake, why would you do this to yourself!?"

Jake's pain is too intense for him to respond. He's so pale he looks like he might pass out.

Athena says to Allen, "Can you do something?"

Allen sighs, nods and bends over Jake's ankle, saying calmly, "Jake, I'm going to try to heal this for you, okay?"

Through his pain, Jake blurts out, "Okay! Please do whatever you can!"

Allen places his hands on Jake's ankle; his blue-green eyes glow a light green color. Healing energy shoots out of Allen's fingertips into Jake's broken ankle slowly mending the bones back together. The color starts to come back into Jake's face as the pain dissipates. He stops crying, and Francisco sits with him on the floor as Allen removes his hands from Jake's ankle and leans against a wall to recover from the intensity of the healing session.

The exhaustion makes Allen feel dizzy. Athena rushes to him and holds him as he dozes off. She whispers to Francisco, "You should take Jake to the ER just to get him checked out." Francisco nods and says, "Good idea."

Jake can stand, but Francisco has to help him hobble out the door.

Fifteen minutes pass before Allen opens his eyes. He looks at Athena and moans. "My head is ringing a little… Is Jake okay?"

Athena replies with a tear in her eye, "Yes, my love. It looks like Jake only has a sprained ankle now, thanks to you. Francisco took him to the ER just to make sure everything's fine."

In the car, Francisco says, "What's going on with you, bro? I've known you pretty much all my life, and I've never seen you act this way. I would never have thought you would try something so stupid!"

"I'm sorry, man. I don't know how I got to this point," says Jake.

Francisco punches his fist hard on the steering wheel and screams, "Damn it, Jake! I'm like your brother! You know you can talk to me."

Jake stares straight ahead as Francisco honks his horn at the driver in front of him who is slowly moving out of his lane. "I don't get it. You're living like a king… and you have one of the hottest girls in the world. Not just in Miami, but in the world, and you want to blow all of—"

"I know," Jake blurts out. "I'm sorry. I know we're the luckiest sons of bitches that ever walked the face of the Earth. And I almost ended my life…"

Francisco asks, "Why?"

"Do you know Becky Honeycomb?"

Francisco nods. "Yeah, so what about her?"

Jake looks down and mumbles, "She's pregnant, and it's mine. I don't know what to do, bro. I'm just a teenager who's never done anything with my life. All I know is partying.... I don't know one thing about being a father. I feel pathetic right now."

Francisco is speechless.

Jake continues, "I'm sorry, Fran, I really am. And today in school, you know who I have in my class? Becky! I heard some girls and guys talking about me behind my back, and a few of them were giving me bad looks. I heard one girl say, 'This guy is a freeloader living in a nice mansion, driving a nice car and wearing expensive clothes. And to top it off, he's dating one of the hottest girls in Miami!' How am I supposed to feel now that I'm going to be a father? I can barely take care of myself. My dreams are gone, man. No more Your Last Resort restaurant! No college, and probably no Samantha! Dude, my life is over."

Francisco screeches to a stop at the side of the road and declares, "No, it's not, Jake! We're brothers, and we'll get through this. I want you to take a paternity test."

Jake stammers, "A wha… a what?"

"I want you to be sure that this kid is yours."

Jake laughs cynically. "You think Becky Honeycomb's playing me?"

Francisco shrugs and replies, "Who knows, bro. She sees you're living the life and thinking you're Mr. Millionaire Mack Daddy or something. You're going to have a paternity test done."

"Okay… but when it comes back saying I'm the father, I'll have to deal with it."

Francisco says with pride, "Jake, if you're the father, then I'll be his uncle. Better yet."

He imitates Marlon Brando in the Godfather: "I'll be the best Godfather that little bambino would ever have."

Jake chuckles. "All right, dude. Let's do it."

Francisco does the warrior's salute and says, "Cool, it's on and popping. Let's get you x-rayed and make sure you're all good… And tomorrow I'll talk to Becky Honeycomb for you."

"No!" yells Jake. "I'll talk to her tomorrow."

Back at the mansion, Allen's in bed, but he's feeling better. Athena appears in his room with a tray of food - chicken noodle soup, crackers, cookies and milk.

Allen gulps down the soup and Athena laughs. "I guess healing Jake's broken ankle has given you an appetite."

Allen smiles, wipes his mouth on his sleeve, and burps. "Thanks! I feel better now."

Athena wrinkles her nose and feels his forehead. "You still have a slight fever, superhero. I think you should stay in bed, and I'll check on you in the morning."

"Yes, mother," says Allen with a grin as he plants a kiss on Athena's forehead. "You're the mother of my future children, but you can be mine for now."

She playfully hits him on his shoulder, and smiles. "Good, now it's time for me to do my homework… I also have to write in my journal about how to make the public school system better."

Allen teases. "Mother Athena is helping to make the South Beach public school system a better place for teens."

Athena declares, "You bet I will. I'll have my publicist set up a meeting with the school board and superintendent once I have my diploma."

Allen winks at her. "Little Miss Ambitious."

Meanwhile, at the hospital, Francisco sits patiently in the ER waiting room. An hour later, Jake hops out on a pair of crutches with his foot in an ankle brace. He announces, "It's only a sprain, not even a hairline fracture."

Francisco jumps up and screams, "Yes!"

The other people in the waiting room look at him like he's a crazy person.

Francisco puts his arm around Jake. "Brother, you're already in the good news department. And… after we talk to little Ms. Honeycomb tomorrow I'm hoping there'll be two good things you've heard within twenty-four hours."

Jake mumbles, "I hope so, Fran… I really do."

***

Uncle Zadok and Aoki have just returned from Greece, and when they enter the mansion, Uncle Zadok yells out, “Children, Uncle Zad and your amazing Aunt Aoki are home!”

Athena walks to the staircase and looks down below at her favorite uncle. “Hi, Uncle Zadok and, Aunt Aoki, how were your extra days in Greece?”

Zadok looks up at Athena with a huge smile. “Niece, I can’t thank you enough. Now bring your beautiful self down here and give me a hug.”

Aoki giggles. “Leave the girl alone, Zadok. Athena’s probably busy with homework.”

Athena grins and says, “It’s okay, I’ll come down…”

Athena hugs Zadok and kisses him on the cheek. Then she hugs Aoki and says, “I love that scent… is that—”

“Yes, it’s the perfume you wear, Athena… I noticed you had a small bottle of it in your bathroom on the yacht.”

Athena gleefully nods. “Yes, I left it there. I brought several bottles with me to keep in the chateau and the boat.”

Aoki says, “I loved the scent, so I had to try it on… and I loved the well-crafted butterfly-shaped bottle.”

Athena turns red in the cheeks. “Thank you. I found out about it from a girl at my school… Mercedes. Do you remember her? Josh’s girlfriend?”

“How is that boy doing?” asks Uncle Zadok with concern.

“I think he’s fine from what Allen’s told me.”

Uncle Zadok says, “I hope so. That kid has been through some rough times in his life.”

Allen hears his aunt and uncle and runs downstairs. “I see you made it home.” He kisses Aoki on the cheek and bends down to give Uncle Zadok a hug.

Zadok says, “Nephew, are you sick? I hear you sniffling. I’m surprised that a strong young buck like you is sick. I have never heard of an Atlantean being sick. I don’t think I’ve ever been sick except for that one time!”

“Zadok, just relax, baby,” says Aoki.

Zadok laughs and says, “Sorry about that, neph. I’m sure you’ll be fine.”

"Yeah, I should be one hundred percent by tomorrow," says Allen, who is clearly in high spirits.

Uncle Zadok asks, "Where are my other two nephews? Tweedledum and Tweedledee?"

Aoki slaps him on the back of his head. "Stop it!"

Zadok grins mischievously. "You know I'm joking, honey. Speaking of you know who… You know what I just saw on your internet website thing? Those boys need to learn how to dance, especially if they have two stunning ladies like the Star Island Twins. Whoo Whee! If I was only two-hundred and seventy-five years younger, boy I tell you. With those girls, I would jitterbug with them all night on the dance floor."

Athena giggles and says, "That's why it's good to have you back, Uncle Zadok. You know how to keep the atmosphere positive and lively."

Uncle Zadok asks, "They're out with the socialite girls, huh? Well, they better give those foxy ladies some room to breathe before the girls kick those guys to the curb. They'll be following you two around like puppy dogs for the rest of their lives if they don't."

"Follow who around like puppy dogs?" asks Jake as he hobbles in on his crutches.

Zadok chuckles and whips his wheelchair around without noticing Jake's crutches. He rolls into the elevator with Aoki and says, "Gotta get some rest… Jet lag you know. Goodnight, boys! Goodnight, Athena."

The teens yell back, "Good night, Uncle Zadok. Good night, Aunt Aoki! Sleep well!"

Francisco walks in behind Jake laughing. "I'm sure Unc had a great time in Santorini like we did."

As soon as the elevator door closes, Jake says, "I'm really sorry, guys… about everything. I didn't mean it, honest. I let you all down…"

Allen hugs Jake who starts to cry. "I promise you no matter how down and low I'm feeling, I'll be here for you."

The gang huddles around Jake.

Allen says, "It's okay. Do you know what heals all wounds and sickness?"

"No, what's that?" asks Jake.

"It's love," replies Athena, answering Allen's question.

They catch each other's eye and wink at each other.

Allen shouts, "Who are we?!"

The teen warriors shout back, "Atlantean Superhero Ballers!"

Allen repeats, "Who are we?!"

"Atlantean Superhero Ballers!" They hug and high-five each other.

Jake says, "I feel much better now! Allen, Athena… I have to tell you something."

They look alarmed and say together, "What is it?"

Jake looks at the floor and mumbles, "Becky Honeycomb is pregnant."

"What!?" shrieks Athena, almost knocking Jake off his crutches.

Jake whispers, "I'm so sorry about all of this."

Athena is pissed off and red hot. Allen says soothingly, "Calm down, babe."

Athena scowls. "I want to grab a rope and do the job for you."

Allen and Francisco yell at once, "Whoa! Whoa! Athena."

"Do you realize you have a beautiful, sweet girl who totally loves you?" Athena asks Jake as she glares at him. "Not only that… I think she wants to marry you one day."

"Really?" asks Jake with a surprised smile.

Athena growls, "Don't you smile at me, Jake… I'll give you another missing tooth, mister! You're lucky I love you and think of you as a brother, Jacob. I love you too much to want to kill you." Athena frowns. "I'm going to walk away and breathe."

"What are you going to do, bro?" asks Allen.

Jake says, "I think Francisco's right. I'm going to ask for a paternity test before doing anything."

Allen asks, "You don't think it's yours?"

Jake sadly replies, "I do… but—"

"Allen, we need to be for sure, bro," blurts out Francisco. "We don't know anything really about Becky Honeycomb. I think Jake should have a paternity test done and soon."

Allen nods. "Yeah, I agree with Francisco." He looks at Jake. "Hey, bro, we're all here for you." The boys do the warrior's salute.

Allen says, "We're warriors, baby. Now I know why you pulled that stunt earlier. Please, Jake, for all of us, talk to us first, man… before you let the whole world crash down on your head. We're here to help shield you from that. Hell, you have a shield in the Warrior's Room if you need some protection."

Jake laughs. "I'll keep that in mind… and if I am the father, I might need that shield for protection from Becky's morning sickness, so she won't puke on me."

The boys laugh. Jake smiles a little. "Thanks, guys. I feel a little better. I'm going to talk to Becky in the morning… Now I'm going to take a nice long, hot shower and wash this insane day away. I also need to email a few people to see what I missed in class today."

Allen nods. "Okay, dude."

Jake jokes, "Damn! Now I'm like Uncle Zadok, I have to take the elevator… Being crippled sucks."

Allen and Francisco simultaneously say, "Watch it now!"

Allen teases. "Uncle Zadok will roll up on a brother if he hears you say that. He'll river dance all over you with his phantom legs."

Jake smiles and says, "Thanks again, guys… I'm going to apologize to Athena before I go to my room."

Joking, Allen whispers, "Okay, brother. Be careful. You saw what she did to Dorgan's bodyguard after the football game."

Jake grimaces. "I know and thanks for reminding me. Keep your guard up at all times." Jake winks and says from the heart, "I love you, guys."

Francisco and Allen both wink at him. "Back at cha."

Jake takes the elevator and hobbles to Athena's bedroom. He knocks on the open door. "Athena?"

She doesn't invite him in or get up, but instead stays seated in front of her vanity mirror combing her hair. "Jake, I'm not mad at you. Well, I am mad at you because you've been acting stupid and childish lately."

Jake mumbles, "I know, Athena, and that's why I wanted to apologize to you. I respect you more than anyone I know, and I'm sincerely sorry for the way I've acted."

"If this baby is yours, you know that's the end of you and Samantha."

Jake looks at the floor and nods. "I understand."

Athena sighs and says, "I want you to realize that the twins are like my sisters now. I will not lose contact with them because of your actions. I feel sorry for poor Francisco. Do you have any idea of what he'll have to do to smooth things over with Suzy?"

Jake says, "I know Francisco shouldn't be involved."

Athena becomes a little irritated. "But he is. Don't you get it, Jake? They're twins, like you and Francisco. They do everything together, and if you're not with Samantha, it's going to be really awkward for Francisco."

Jake replies in a sad voice, "I never thought about it like that. I've only thought about my situation."

Athena looks at Jake lovingly. "No matter what happens, I support you. We're family."

Jake smiles and whispers, "Thanks for your support, Athena."

Athena smiles reassuringly. "You'll get through this. It'll make you stronger."

Jake sighs. "I hope so…"

CHAPTER EIGHTEEN

THE ANOYMOUS NOTE

The next morning, Uncle Zadok prepares a breakfast feast for his favorite kids. When everything's ready, he yells into the intercom: "Come and get it while it's hot!" Francisco and Jake throw on their clothes and race downstairs. Jake looks and feels like he's ready to fight a war he's never fought. He ponders while he runs into the dining room. *I had my tooth knocked out. I fought Gargoyles and crocodile-headed bodyguards. I will face my worse and scariest foe yet, a pregnant teenager by the name of Becky Honeycomb.*

Allen waits upstairs for Athena, who is putting on her pink robe and matching slippers. As she walks out of her bedroom to join him, he wolf-whistles. "Whip whoo! Well, look at you."

He extends his arm to escort her downstairs.

Athena smiles at him. "I feel spectacular today… and I have a feeling that today is going to be a great day for everyone."

Allen sighs. "I hope so, especially for Jake…"

Jake is happily eating his pancakes, omelet, and sausage smothered with maple syrup when he glances over his shoulder and sees Allen escorting his girlfriend to her seat.

Athena smiles at Jake and says, "You look terrific this morning, Jake."

Through a mouthful of pancake, he declares, "I feel awesome! Today, I face my demons."

Uncle Zadok frowns and says, "Let's not talk about Reptilians and Gargoyles at this time in the morning."

The teens laugh and Francisco winks and says, "That's a good one, Unc."

Zadok looks across the table at his warriors and asks, "How did we sleep?"

Everyone replies, "Great."

Allen says, "I don't even have the sniffles anymore."

Zadok shouts, "Good!" and pounds his fist on his chest. "That's the African Zulu and Atlantean warrior stock in you, neph!"

Everyone cheers.

Aoki says sweetly, "Honey, calm down; you've been worked up ever since you started cooking this morning."

Zadok chuckles. "You're right, my love. Okay everyone, eat up and let's have a wonderful day!" He lifts his coffee cup, and the teens raise their juice glasses. "Cheers!"

The teens finish their breakfast and rush upstairs to get dressed for school. Jake wears a white silk shirt with gold buttons, black shorts, and white sneakers. He tops off the ensemble with black shades. Francisco wears a red, short-sleeve shirt, white slacks, and blue sneakers. He looks in the mirror, makes a finger gun and says, "I'm killing everybody Americano-style."

Allen wears a pair of tan cargo pants and a white short-sleeve linen shirt with white sneakers. Athena puts on a white halter dress she created to look like the iconic dress Marilyn Monroe wore in *The Seven Year Itch*. She accessorizes it with white flats, big gold hoop earrings and multiple bangles. They all wear their crystal necklaces.

Zadok and Aoki are in the foyer waiting to see the fashion parade as the teens leave for school. Zadok watches Athena descend the stairs like the Goddess she is. He clutches his heart and shrieks, "Oh, Elders of Zion please help me! Save me!" Athena almost falls down the stairs laughing so hard.

Allen says with a smirk, "Unc, you have to stop that. You have high blood pressure, and we don't want Athena spiking your heart rate up."

Zadok boasts, "Neph, haven't I already told you that I come from Atlantean Zulu stock? I'm just fine, thank you very much. Now get to school."

As the teens walk outside, Allen asks, "Are we're going together or solo?"

Athena replies with a bit of swagger, "I'm feeling so… lo, like I said, today feels spectacular. The last one to school is a rotten egg."

Jake hobbles on his crutches to Samantha's black Maserati as Francisco digs for his keys in his pants pocket. He yells, "Ah man! These pants are too tight!"

Allen shouts, "You've been gaining some weight… starting to look like Uncle Zadok!"

Francisco growls, "Not funny, bro. I'm not going to get big like Uncle Zadok."

They all make it out of the driveway, and as Jake zooms by in the Maserati, he says telepathically to Allen, *You can't beat this Italian vehicle, my brother. Woohoo!*

Jake shifts gears and approaches Athena. She says telepathically, *You may have that expensive car, but you don't have the extras I have in mine. They're worth more than that piece of metal.* She blasts her music and weaves through traffic, shifting gears like a professional racecar driver.

Francisco's trailing behind in his Camaro shouting telepathically, *Not fair, guys! I couldn't grab my keys.*

You snooze you lose, Fran, says Allen with a laugh.

Francisco replies in his Tony Montana voice, *I see you, Allen. I'm right behind you. Say hello to my little friend.* He slams his foot on the pedal and passes Allen.

Allen sighs and says telepathically, *Alright. I'll let all of you hot rodders shine. Maybe I should have a little more horsepower in my whip.*

Francisco laughs. *Yeah, maybe you should.*

Athena's ahead of Jake as they approach the school. They stop at a red light before entering the school parking lot, and Jake looks at Athena who is impatiently waiting for the light to turn green. When it does, they both punch their gas pedals; their car engines sound like sixteen hundred horses wanting to be released from the starting gate. Their tires burn rubber creating a cloud of smoke. Athena pulls into the school parking lot still ahead of Jake. Allen pulls in behind Francisco. He sees Athena cheering.

She jumps up and down yelling telepathically, *Once again, I won!*

On their way to the lockers from the parking lot, Athena does a supermodel strut and gloats, "Who's the only racecar driver you've ever met who looks this glamorous while she's kicking everyone's ass?"

Allen replies graciously, "Only you."

Jake says, "You know what we should do after we kick some monster ass, but before you two get married this summer? We should settle this once and for all by having a race on a real racetrack."

They all shout, "You're on."

Jake breaks away from the group and walks to his locker. On his way, he hears snickers and whispers. "Yeah, Jake O'Connor is the baby daddy." He sees Becky talking to her girlfriends and motions to her.

Becky excuses herself from her girlfriends who are giving Jake the evil eye.

Jake whispers, "Becky, I'll be here for you if the kid is mine. There's one thing we have to do first."

She smiles and touches his face. "What's that, sweetheart?"

Jake moves her hand away, and says, "I want a paternity test."

Becky protests. "What Jake? You think I go sleeping around? Is that it? You think I wanted to be pregnant by you! I will not have a paternity test! It's your responsibility to take care of your child!"

The students in the hallway stop what they're doing to watch the fight. Jake can hear a few girls adding their two cents. "Umm-hmm! *You go, girl.* You tell him like it is with his *trifling* ass!"

Francisco hears the commotion and runs over to stand next to Jake as he shoots back, "You know what, Becky! We'll see if this baby is mine!"

Francisco says, "Yeah! We'll have a lawyer on this pronto!"

Jake snarls at Francisco, "Fran, please. I got this!" he glares at Becky and says, "Yeah, it's exactly what my brother, Francisco said… If you want to play hardball baby! I'll have my lawyer see about this!"

Becky looks like she might burst into tears. "Fine!" she yells and storms off.

"I'm a little worried. Are you okay, Jake?" asks Francisco.

Looking sad, Jake nods. "Yeah, I'm fine." He puts his backpack over his shoulder and hobbles on his crutches to class. Francisco telepathically says, *No matter what, bro, I would be proud to be an uncle.*

Jake smiles slightly and says, "Thanks, dude."

Later that day, as Jake is putting his backpack in his locker to go to lunch, a linebacker intentionally bumps him hard and knocks him down. The linebacker barks, "Watch where you're standing cripple."

Jake gets up and sighs, says to himself, "What did I do to that guy?"

He hobbles on his crutches to the quad to see Allen and Francisco. One of The Party Boys sees them and announces over the microphone, "It's Francisco and Jake, The Star Island Twins' boyfriends!" They can hear cheers and boos coming from the students.

Some girls yell out, "Two-timer, what a poor excuse for a father you'll be!"

Allen looks at Jake and says with encouragement, "Don't worry about it, bro."

The DJ plays the twins' song. Francisco runs up to the DJ and asks, "Hey, guys, could you cool it with the twins' music? Maybe play something else?"

One of the DJs displays the okay sign.

Jake grimaces and looks at Allen. "It's only a matter of time before Samantha finds out about what I did," he whispers.

Allen pats him on the back and says, "Hang in there, brother, and we'll see how this plays out."

Jake replies, "Thanks, Allen. You're definitely more mature than I am. You always know what to say, even if it's the simplest thing."

Allen smiles. "I don't know if that's true, but things can only get better compared to where you were yesterday."

"True that, my brother."

They see Athena across the quad, and Allen telepathically jokes, *How are you hanging in there not being around me during lunch?*

Are you sure it isn't the other way around? Athena quips.

I confess. It could be a little bit, Allen laughs.

Athena says flirtatiously, *Don't worry; you'll see me after school.*

Allen begs like a kid wanting candy, *Really? Can I? Can I?*

Athena giggles.

The bell rings, and everyone disperses. Jake walks to his locker and notices a note folded in half, taped to it. He reads the note which is written in a girly curlicue script.

> *Dear Jake,*
>
> *I feel sorry for the torture you're going through. I'm not going to let Becky Honeycomb get away with deceiving you. I see how nice you've become. Becky is not pregnant with your child. She thinks because you live in a nice house, and wear expensive clothes, and driving a nice car that you can take care of her and the baby. The jerk that bumped into you earlier is the father. He's jealous of you because he knows he can't take care of the baby. And, to top it off, he might not even graduate this year. He's a Neanderthal. Why do you think Becky made a scene when you mentioned a paternity test? I think it's terrible that she's pinned this on you. I wish you the best with your life.*

The note is not signed. Jake screams with joy, "Yes!" and jumps in the air almost landing hard on his sprained ankle. "Ouch! Oh happy day!" A couple of students stare at him like he's nuts. Jake smiles and shouts, "Hey everybody, stop being so damn nosy and stop believing everything you hear!" Jake hobbles into his science class whistling like he's the happiest guy in the world.

Becky's sitting in her seat waiting for Jake. When she sees him hobble in, she smiles and says, "Our baby won't stop kicking. I hope I don't get sick today." She looks down at her belly and rubs it meaningfully.

Jake says quietly with a slightly menacing tone, "You have the wrong guy."

Mrs. Jones hears him and says, "Jake, please."

Jake nods at Mrs. Jones and then whispers, "Becky, I know you're pregnant by that caveman linebacker."

Becky covers her mouth in shock.

"What? You didn't think I'd find out?" asks Jake with disgust.

Several students behind them hear the conversation. One girl gasps and exclaims, "Oh my God! Becky Honeycomb! You conniving vixen."

She quiets down when Mrs. Jones looks across the room to see who's talking instead of dissecting their frog.

The students can't contain themselves; comments and opinions spread like wildfire. "Becky Honeycomb lied to make Jake think he's the father of her baby… What a slut!"

The teacher looks around and bellows, "All right, class, I won't stand for this!"

Becky starts to cry. She gets up and rushes out of the classroom. As she flees, she says through sniffles, "I'm sorry, Mrs. Jones. I don't feel so good."

The bell finally rings and as the guys and girls file out some of them pat Jake on his back. They say, "I knew it all along."

Jake says with irritation, "That's not what most of you were saying to me earlier. Now you're all nice to me again as if nothing ever happened. You already had me tried and hung!"

Jake telepathically tells the ASB, *I have exciting news, I can't believe it! I'm a free man!* Francisco shoots back telepathically, *It's a celebration bitches! I'm talking about Jack Um and champagne!*

Jake says telepathically, *Not yet, guys… Let's celebrate after Athena graduates and after Allen finds the crown and becomes King. I still have to figure out what to do about Samantha.*

Athena says telepathically, *Jake, you were lucky. Now do the right thing.*

Jake transmits, *Don't worry, Athena. I will own up to my mistake.*

After school Jake texts Samantha: *Hey babe, can I bring your car to your home and see you?*

Samantha replies with a smiley face. *Sure you can handsome.*

Jake drives the Maserati to Star Island. His eyes well up with tears as he pulls into the long driveway. He wipes his eyes and thinks. *I have to man up and tell Samantha what happened. It's going to change everything for Francisco and me if Samantha doesn't accept my apology for cheating on her.*

Samantha walks outside to greet Jake with a kiss. "Hello, pretty boy… I'm so happy to see you."

Jake replies with a slight smile, "Me too gorgeous… me too."

Samantha looks Jake in the eyes. "What's wrong, Jake?"

"Can we go out back to your dock and talk?" asks Jake.

Samantha nods. "Yes, let's get some fresh air and chat on the boat." They walk outside and stroll across the lawn toward the boat dock.

Suzy walks out after them. Smiling ear-to-ear, she yells, "Hey, you two! I'll see you later. I'm going to see my man at his home."

Feigning nonchalance, Jake says, "You're going to... going to see Francisco?"

"I am going to see my guy and hang out by the pool and have some of Uncle Zadok's famous soul food and sweet tea."

Samantha says, "Have fun!"

Suzy puts on her mirrored shades, turns back toward the house and sashays in her stiletto heels across the lawn to her red convertible Ferrari. Jake and Samantha smile at each other as they listen to the powerful Ferrari engine start up and then roar ferociously down the long driveway.

Samantha says, "I just love how your family gets along with my sister and me."

All of a sudden, Jake breaks down and cries. "Samantha I'm so sorry about a terrible thing I did. I almost killed myself because of it." He drops to the grass and rolls into a fetal position.

Shocked, Samantha sits down in the grass with him and hugs him. "Jake, whatever it was. It doesn't matter to me. I don't care about what you did. I love you, so let's forget about what ever happened and move on."

Jake dries his eyes with his shirt sleeve and looks at Samantha lovingly. "Are you sure? It could change things between us."

Samantha starts to cry while they hold each other. Through her tears, she looks deeply into her boyfriend's eyes and says with a loving but firm resolve, "Yes, I'm sure of it. I love you, Jake. Let's keep the past in the past and start from this moment. We will not keep secrets from each other ever again. And whatever happened... can't happen again... Okay?"

Jake smiles a little and says, "Okay, my love."

CHAPTER NINETEEN
PROM SHOPPING

Several months have passed... At breakfast one morning, Athena says to Allen, "This coming weekend is the prom. I don't care who knows who I am now. Finals are over, and I'll be graduating next week."

Allen takes a big bite of his strawberry waffle, and mumbles, "Yeah, it'll be fun!"

Francisco laughs and says, "Yeah, bro. It's going to be fun for all of us, but too bad Jake and I aren't seniors so we could take the twins to South Beach High. Oh well... they're going to take us to their prom!"

Allen replies, "After what happened last time, I'm not sure that's such a great idea. Everyone at the prom will be focusing on you two."

Athena playfully teases. "Aww, my handsome guy feels that his thunder is going to be taken away if Francisco is there with Suzy and Jake with Samantha."

Allen smirks and says, "No way...but I must say, I'll be the most envied sophomore, going to prom with my beautiful socialite senior girlfriend."

Francisco and Jake point at Allen, as Francisco yells, "See, I knew it, you do like the attention you get being with Athena... especially if the whole school knows who she is!"

Allen says, "No... not really, it's not at all like that. It would be cool for everyone to know that the shy kid with no muscles is now the total opposite and he has one of the hottest girls in the world as his prom date. Plus, I'm the one who was invited."

Athena giggles as she says, "I can see the headline in our school newspaper: 'Allen King Dating the Stunning Australian Greek Socialite Athena Dranias, Known to All of Us as Audrey Monroe!' The Fairytale Story Unfolds!" Athena keeps giggling to herself as she takes a dainty sip of tea and nibbles on her scrambled eggs.

Uncle Zadok is quiet; he's proud of his teenage kids. Aoki looks at Zadok with pretend shock. "What is this, Zadok? You're actually being quiet for once." The teens look at Uncle Zadok, who is a little teary eyed.

He sniffles and says, "I don't want to ruin the warriors' moment. They're going to their first prom together, and Athena's graduating next week. I feel like I've known Athena all my life, but it hasn't even been a year! Soon the kingdom will be ours again, and she'll officially be my niece."

The teens look at Zadok and say, "It's okay, uncle."

Allen says, "Uncle Zadok, you deserve it. You believed in me and all of us more than we believed in ourselves at times."

Zadok exclaims, "Really, Allen? You *mean* that?"

Allen nods and smiles. "Of course, I do." He looks around at his family. "We all do."

Zadok says, "I'm sorry to sound so emotional like I'm having hormonal issues, but Damnit, I wish I had my legs so I could kick some Gargoyle ass!" He slams his fist hard on the dining room table making his plate fly up in the air. It comes down on his lap splattering maple syrup and scrambled eggs on his bald head, shirt, and pants.

Zadok chuckles and everyone laughs. He says, "I'm sorry. I just got excited! And I'm the one who has always said that we should never talk about monsters at breakfast. I'm a little overwhelmed and proud, knowing that you (the Atlantean Superhero Ballers) are so close to whooping some monster ass just got me all riled up. Sorry, troops."

"It's okay, Unc, we understand," says Allen.

Athena shouts, "Uncle Zadok, we love you!"

"I love you too, Princess," Zadok replies in a tender voice.

Athena points a trigger finger at him. "Watch it now!"

Zadok laughs boisterously. "Athena, girl, you're funny. You got me on that one."

The teens finish breakfast before driving to school in two separate cars. Jake drives with Francisco and Athena with Allen. Five minutes before the bell rings for class to start, Allen says to Athena, as they're walking to their lockers, "I'm so excited that we're going to go shopping together after school to look for our prom outfits. It feels kind of like we're going to go shopping for our wedding outfits."

Athena's eyes grow big. She grabs Allen by his arm and whispers, "Ooh! I can't wait, handsome prince! I'm going to find the most incredible... No... I'm going to collaborate with one of the most iconic designers to make the most lavish one-of-a-kind bride's gown and bridesmaid dresses."

"Oh no, I see bridezilla in the making." teases Allen.

Athena says, "Allen King, this will be the first and last time I'll get married. So, if I become a bridezilla, so be it. I'll make this the wedding event of the century!"

Allen kisses his girlfriend. "Okay, whatever you want. I need to grab a few things and go to class. I love you." He breaks away from Athena and runs to his locker.

Athena pouts like a brat and thinks. *Hmm... he had to take off right as I was getting to the good part... talking about my wedding gown.* She puts her backpack in her locker and strolls slowly down the hallway as students run past her. Athena pretends that she's walking down the aisle in Atlantis. She hums the wedding march until the bell snaps her back to reality.

Allen telepathically says to her, "On prom night, maybe we should have dinner with Francisco, Jake, and the twins before they leave since it'll be just the two of us at your prom."

Athena transmits telepathically, *Yeah, that sounds like a lovely idea, mate.*

Allen laughs, and teasing. *Mate? You've been in Miami for almost a year now, and you still can't shake your Aussie lingo when you say certain things.*

Athena proudly retorts, *That's me... I love my Australian accent and our own way of saying certain things.*

Allen says, *I love it as well. Let's tell the guys during lunch.*

That sounds like a plan, man, says Athena.

At lunchtime, the Party Boys are experimenting with new music for prom. They're planning to DJ their formal dance for the first time. The group asks the students to applaud for each song they hear so they can determine which songs people like best.

As Athena enters the quad, several students point and stare. They recognize her from the videos of her in Greece that have been posted online. It suddenly all clicks in the students' minds like a light bulb going on, when they see Francisco, Jake, and Allen join her.

Jake says, laughing, "I think the entire school knows now."

Several girls scream, "It's the Greek socialite!"

A guy yells, "Athena, you rock!"

And another guy shouts, "Wow! I have her in my physics class!"

They all take pictures and ask for autographs.

Allen yells, "Chill out, you guys, she's one of us! You should feel happy and proud; we have someone of Athena's caliber going to high school with us." Allen whistles for one of The Party Boys to turn the music down and toss him a microphone. Allen grabs the mike and says, "Athena is the same as Audrey Monroe, and she takes classes like a normal student with quite a few of you." Students cheer and Allen pleads, "Please let her enjoy her last week here. She's graduating as a Pirate!"

The students yell, "Pirates! Athena! Pirates, Pirates, yeah!"

Athena says to Allen telepathically, *Give me the microphone.* More students gather around as Athena announces, "Students of South Beach High, I'm here for you. I've been researching to help make our school a better place. For one, we need better food in our cafeteria."

The students scream, "Yeah!" A few shouts, "She understands what we need. How cool is that!"

Athena looks around at the crowd. "We need equal opportunity for all students. Do you know that thirty-five students from our senior class won't graduate this year?" The students are quiet as they listen to Athena's speech. "It's true. Look around you." The students do.

Athena continues. "There may be someone standing next to you who can't even read a book let alone do a math problem. That's a problem. We need to help each other. I know there's peer pressure to act cool, but it isn't cool, guys. There will be another ten to fifteen students who will end up becoming pregnant and dropping out of school next year. These are staggering but accurate statistics." Becky Honeycomb is in the back of the crowd listening and pretending that she doesn't hear what Athena is saying.

"You don't have to drop out. I'm starting a program to help those who need it to stay in school so you can receive your diploma. There's one too many of us who are failing ourselves and society. I am not here to preach to you. I'm telling you the truth. If you believe in what I'm saying, then let me hear you say, 'We can succeed!'"

The students scream, "We can succeed!" They applaud and chant, "Athena! Athena!" as they surround her for a group hug. They have forgotten that she is a rich and famous socialite. They see her as a normal teenager who wants to help them.

The bell rings, and the crowd departs. Athena and her warrior family notice Principal Jenkins and several teachers staring at her. Principal Jenkins stares at Athena for a moment. The teens stand dead still in silence. He starts to applaud along with other teachers who heard her speak.

Principal Jenkins walks over to Athena and says, "Young lady, that was the best speech I've heard since I marched to the Lincoln Memorial to hear Martin Luther King Jr. speak with my parents when I was very young. You spoke eloquently, giving your peers hope. That's one thing I always wanted to do as a principal. I can't reach them like you just did. You speak their language, and they understand you. Ms. Dranias, you sounded as if you were valedictorian giving the final remarks at your graduation. If I had the power, I would make you an honorable valedictorian."

"Well, thank you, sir!" says Athena.

Principal Jenkins replies, "I understand why you had to take a pseudonym… being as famous as you are. I see no harm in it, and you will still graduate with your class, under one condition…"

The Teen Warriors look at Athena, wondering what Principal Jenkins might say.

He politely asks, "Do you mind if I take a picture on my camera phone with you and get your autograph?"

Francisco says telepathically, *Here he goes again… he's a real groupie.* The teens contain their laughter.

"It would be my pleasure," says Athena with a smile.

Principal Jenkins gives the camera to Francisco on purpose. "Here you go, son. Make sure you get my good side."

Francisco mutters, "Your good side should be your ass since you act like one."

The Principal talks like a Ventriloquist through his smile. "What was that, son? You know I can put you in detention for being tardy right now."

Francisco grins and replies, "I definitely shot your good side, sir. You look great. "

Principal Jenkins looks at his camera phone with delight. "That's a good picture, Francisco." Principal Jenkins thanks Athena for the autograph and picture. He straightens his posture and snaps his fingers. "Let's go, get to class right now!"

The teens say, "Yes, sir," and quickly walk to their classes.

A few classes pass by, and school ends for the day. Allen telepathically says to Athena, *I'll meet you at the Rover.*

Athena transmits, *Okay, I'll be there.*

Jake says telepathically to Francisco, *I'm running to your car now. We need to get to the mall and find the perfect outfit before everyone else buys our sizes.*

Francisco transmits with excitement, *I'm right behind you.* They hop in Francisco's car and speed out of the parking lot.

Athena poses against Allen's Range Rover and coos, "Hello, handsome, you ready to go prom shopping?"

He nods happily. "Yeah, I'm ready to go shopping with the future, Mrs. Athena Dranias King. The new heroine for literacy and the savior of discouraged students, descended from the heavens to help them stay in school and graduate!"

Athena says, "You know what we should do once we're married? We should travel the world doing charity work like helping people living on skid row and building schools every summer."

Allen leans into Athena for a kiss, and confesses, "That's why I love you. You think about others more than you do about yourself."

Athena smiles mischievously. "We have to give in order to receive. And right now, I want to receive that sexy prom dress. So, let's get this vehicle a moving. Chop-chop,"

Allen grins. "Okay, no problem."

They pull out of the parking lot driving to the mall. Allen enters the valet parking in front of the mall. Athena jumps out, pulls out a credit card, and says, "Okay, future King of Atlantis, here's the black card. I'm off to my favorite store."

"Oh… I love that store!" says Allen.

"Then I guess we're shopping together," replies Athena.

Allen is thrilled. "I guess we are."

They enter the store and are greeted by the store manager. "Good day, my name is Claus… What are we looking for today?" he asks in a thick German accent.

Athena replies, "We are shopping for a few things."

Claus replies, "I am of service and you two are a gorgeous couple."

Athena blushes and says, "Thank you."

"Do you have any new suits in stock?" asks Allen. "We're both looking for something special for our prom this weekend."

Claus smiles and exclaims, "Oh, you have your prom. Let me show you the new black suede suits." He looks at Athena and says, "And for you my dear, we have new dresses and gowns." He escorts Athena to see the new gowns.

She sees a unique red-and-black beaded gown and gasps in awe. "I have to try that!"

Claus grins with joy. "I knew you would love that. You have such fabulous style!"

Athena graciously replies, "Thank you."

He then shows Allen the new suits. Allen says, "I'm not really a suede kind of guy."

Claus says, "Believe me, this is something different. I haven't seen anything like it." He grabs a jacket, hands it to Allen and says, "Feel that."

Allen nods with approval. "You know, Claus, this doesn't look so bad after all."

Claus claps and says, "The fabric is breathable. You won't sweat a bit in it while dancing at your prom."

Allen thinks about it for a moment and says, "Okay, let's see how it fits." Allen walks into the dressing room and comes out looking like a model. He says, "Claus, I love it. It feels nice, and it's cut perfectly."

Claus says, "You look great in it."

Allen nods. "Thank you." He walks over to Athena who looks stunning in the red-and-black dress. She's jumping up and down giggling with excitement while admiring herself in the mirror.

Allen gives her a thumbs up, and then does a model turn and asks, "So what do you think?"

Athena stops in her tracks and gazes at Allen. "Wow! My handsome, Allen King, looks super-hot in that suit."

Allen replies seductively, "You look amazing, babe. On our wedding night, I would want you to wear that so I could slowly take it off you."

Athena replies with passionate eyes, "I can't wait for that to happen on our wedding night." She walks up to Allen purring like a cat and kisses him on the cheek.

Allen says, "I think this was the easiest shopping we've ever done. You sure you don't need to look at any other gowns or dresses?"

Athena smiles big and nods. "No, I'm fine. I feel like I'm at the Waterball Games right now in my red-and-black dress cheering my man on as he scores against his opponent."

Allen whispers, "If I was playing on the Baller squad right now, I think I would be distracted looking at your sexy ass."

Athena says in a soft voice, trying not to be too naughty, "We better stop talking like this. We made an oath, no sex before marriage, remember?"

Allen nods. "Yeah, I know. After we're married it will feel more meaningful and special."

Claus walks up to them and asks, "How is everything?"

Athena says, "We'll take everything! You can ring us up."

Claus takes Athena's black card and walks to the register as two older ladies stroll in. They stop and stare at Athena and Allen, and one of the ladies asks, "What's the occasion? You two look gorgeous."

Athena cheerfully answers, "Thank you…We're going to the prom."

The lady winks at Allen and looks at Athena. "Darling, you have an attractive young man with stunning eyes. If I were only ten years younger, I would give you some competition." She laughs at her joke and says, "Enjoy yourselves, toodles."

Athena smiles and whispers to Allen, "Ten years… more like forty years."

Allen gives Athena a hug and a kiss on the forehead. "Calm down, tiger, no need to bring out the claws. You have nothing to worry about."

Athena replies with a smirk, "I know, but I still like to mark my territory."

Allen telepathically asks Francisco and Jake, *Hey, are you two at the mall yet?*

Francisco transmits, *We're in a store right now. We wanted to see what they have before hitting up the store you and Athena probably went to first.*

Allen smiles and says telepathically, *Athena and I are here right now. We're going to leave in a minute and probably go somewhere to grab a bite to eat.*

Francisco transmits, *Jake and I are going to meet with our girlfriends later. They want us to check out what they bought for prom and meet their parents before they fly off to Dubai.*

Allen remarks, *They're definitely independent.*

Francisco transmits, *Yes, they are, their parents are never home.*

Allen says, *Okay, our bags are ready, it's my job to carry them and escort my lady to lunch.*

Francisco and Jake say at once, *We'll see you at home.*

Allen and Athena walk out of the department store.

"You're such a gentleman, carrying our bags to the valet," says Athena with a big smile on her face.

As Allen walks ahead to the valet stand, Athena stops to remove a piece of gum stuck to the bottom of her shoe. A burly security guard approaches Allen as his car is pulled into the valet area.

CHAPTER TWENTY

RACIALLY PROFILED

Allen hands his valet ticket to the valet guy and walks to his car as the security guard accosts him. "Let me see your identification, boy!"

Shocked, Allen replies, "Excuse me?"

The security guard says, "I have reason to believe that the car you're driving was stolen."

Allen mutters, "You're kidding me, right?"

The security guard snarls, "I didn't ask for any back talk." He grabs his radio and says, "I got him." Three cop cars immediately screech into the valet area with their sirens and lights on.

Athena runs up looking confused and alarmed. "What's going on?" She looks at Allen and mouths, "Are you okay?"

The security guard steps between Athena and Allen. "Ma'am, step back. I have reason to believe that this boy has stolen this vehicle."

Athena screams, "What do you mean this boy!? This person happens to be my boyfriend, and that's his car!"

Allen peers around the guard's body and says in a calm voice, "Athena, don't worry about it. I'm fine. This will all be sorted out."

Allen hands his driver's license politely to the guard. "Here's my ID. You can check my registration in the glove box to verify that I'm the owner. My name is on the registration."

A police officer walks into the middle of the conversation. "We have a report that the car is stolen, and you have some type of gold crystal necklace around your neck that was also stolen."

Allen gasps in a fury. "What!"

Athena is livid. "You're harassing my boyfriend because he's Black! I will sue the police department and this mall for harassment!"

The police officer says to Allen, "Come with us to the station so we can verify that the car and necklace I see around your neck are yours."

Allen says telepathically, *Athena, I can't do anything; if I show any signs of having superpowers, it would bring unwanted attention and let everyone know that I am the Teen Warrior people have been talking about.* Athena shakes her head and transmits, *I understand, but this doesn't look safe to me.*

Allen says to Athena out loud, "Meet me at the police station."

The police officer cuffs Allen and puts him in the back of the squad car. He then looks at Allen's registration, smirks coldly, and says in his Southern drawl, "Well, I do believe this is the boy's car." Smiling lecherously at Athena, he hands her the keys and takes off with Allen.

Fuming, Athena telepathically says, *Francisco and Jake I hate to tell you this, but Allen's been falsely accused of stealing and he has been handcuffed and taken to the police station for questioning.*

Upset, Francisco telepathically replies, *What kind of bullshit is that?!*

That is absurd, Jake adds.

Yeah sis, that sucks. We're on our way, says Francisco.

Athena calls her publicist, Nicole, to get her a lawyer ASAP and have them ready to spring Allen out of jail. The publicist immediately calls a lawyer for her.

Irate, Athena transmits to Jake and Francisco, *This smells scaly… It looks like Drogan Reptilly has something to do with it.*

Francisco is pissed off. *I would love to rip his tail off again and use it as fishing bait for sharks.*

I second that, says Jake.

Still, in shock, Athena follows the police cars to Miami Central Division. She transmits to Jake and Francisco, *This station is close to the docks. It's looking more and more like what I thought… It must be Drogan!*

Allen is taken into the interrogation room with two-way mirrors. A heavyset officer walks in and barks, "Boy, you're Allen King? Yes?"

Allen politely replies, "I'm Allen King, and I'm not a boy."

The officer slaps his hands on the table. "Don't you get uppity with me! You think because you live in a mansion and wear those nice threads, you're someone important, huh?"

Allen smirks and replies, "I'm more important than you will ever know. You don't have anything on me, and if you don't give me my necklace back, you're going to be working somewhere far from here, like Alaska."

The incensed officer leans toward him. Immediately a voice yells through the speaker, "Enough, now leave us!" The officer walks out. Drogan walks in minutes later. He grins as he sits down across from Allen.

Allen says with a sigh, "I'm not surprised to see you bend so low and have me racially profiled by dirty cops and security guards."

"I told you we'd meet again, and now we're meeting on my terms," snarls Drogan. He dangles Allen's necklace in front of him. The chain quickly turns red hot in Drogan's hand, forcing him to drop it to the floor. Suddenly and unexpectedly, a thunderstorm forms above the precinct.

Allen scowls. "Your scaly Reptilian hands can't handle this Alien jewelry." The necklace materializes back onto Allen's neck.

With a note of admiration, Drogan says dryly, "Apparently, you do have great powers. When I walked in on your vacation in Greece, you summoned an invisible wormhole and teleported me into the Aegean Sea with my men. Three aggressive bull sharks met us. I narrowly escaped, but four of my ten bodyguards were eaten alive."

Allen roars, "How fortunate for you that you're still alive. You want to know about my powers, evil Hybrid!? I'll show you power."

Allen stands as a lightning bolt strikes the police station causing a power outage, making the lights go out, and the video camera in the interrogation room shuts down. The emergency generator kicks in and the lights turn back on. Drogan is splayed out on his back on the floor, choking for air as Allen's heel presses down hard on his neck, pinning him to the floor. The Hybrid Reptilian can't breathe. Allen booms with rage, "The only way to kill a serpent like you is to smash it in the head."

The Atlantean warrior lets the villain up. Drogan gasps for air while declaring calmly, "This summer I'll summon the Gargoyle and finish you off… and then I'll take your girlfriend, Athena, for my wife and I will join the pantheon of Greek Gods. Her family might accept me more than you."

Allen becomes more heated. "You really think Athena's family would accept you after you kidnapped and held her hostage on your boat? You pathetic fool! Athena isn't meant for you! I would love to kill you now but killing you and the Gargoyle together will be even sweeter. I'll be killing two birds, or should I say, two monsters, with one stone. You know why you can't wear this necklace, Drogan?"

"Why is that?" asks Drogan sarcastically.

Allen sits back in his seat as he keeps his eyes locked on Drogan. "You're an idiot you know that, if you still had Reptilian and Nomadic Indian blood in you, you would have been able to wear the necklace just as your grandfather Damius did. But not you! You want to have all the power and you actually thought you could mix my Atlantean DNA with your Reptilian blood. Still, that's not the reason why you can't wear the crystal necklace. You had to add Gargoyle blood to the mix. The Alien race's true enemies are the Gargoyles, not the Reptilians. The only way you could wear this chain without burning your neck, you would have to drain all your blood and then find a way to infuse yourself with your original combination of Reptilian and Nomadic Indian blood. You can't do that, can you? You love the rage of the Nomadic Indian and the Gargoyle blood. It's a drug to you now. I can see it in the Atlantean eyes you replicated from my DNA."

Drogan says menacingly, "Either way, Atlantean when this summer comes, you better be prepared, because there will be a war, and I'll make sure someone you love will die."

Allen's eyes glow fire engine red as he hits the iron table splitting it in half with his fist. Drogan laughs as the heavyset officer he paid off comes in to check on the cross-examination.

Drogan replies in a calm manner, "You can let this young man go. He has nothing of mine."

Allen closes his eyes and opens them. They have changed back to his blue-green color, and the thunder and lightning have stopped. Ignoring the cop, Allen gets up and walks out. He knows that the police and the security guard who harassed him are merely pawns working for the evil

Hybrid. As Allen steps out of the station, he sees Athena with her publicist and lawyer.

He says to her in a loving voice, "Hi, sweetheart, I'm fine."

Athena wipes a few tears from her glistening cheeks and says, "Thank Heavens, Allen." She grabs him and gives him a huge bear hug. "I'm going to destroy this police station and sell it piece by piece. Better yet, I'll turn the building into a school and create a literacy program for the Black youth they harass for no reason."

Allen smiles and says, "I'm fine."

"Okay, my prince. I'll let Francisco and Jake know," says Athena.

Allen says, "It's okay. I'll tell them."

Allen telepathically contacts them and says, *Hey, guys. I'm okay.*

Jake asks telepathically, *Are you sure?*

Allen answers, *Yes, I'm sorry to take you away from your shopping. Please go back and finish what you were doing. I'm fine.*

Athena's lawyer asks, "Are you all right, son? I'll take this whole precinct down and have the Chief of Police working at a fast food restaurant by the time I'm done."

Allen nods. "Yes, everything's fine. Thank you, sir, for coming, I just want to go home and be with my girl."

The lawyer shakes his hand. "Here's my card if you ever need anything."

Allen graciously replies, "Thank you."

The publicist, Nicole hugs Athena and says, "Okay, Athena. You know I'm here if you need me."

Athena nods. "Yes, I know, and thank you for being by our side last minute."

Nicole winks. "That's what I'm here for. I like to end the drama before it starts. It looks like everything's fine... Kind of like how the storm that appeared out of nowhere a few minutes ago has suddenly disappeared."

Athena smiles. "It's sunnier days ahead."

Allen gets in the passenger seat of the Range Rover, and Athena drives them home. Still fuming she says, "This had to be the work of that rich Australian slimeball, Drogan Reptilly."

"It was," mumbles Allen.

Athena slams her fist on the steering wheel. "Allen, we need to kill that son of a bitch, and we need to kill him now before he does some serious damage to us!"

Allen sighs and says, "I can't… not yet, Athena… You know why."

Athena shouts, "To hell with Josh! If he turns into Destroyer while we're retrieving your crown, I will not risk your life or anyone else's to save him!"

In a sad voice, Allen says, "I know how you feel but we just can't. The game is still being played. You know that!"

Athena is about to burst with anger. She takes a deep breath and silently counts backward from ten to one. "Okay, Allen. We're not going to let this guy ruin our week, or our prom or my graduation."

Allen whispers, "We won't see Drogan again until a few more weeks. I need to go to the chess room and glance at the chess pieces. It might give me a clue to see what could happen next when we encounter Drogan again. It's been months since I've been there. It's time to go back now… You'll be fine. You know how to reach me if you need me."

Athena stops at a red light and leans over to kiss Allen before he teleports through a solid blue rainbow cloud. There aren't many cars around making it easy for him to teleport out without being noticed.

Allen lands in the Warrior's Room in front of his armor. He stares at his golden spear, shield, and lasso. He touches the tip of his golden spear, whispering to it, "Before this summer ends, we will shed blood together. I would love nothing more than for us to tear out the heart of the Hybrid and Gargoyle at once."

He presses harder at the tip, drawing a little blood. Allen tastes it and says softly, "I will soon taste Destroyer's blood and drain the rest of Drogan's blood from his hollow heart."

Allen walks up into the chess room, and surprisingly, his grandfathers aren't there to greet him. He's alone without his spiritual guides. He puts his hand on his chin and observes the illuminated chess pieces. He notices that Josh's chess figurine seems to have moved a few squares toward the dark side of the board and is now standing between Drogan and Destroyer's game pieces.

He analyzes the chessboard and ponders. *Okay, now I see Josh is succumbing to the dark side. I don't believe it. I know his heart has light in it.*

Josh can't be deceiving himself or me. He's a good kid trying to make the best of his situation.

Allen observes one of Drogan's pawns moving closer to Francisco and Jake. The pawn looks as if it is about to grab his sword to kill either one of them. However, it's still a few moves away. Francisco and Jake could easily destroy it since their chess figurines are knights. Athena's queen figurine is still fine. She looks strong as ever standing by Allen's side.

Allen leans back on the bench as he ponders a countermove. He thinks about what Drogan said that he will make sure someone Allen loves will die. Allen sees that if he moves his king to a diagonal position, it will put him in front of Josh, leaving Drogan or the Gargoyle to flank him. Allen ponders. *I can't physically touch the chessboard. If I do, the results might not be in my favor.*

He sighs and thinks. *I know the game is played out on the battlefield, and the chessboard is merely a simulation of various possibilities.* He leans forward and whispers, "If Athena makes a move to the right taking out Drogan's queen on the chessboard after I make the move taking out his bishop that might give me the opportunity I need to kill Drogan since he's so smitten by Athena." Allen nods with a confident smile. "Yeah, it might work. I have to see what happens when we fight again. Destroyer isn't the evil king of the chessboard anymore, Drogan is."

He stands and opens the curtains. His grandfather King Leon and great-grandfather General Lionel are there. Allen smiles and says, "I didn't think you were around."

King Leon says, "We're always around for you, my grandson."

General Lionel chimes in: "We both thought it would be best for you to figure things out for yourself. You are an Atlantean General and a Prince, and soon. You will be King; you will have to make quick and decisive decisions on the battlefield…You already know that it will not be an easy task, but you have one great advantage over your enemies."

Allen asks, "What's that?"

"You have goodness in your heart and loyal friends who will fight with you to the death," replies General Lionel.

Allen says with pride, "Thank you, great-grandfather. I must prevent any casualties on my side."

King Leon says, "I have no doubt that you will prevail. We know you have tasted the powerful liquid of the Greek Gods. You are the chosen one. That's why I know you are special and meant to be the one to restore our kingdom and keep Earth safe from evil. You are well aware each time these Gargoyles come to this world. Their carbon footprint heats up the Earth's atmosphere. I am proud of you. May the Elders of Zion keep you and your friends protected."

Allen does the warrior's salute simultaneously with his grandfathers and then walks back down into the Warrior's Room and toward the King's Chamber. He sees Jumper, Bucky, and Dance II. They're delighted to see him. Allen walks to the opening of the pool, which connects to the ocean.

He says cheerfully, "Hello, my loyal friends. How have you been?"

The sea animals jump around in delight upon hearing Allen's voice. Jumper leaps so high he comes close to the ceiling. He does a triple somersault and lands flawlessly back into the water. Dance II and Bucky smile like they are applauding for Jumper. Dance II jumps onto the edge of the pool for Allen to stroke his head.

Allen says, smiling, "I'll be seeing all of you again in a few weeks. We will be victorious in restoring our kingdom."

Bucky bucks up and down in the water with glee.

Allen can hear the shark's thoughts: *I would love to taste another Reptilian or better yet a Gargoyle. That would be something to tell the sharks in my clan.*

Allen nods. "I hope you'll have both of your wishes. I'll see you soon, my friends."

He summons the wormhole, teleporting in a magnificent red, yellow, green, and blue cloud back to the mansion. He cheerfully slides down the wormhole like he's surfing, feeling the exhilaration as his dreadlocks fly in the air.

He yells out, "Woohoo!" going full speed and then slowing down as he enters the mansion. He's made it home for dinner.

CHAPTER TWENTY-ONE

Prom Night And Engagement Proposal

Allen walks into the dining room where the family is eating. No one's mentioned anything to Uncle Zadok about the incident with the cops or Drogan. Athena's happy to see that Allen appears calmer. She puts her hand on his chair, patting it. "Well, sit down, Mr. King and have a bite to eat. It looks like you enjoyed rainbow surfing."

Francisco talks with a piece of tri-tip in his mouth. "We should do that before we go into action. We need to prepare and loosen up before going to that volcanic island in Hawaii."

Jake nods. "Yeah, dude that would be gnarly, bro."

Francisco looks at Jake and teases. "C'mon, Jake, just because you have blond hair and blue eyes don't mean your gnarly ass can surf."

Jake laughs sarcastically. "Ha ha ha, Fran… It would still be fun."

"I agree, that does sound like a great idea. I would like that as my graduation present. We should all go rainbow surfing," says Athena.

Allen nods with delight. "Okay, it'll be practice and fun. We should do it in our warrior's outfits."

Athena replies excitedly, "Which reminds me… After dinner, I'm going to make a few alterations in our outfits."

Uncle Zadok says, "Wait a minute now! The warrior's uniform has been traditional for centuries. What kind of alterations are you talking about?"

Before Athena has a chance to answer, Allen says to Francisco, "Is the Grey Poupon next to you?"

With the manners and accent of a British aristocrat, Francisco answers, "Why yes, there just happens to be a jar right next to me."

Uncle Zadok looks at Allen and Francisco like they're going bonkers. Athena and Jake observe the rest of the family. They know Uncle Zadok's thinking that he missed out on something. The teens start to laugh hysterically. Francisco looks at Allen and Allen looks at Uncle Zadok as everyone points their fingers like guns at each other, and yells, "Watch it now!"

Allen winks and says, "Gotcha, Francisco!"

Puzzled and a little irritated, Uncle Zadok says, "Alright alright! Now cut out the foolishness and let's eat."

The teens reply, "Yes, Zir!" through fits of giggles.

Still wiping away tears of laughter, Francisco says, "Allen, we still got our shopping in at the exclusive stores."

Allen asks, "Oh yeah, what you get, brother?"

Francisco says, affecting a snobbish attitude, "I met this really cool store manager by the name of Claus, and he hooked me up with a one-of-a-kind black suede suit. I need a few alterations since I'm a little shorter than the sizes they have."

Athena and Allen laugh as Allen telepathically says to Athena, *Claus is the man.*

Yes, he is, Athena replies telepathically.

Teasing, Allen says to Francisco, "Let me guess, it has very breathable material, and you won't sweat a bit in it while dancing the latest dance craze at prom?"

Francisco gasps. "How did you know?"

Allen smiles. "Duh, we were in the store before you, remember?"

Francisco nods and replies, "Oh, yeah, that's right, so you have the same black suede suit?"

Allen nods with a smirk. "Yes, and I didn't need any alterations."

Athena says, "That's because your supermodel body was built for ready-to-wear."

Francisco asks, "Ready to who?"

"Ready-to-wear, straight off the rack," explains Athena.

Francisco plays it off, and says nonchalantly, "I knew that."

"No you didn't, Fran," says Jake, laughing.

Francisco scowls. "And neither did you… So what!"

Uncle Zadok says, "Well, at least you catty lads didn't… never mind… So you both have clothes for the prom?"

Jake says, "Yes. I'm wearing a white suit with white leather shoes I can slip into… young Sonny Crockett style."

Kidding, Francisco says, "So when are you going to give up that Sonny Crockett act?"

Jake retorts, "The same time you give up your Tony Montana act!"

Francisco yells, "Oh, yeah!" as he leans across the table toward Jake.

Jake leans toward Francisco like they're about to have a face-off, and yells, "Yeah!"

They laugh and turn toward Uncle Zadok. Francisco impersonates him. "Watch it now!"

Jake follows suit. "Gotcha!"

Uncle Zadok shouts, "Now, damn it, boys! Stop with the childish antics." Zadok lets out a huge burp and laughs boisterously. "Gotcha! I'm the king of the 'watch it nows' and 'gotchas.' You got that!"

Everyone laughs and says. "Yes, Zir, we do."

Uncle Zadok scowls and asks, "What's this yes, Zir thing all about?"

Allen says, "Uncle Zadok, haven't you ever heard of Pharrell from *The Neptunes?*"

Zadok replies, "*Pha-who?* I've heard stories about King Neptune when I was a kid in Atlantis. Zadok I invited him to a Waterball Game. They were good friends."

The warriors look at each other with their mouths open.

Athena gasps in awe. "I'm beginning to believe every myth out there might be true. Everyone thinks the Greek Gods are a myth… Ha!"

Uncle Zadok says, "Well, that's the story I heard. We'll tell these tales to the new generations of Atlanteans when we have a thriving Kingdom again."

The family finishes their dinner and dessert before going into the entertainment room.

Francisco announces, "Hey, guess what I saw on my cell phone? Someone posted it online only a few hours ago…" Francisco shows a video of Athena's impromptu speech at their high school. He points out that the video has already received over two million views, and that the Mayor of Miami and various celebrities have endorsed Athena's efforts.

Overwhelmed, Athena says, "Wow! I never imagined this!"

Allen says lovingly, "Well, babe, you have the heart of a saint. Now, Miami and the rest of the world are seeing you as you really are, not just as a socialite, but as a student and humanitarian."

They watch people online asking where they can donate money to the South Beach Miami High School Literacy Fund. Many of them are saying that they want to help kids stay in school.

"This is so exciting!" shouts Athena. She jumps on Allen, wrapping her legs around him. "I love you, Allen King. Look what's happened to me by being with you… I'm attending a public school, and people are seeing me in a different light. I'm so happy we're all making a difference. I need to call my publicist so she can set up an account for the new charities we're going to start. And I'm going to make something special for you boys before we go to Hawaii and kick some Gargoyle ass. There's so much to do before prom." Athena runs upstairs.

Uncle Zadok says with pride, "Now that young lady is a firecracker. You're fortunate to be with her. Man, I tell you!" He beckons Allen with his index finger.

Allen leans down and asks, "What's happening, Unc?"

Uncle Zadok kisses Allen on the cheek. "I'm happy for you and thank you for just being you."

"No problem, Unc," says Allen with a grand smile.

Zadok says, "I'm not soft or anything. I really love all of you." He proudly pounds his fist to his chest and yells, "Hail Atlantis!"

His nephews do the warrior's salute and echo, "Hail Atlantis!"

The time has come for prom night. Allen gets out of the shower, puts on his necklace and telepathically asks Athena, *Are you getting ready?*

She telepathically says, *Yes, it's going to take some time. Just pretend it's our wedding day.*

Allen smiles and transmits, *Okay, my love…*

Athena has a makeup and hair team, a manicurist and pedicurist in her bedroom helping her get ready for the prom. The hairstylist is playing with her hair, experimenting with different looks. They all know that she is a huge fan of Audrey Hepburn and Marilyn Monroe, even though they had different looks and styles. Audrey was petite and elegant, while Marilyn was voluptuous and seductive. Athena feels she is somewhere between the two. Her publicist, Nicole, is also there and is conferring with the hair and makeup people about Athena's look, but Athena will make the final decision.

Jake and Francisco walk into Allen's bedroom.

Jake asks, "Are you ready for your first prom?" Allen replies a little anxiously, "Yeah, I think we're going to have an awesome time. It feels a little like we're getting married though."

Francisco understands. "You're feeling a little tense huh, bro? We're getting closer to the moment."

"Maybe just a bit," confesses Allen. "It's hard for me to think about getting married when I have to avenge the damage that has been done to my family and restore our ancient kingdom. I can fight Drogan and Destroyer all day, but when I think about getting married… dude, I'm petrified! I know I'm a lucky guy, don't get me wrong… It's just… I never thought I would feel so jittery."

Allen brightens up and says, "Check this out, guys." He holds up a one-of-a-kind gold engagement ring festooned with ten-karat diamonds.

Francisco says in awe, "Now that's a ring, bro!"

Jake says, "Wow, Allen, I agree with Francisco. When are you going to pop the big question since we all know it's going to happen?"

Allen says, "I know it might sound cheesy, but I was thinking about when we have our first slow dance on the dance floor at prom. I have everything set up with The Party Boys. They're going to put a spotlight on us…"

Jake shouts, "Whoa, dude! That sounds amazing. In the middle of the prom. Fran and I will have to crash it just for that."

Francisco says, "Wow, Allen… that will be something to remember! I'm so happy for you. I feel like Jake, and I should be there, we want to be the first to congratulate you two."

Allen nods as he blushes. "No, that's okay, guys. You enjoy yourselves and have the most epic night at the twin's prom."

Jake says, "Yeah, maybe you're right… We're proud of you, brother."

The guys hug each other. Francisco gestures to himself and says, "What do you think? I'm looking good? I see you have your suit hanging on your closet door."

Allen smiles and says, "You look great, Fran…"

Allen glances at the time on his phone and says, "Hey, guys. I'm sorry, but I don't know if we're going to have time for dinner. Athena is still getting her hair and makeup done. I don't think she's touched her gown yet. She's probably still in her robe. You know how long it takes girls to get ready."

"Yes, I do, my man," says Jake in his Southern drawl. "You want a swig of Jack Um?"

Allen shakes his head. "No thanks, I'm good, bro."

Jake replies, "Alright, but I think you need it more than Francisco and me. We don't know what kind of preppy stuck-up dudes going to be hating on us since we go to South Beach High, a public school dump in their eyes."

Francisco says with assurance, "We'll be all right, Jake. The old days of kicking assholes asses are over unless there are monsters who want to rule our world."

Grinning, Jake winks at Allen. "I don't know… the preppy guys might be scarier." The guys laugh and head downstairs to their limo.

A few hours pass by, and finally, Athena is almost ready. She telepathically says, *Allen, meet me downstairs in fifteen minutes.*

Allen replies, *Okay, I'll be there.*

Uncle Zadok and Aoki are downstairs in the entertainment room watching Denzel Washington's, *The Devil in the Blue Dress.* The bluesy music blares out into the house when Allen opens the entertainment room door. He shouts, "Uncle Zadok!" Zadok doesn't hear him. Allen telepathically says, *Uncle Zadok,* as he telekinetically vibrates his uncle's crystal.

Zadok feels it as he puts the movie on pause and turns on the lights with a remote control. Aoki and Zadok turn around, and Zadok says proudly, "Let me look at you, nephew."

Aoki says, "Allen, you look marvelous!"

Allen's eyes beam with delight.

Zadok says, "I need to grab my camera. Aoki, baby, where did I put my camera?"

She points, giggling. "Honey, it's on your chest. You have it strapped on, remember?"

Zadok looks down and sees his camera. "Well, there it is." He gets into his wheelchair and turns toward Allen. "I have to take a picture of you right now, nephew."

Allen does an Atlantean Water Baller athletic pose. Uncle Zadok protests, "No, no, don't be cocky, neph. We already know you're the man. Just look natural."

Allen sighs. "Okay." He puts his hands in his pockets and smiles.

Zadok nods and says, "That's it!" He shows the digital picture to his nephew who loves it.

"That's nice, Unc. Thanks."

Zadok winks. "Now let's go find the Goddess."

Allen replies like he's almost forgotten. "Right, I need to be on cue. She said she'd be at the stairs in fifteen minutes."

Aoki walks to her nephew, declaring, "Allen, you still have a lot to learn about girls; fifteen is going to be more like thirty." Aoki grabs Allen by his arm and escorts him out. "But you better stay close to the staircase just to be sure."

"Yes, ma'am," replies Allen.

Uncle Zadok follows behind them. Allen walks to the bottom of the staircase and waits patiently.

Five minutes later, Athena telepathically asks, *Are you ready for me?*

Allen happily replies, *I sure am.*

First, her publicist and manicure girls walk downstairs. Nicole says, "Well hello, good-looking."

"Hello," Allen says, a little shyly.

A few seconds later, Athena walks to the staircase. Nicole and Zadok take several pictures. Athena looks stunning in the black and red gown. She walks down the stairs like she's floating. Allen grins from ear to ear, playing with the ring case in his pants pocket.

He thinks. *I want to ask Athena to marry me right now, but I have to be patient and wait for the perfect moment at prom.* Athena walks to Allen who leans in for a kiss.

Athena raises her index finger and says, "Not yet, prince, you have to wait for the right moment."

Allen chuckles. "Well, excuse me, girlfriend."

They both laugh as Nicole and Uncle Zadok take pictures of the couple.

Zadok declares, "You two take gorgeous pics. It looks like a fairy tale."

Nicole nods. "I agree." She sheds a tear. "I never cry, but this is so romantic. This beats my bat mitzvah, two proms and three marriages put together, just this moment."

Athena says with a smirk, "Oh don't be so dramatic."

Nicole replies diva-like, "Darling, you know I live for magical moments like this."

Athena says with seriousness, "Remember, no pictures to be leaked yet. Not until after a few more weeks, okay."

Nicole winks. "Got it." She shimmies out the door.

Allen offers Athena his arm and says, "Shall we?"

Athena takes his arm and smiles. "We shall."

They walk like a royal couple to the front door, which automatically opens. They step out onto a red carpet, which leads them to their limo.

CHAPTER TWENTY-TWO

The Prom King And Queen Fiasco

After Allen and Athena climb into the limo, Allen grabs a box he'd stored in the limo earlier. He pulls out a red corsage and slips it on Athena's wrist.

Athena sheds a tear, and whispers, "Allen King, you think of everything. I love you... to hell with the makeup." Athena kisses her dream guy.

Allen says, "You helped mold me into the gentleman I am."

He then gestures to two bottles of the Star Island Twins' nonalcoholic champagne on ice.

Athena shouts happily, "Allen, you're one of a kind. Let's get those bottles popping!"

Allen says, "Okay." He opens the sunroof and pops the champagne cork out onto the lawn. He pours two glasses and they both shout, "Cheers!"

Athena says a little sheepishly, "I'm sorry about being diva-ish and making us late so we couldn't have dinner with the boys and the twins."

Allen replies with passion, "I'm happy it's just the two of us."

Athena wonders out loud, "What's going to happen when we get married? Won't they be lonely without us?"

Allen nods. "I don't think so, they can still stay in the mansion. We'll be restoring the kingdom, going to school, and doing charity work. I think it's going to be an interesting year next year."

Athena lifts her glass. "Cheers to that." They tap their champagne flutes.

Allen stands up in the limo and grabs Athena's hand. "Stand with me."

"But my hair," says Athena, touching it.

Allen smiles. "Just for a minute."

Athena stands, and Allen yells at the top of his lungs, "I'm going to be the King of the World!"

Athena screams, "I'm going to be the queen!"

The handsome couple notices people are honking and cheering.

They arrive, and the chauffeur opens the door for them.

The prom is being held at a country club, and Principal Jenkins and Mrs. Ramirez are chaperones for the night. Principal Jenkins says good evening to the prom guests. Mrs. Ramirez exclaims, "Now don't you two look like you will be voted king and queen for the evening. You're both are stunning."

Allen and Athena politely reply, "Thank you." They walk in saying hello to other faculty members.

Allen says telepathically, *I totally forgot about they vote for king and queen at proms. How appropriate is that? We might be king and queen before we're actually king and queen.*

Athena telepathically shouts, *Who would have thought that! I'm so excited.* She squeezes Allen's hand a little tight.

He replies with a grin. "Whoa, sweetheart. You don't know your strength."

Athena giggles. "Sorry." The super couple enters the banquet room, making everyone stop for a moment to gaze at them.

Several girls walk up to them and declare, "You two are the king and queen. I'm voting for you two." A few guys leaning against the wall give Allen the thumbs-up and a head nod.

Allen nods back.

The Party Boys see Allen walk in, and the DJs smile at him. Allen looks at his watch, letting the guys know that when they play a slow song, he will be on the dance floor proposing. The anxious teen takes his girlfriend to the bar and orders two sodas.

Josh and Mercedes, another handsome couple, walk in, and everyone in the room erupts with, "Josh! Josh! Josh!" He waves and they walk to the bar where Athena and Allen greet them.

Mercedes stares at Athena in awe. "You look gorgeous, and I love your dress!"

Athena smiles and says, "Thank you! You are also stunning!"

Josh asks a little sarcastically, "How are you doing, Mr. King?"

"I'm good, Mr. Stone, and how are you?" replies Allen.

Josh mutters, "Same old, you know, trying to prepare for life and death struggles against the devil inside you. Sorry if I sound rude. I'm feeling a little angry."

Allen says reassuringly, "You can fight this, Josh, I believe in you."

Irritated, Josh says, "You believe in me more than I do in myself right now. It's harder than you think, but the ancient Nomadic Indian chants are helping me. That's the positive thing I can say… Will you excuse me? I need to get to my date."

Josh grabs Mercedes by her arm and pulls her away from the bar.

Athena watches Josh and telepathically says, *You see, Allen, there's no helping him. He's a lost cause.*

Allen replies, *No, Josh isn't, Athena. Nothing has happened yet. I still have faith in him.*

With his acute hearing, Allen can hear Mercedes complain, "Josh, you're acting a little annoying right now."

Josh mumbles, "I'm sorry. I needed to walk out. When I'm close to Allen, something inside me makes me want to hit something. I feel better now, okay."

Mercedes kisses him on the cheek. "Okay."

Allen doesn't say anything to Athena. He doesn't want to give her any reason to talk him out of helping Josh.

Principal Jenkins steps into the DJ area and taps the microphone. "Attention! Attention, students of South Beach Miami High! I want to thank you all for coming, and I want to thank Mr. Frye for letting us use his magnificent country club for this event. I want every one of you to be on your best behavior, and to act like proper young ladies and gentlemen."

A few guys in the back laugh after coming out of the bathroom where they were obviously smoking something not legal. Principle Jenkins sees them and says, "We have our eyes on everyone, and I expect all of you to leave this property the same way you found it. So now let's have a good time and enjoy yourselves."

He gets off the microphone as a random voice yells out, "You suck!"

The Principal immediately turns to see who it was, and a faculty member points out the culprit. One of the football coaches grabs him and escorts him out the door.

A couple of students laugh out loud. "What a tool." A few others on the opposite side of the dance floor say, "He got busted so quick smelling like sticky icky."

The music starts, and the teens begin to dance.

Allen looks at Athena and says, "Shall we dance, milady?"

She smiles. "I would love to."

The Party Boys play popular dance club songs, mixing in the Star Island Twin's music. Athena and Allen scream, "Yeah, that's our friends."

They continue dancing as students hear on the other turntable the sounds of teens chanting, "Athena! Athena!" The socialite yells cheerfully, pointing to herself, "That's me!"

Allen gasps with excitement. "Wow! The Party Boys have outdone themselves."

Later on in the evening, Allen and Athena grab food on the buffet and sit at a table. He notices Josh talking to his linebacker friends a few tables away. He eavesdrops on the conversation.

"Hey, Josh. I'm going to be a Gator with you, bro. I can't wait to block for you on the line."

Josh replies, "You got it, brother. We'll be a great team for sure, but I've actually been considering playing for The Canes… right here in Miami."

Allen hears Josh's heart rate speed up – it's beating hard and heavy. He notices that the quarterback's eyes are starting to glisten and turn red. He's slowly becoming angrier as the full moon approaches. Josh will feel the fiery rage of his Nomadic Indian and Reptilian blood, which will summon the Gargoyle. Allen stares at Josh in a daze as Athena talks to him.

He slowly zones back in. "Huh?"

Athena looks at Allen and snaps her fingers in front of his eyes. "Allen, are you okay?"

He nods. "Yeah… yeah, I'm fine. What's going on?"

Athena scowls. "You, is what's going on. Is there anything you want to tell me?"

Allen replies coolly, “Of course not.” He continues eating his food and then glances at his watch. The time has come for the slow dance. Allen gestures to the DJ, letting him know that he’s on.

“I feel like dancing, don’t you?” he asks Athena in a soft voice.

Athena nods with a smile. “Sure thing.”

They walk to the dance floor as a slow romantic song comes on. Allen takes a deep breath and proclaims, “Athena, you have made me the happiest guy in the Universe. I know I’m just a teenager, but you’re helping me become a man.”

Athena looks deeply into Allen’s eyes as they move to the romantic song. “Allen King, I love you with each breath I take. I’m all yours, body, mind, and soul.” Athena feels the spotlight shining on them. “Allen King, what is this?”

Allen stops and drops down on bended knee. He pulls out the engagement ring and asks, “Athena Dranias, will you marry me?” The engagement ring sparkles like a crystal ball.

Athena gasps and says, “Yes, Allen, I will marry you.”

Allen puts the ring on her finger, stands, lifts his fiancée up, and swings her around as the students, principal, and faculty members cheer them on. Everyone congratulates them as The Party Boys shout out, “Now, let’s get this party started.” They start playing music.

The students pick up Allen and Athena and carry them around in a circle as they hold hands laughing and cheering.

Allen sees Josh standing by the dance floor gazing at him with a blank stare. He suddenly hears. “Your brothers are here.” He looks around and sees Francisco grinning up at him. He’s there with Jake and the twins. Allen yells with elation, “Athena, look!”

“Did you think we would miss our brother’s proposal to our soon to be sister-in-law!” shouts Francisco like he’s out of his mind.

Jake proclaims, “We would never, and once we told Suzy and Samantha, they grabbed us, and we hightailed it out of that boring-ass prom. It was nice having caviar and great food, but nothing beats a South Beach Miami High School party, baby!”

“You got that right, Jake,” says Francisco.

The prom-goers enjoy themselves. They wait to see who's chosen for king and queen. The votes are tallied, the student body president announces, "The new king and queen of South Beach Miami High are... Josh Stone and Athena Dranias."

Allen and his friends gasp in shock. "Huh?"

Angry, Athena says telepathically to Allen, *There's no way I'm going to dance with that murderer.*

Allen transmits, *It's only one dance. You have to do it.*

Mercedes applauds. "Yeah, Athena." Mercedes genuinely likes Athena.

Josh is also shocked, but he strolls up to the stage to be crowned as if he knew the two of them would be the chosen couple. Athena hesitantly extends her hand out to Josh, who grabs it tight, pulling her to him. "Hello, Athena, who would have thought this?"

She replies unhappily, "Josh, let's step back a few inches away, okay. I don't feel comfortable being next to you."

Josh grins, mocking in a soft voice, "Now why is that? You love that used-to-be-shy asthmatic fool of a guy I used to punk around last year over this sexy beast, which is moi? You know we would make a perfect couple - the new King and Queen of Atlantis."

Athena stomps her stiletto heel on his foot.

Josh screams angrily, "Ouch! You bitch!"

The crowd stares at him speechless.

Allen walks closer as Francisco steps in front of him. "Allen no, not yet, you see he's still a jerk, but right now we must chill."

Athena storms off.

Mercedes looks shocked at her boyfriend's behavior. Josh's eyes begin to glow redder. Allen catches a glimpse of Josh's front teeth that are now starting to look like vampire fangs. Allen thinks. *I was afraid to see this... the Gargoyle will arrive on Earth soon through Josh.*

Athena has had enough. "I want to leave if that's okay."

Allen understands his fiancée's feelings. "Yeah, let's go."

Francisco says to Suzy, "We're leaving."

Suzy replies, "I don't know what's going on, but let's go to my yacht and celebrate... it's just a cheesy prom anyway."

"Yes, let's do that. That would be perfect. I want to celebrate this night with my friends and family," says Athena.

As they're walking to their limo, Mercedes runs over to Allen and Athena and says, "I'm sorry, it's like something is trying to take over him again."

Allen whispers, "Mercedes, I think it's best for you to stay away from Josh for a while, at least for a month, if you can. Believe me, it's for your own good. Stay away from him until the end of July."

"That's three weeks from now," says Mercedes.

Athena says, "Do you want to hang out with us?"

Mercedes shrugs, and says, "I better not. I don't want to upset Josh any more than he is."

Allen protests, "Mercedes, you're jumping back into that pattern again."

Mercedes, who doesn't want to feel sad on her prom night, says, "I don't want that… Okay, screw it, let's go." She gets in their limo as Josh watches them drive off. His teeth start to grow out from the bottom as he becomes angrier by the minute.

Within an hour, the teens are on the twin's yacht by their home on Star Island.

Francisco says to Allen and Athena, "I hate to tell you this, but the asshole billionaire used to stay three houses down from here."

Allen focuses toward the area using his acute hearing. He doesn't hear a heartbeat or even a squeak inside the empty house. He says with conviction, "Drogan isn't here. The Hybrid may not be in Miami right now."

Athena barks, "I want them both gone before we go to Hawaii."

Allen calmly replies, "Athena, we just can't."

Jake cheerfully intervenes. "Hey, guys, this is our night. Let's enjoy it and pop bottles with our girls." They open a few bottles of champagne and drink out of red plastic cups while listening to the twins' music.

Mercedes says to Athena and Allen, "Thanks again for taking me away. I feel terrible for him, but I don't want another black eye. If it wasn't for Glam Girl Warrior Princess catching me before I hit the floor during the school's Halloween contest, I might not be here talking to you now."

Athena hints, "Well, maybe Glam Girl Warrior Princess is rescuing you from him right now. You have to worry about yourself. You don't want to end up like Tyrone did."

Mercedes shrugs in denial. "Yeah, but that wasn't Josh though. That was someone dressed in a monster outfit that did a terrible thing, and they still haven't caught that killer."

Allen replies with concern, "You have to worry about you, Mercedes. We might have saved you tonight like how Glam Girl Warrior Princess did at the homecoming, but we can't say what's going to happen tomorrow or the next day."

Mercedes nods. "Yeah, you're right, Allen and, Athena… On another note. Do you know that you two are the most gorgeous couple I've ever seen?"

Athena blushes. "Thank you."

Allen proudly announces, "Hey, this is an engagement party, so let's get back in there and party, shall we?"

Athena winks. "Okay, we'll be right there."

She turns to Mercedes and whispers, "Mercedes, you know you can talk to me anytime like we did in the mall during the beginning of the school year. That's what girlfriends are for."

Athena stretched her arm out. "Smell my wrist."

Mercedes smiles. "You're still wearing the perfume?"

Athena nods. "Yes. I love it. I've always been a fashionable person, and I thought I knew every fragrance out on the market. When I saw the butterfly on your perfume bottle, it sparked my interest. Thank you for sharing your lovely perfume with me."

Mercedes replies with joy, "You're welcome."

The gorgeous girls gaze into each other's eyes slowly moving closer almost touching each other on the lips.

Jake yells out, "Hey, you two get up here and celebrate. The twins just went platinum in Europe!"

Athena screams, "Yeah!" She grabs Mercedes' hand, and they shimmy onboard to celebrate with the gang.

Athena slaps Allen's butt and kisses him. Mercedes drinks her champagne and smiles at them.

The night continues on. Mercedes finally says, "I'm getting tired."

"You can take our limo. We're going to stay," says Allen. He calls the driver to take Mercedes home.

CHAPTER TWENTY-THREE

THE TEEN WARRIORS TRAIN FOR ARMAGEDDON

The teens wake up Saturday afternoon hungover. Francisco rolls out of bed trying not to wake Suzy, who has fallen asleep next to him. On his way out of the bathroom, he bumps into Athena and Allen who are way too cheery as far as Francisco is concerned, "Good morning! How're you feeling?"

Francisco squints through bloodshot eyes, and says in a monotone slur, "Aw, bro, I don't ever want to drink again." He walks like a zombie back into the bedroom.

"I think Francisco has outdone himself this time," says Athena with a grin.

Allen replies, "I agree, I think we all have... You ready to leave?"

Athena nods. "Yes."

Allen smirks deviously. "We're going to cheat and teleport back since we don't have our limo waiting for us from last night."

Athena eggs him on. "Let's do it."

He touches Athena's hand as the rainbow cloud comes in with a stunning dark red, yellow, green, and blue hue. Allen feels euphoric as he walks through the wormhole with his bride-to-be. The arch goes over the skyline of downtown Miami. They stop for a moment to gaze at the view.

Athena says, "It's so majestic up here today, and so wonderful to look at all the people down below happily going about their lives..."

Allen hugs Athena from behind, whispering, "I want it to be like this forever with everyone living peacefully and happily, just like they are today. In a few more weeks, I'll make sure they will."

Athena whispers admiringly, "I know you will."

They continue traveling through the wormhole until they land in the foyer of the mansion. Allen finds a note from Uncle Zadok: *I'm sure you all enjoyed your prom night. Aoki and I will be in New Orleans by the time you read this. We're going to the Jazz Festival. I forgot to mention to you, neph, I bumped into a distant cousin of yours when I was in Greece, her name is Raven, and she's half-Atlantean. Aoki and I are meeting up with her and her girlfriend at the festival; you may meet her one day in the future. This weekend I didn't make any meals for any of you to eat. You're old enough to fend for yourselves, so get to it. Ha ha.*

Love,

Zadok and Aoki.

Allen laughs and says, "Athena, you're not going to believe it, Uncle Zadok said in his note that I have an Atlantean cousin. Unc will see her in New Orleans, and I might meet her one day."

Athena remarks with a surprised look, "That's very interesting." They're both too tired to talk about it. They saunter upstairs to their separate bedrooms to rest. An hour later, Allen knocks on Athena's door before walking into her bedroom. She is writing in her journal. Allen asks, "Am I interrupting you?"

Athena replies, "Of course not. I'm just writing about the lovely time I had with you last night, in spite of the ugly incident with you-know-who." Athena rolls her eyes.

"Uh-oh, I knew it would only be a matter of time before Josh's name would come up again," says Allen.

Athena retorts harshly, "I'm not holding anything back. It's bad enough. I have to walk down the aisle with that jerk at my senior graduation. I'd love to get my lasso from the Warrior's Room and wrap it around Josh's neck."

"If he's a threat in two weeks, then it'll be the end of him. I will not risk our safety, especially yours. I know what I must do."

Athena says with seriousness, "I hope so, Allen, because from now on, the gloves are off and somebody is getting the hell knocked out for good."

Allen sighs and nods. "Understood. I think after Monday when we're all out of school, we need to start practicing and preparing for the next two weeks. I know you have graduation on Friday, so we'll skip that day and practice some maneuvers in the wormhole cloud."

Athena says with delight, "That sounds great to me, and I'll have the surprise ready by the time we go into battle."

Allen says, "I can't wait to see it."

A few days later, the Atlantean Superhero Ballers rainbow-teleport to the Warrior's Room to practice their moves.

Francisco asks Athena, "So when are we going to see what you have for us, sis?"

"You'll see it soon enough. Don't you worry." Athena winks.

Allen says, "Okay, ASB, let's get dressed."

Athena replies, "I need my own dressing room," then she instantly changes into her Glam Girl Warrior Princess costume. Allen changes Francisco and Jake into their warriors' outfits.

Francisco yells, "C'mon, bro! You know I always feel violated when you do that."

"I'm sorry, guys, but Athena's right. She doesn't have a dressing room, so this is more appropriate until we rebuild Atlantis and have changing rooms for future warriors."

Athena does the warrior's salute and says, "We will have great Atlantean female warriors in the future."

Jake and Francisco proudly say, "It will happen."

Allen telepathically says, *Okay, ASB. We need to be ready for whatever Drogan and the Gargoyle throw at us. We already know how to flank, but we need to create a cocoon.*

Everyone asks at once, "Create a what?"

Allen stops talking through the crystal and says out loud, "A cocoon, I don't know if Drogan will have ten goons or one hundred. What we're going to do is position ourselves like we did against Destroyer, when we fought him by the arena."

"Okay, I remember that," says Jake.

Allen says with excitement, "But now we all come in together instead of being spread apart." He holds his shield over them. They're close to each other, kneeling with everyone's shield covering their bodies. "Watch this," says Allen feeling thrilled. His golden crystal necklace and emerald ring glow as his eyes turn the same golden color as his shield. The shields become massive and wider, attaching to form a perfect block shape, protecting their bodies inside.

Athena gasps in awe. "Wow!"

Jake and Francisco scream, "Holy—"

"Pretty cool, huh?" says Allen interrupting their expletives. Everyone nods.

Francisco says, "There's only one problem, we can't see outside of it."

"Sure, we can," says Allen, smiling. He makes the shield appear like a one-way mirror. "We can see out, but our opponents can't see in."

Athena says with amazement, "This is a perfect defense against anyone who may try to shoot at us from any direction."

Allen retracts the shields to their normal size and then says, "You got it, Athena. This will be a great asset to us."

The warriors hear clapping as General Lionel and King Leon walk downstairs toward them. General Lionel exclaims, "Great-grandson, we could have used your skills when we battled against our enemies centuries ago. You're the best general I've ever seen, I must say. You've outdone me."

King Leon says with a smile, "And you're very wise, as I have said before, beyond your years."

Allen bows and says, "Thank you, grandfathers."

General Lionel looks at Athena. "I didn't say this the last time you practiced in the Warrior's Room. Your uniform suits you. I'm proud of the new generation. During my time, we did not have female warriors. If we had female warriors…our Atlantean women would have been fierce in battle. It's in our DNA."

Athena smiles and says, "It's an honor to be the first female to train and fight as an Atlantean warrior." General Lionel proudly says, "Change is always good." He looks at Allen and says, "I can't wait for you to hold the crown, my great-grandson. We will show you a few new things that will prepare you for this quest. I think the three of you should practice riding your sea animals."

Francisco is a little alarmed. "With all due respect, I've never even ridden a bike, let alone a dolphin."

General Lionel smiles reassuringly. "Don't worry. You will be ready soon."

Francisco mumbles, "Okay."

King Leon walks to Francisco and says, "You'll have special adhesive on your inner thighs and shins to keep the two of you from falling off when you're quickly maneuvering in battle."

Jake yells, "Cool!" He cheerfully slaps Francisco on his back, pushing him forward. "Sorry about that, Fran…"

Francisco scowls. "Geez, now you're like Allen… you're getting stronger."

General Lionel says with pride, "It's the golden armor you wear. Titum is the alien metal from Zion West combined with the composition of gold alloy on Earth. It enhances your strength. Because of the alien technology, your armor is light and very resilient. Our sea animals wear it as a protective armor on their heads. Athena's armor comes from the Gods of Olympus, so it enhances her strength quite significantly."

Athena smirks and replies with astonishment, "So that explains why I was able to lift up that bitch of a bodyguard and slam her sorry ass on the hood of the limo."

King Leon says with a touch of dismay, "Yes, Athena. I see that when you're among the men, you talk like one."

The guys laugh.

"Yes, and she has balls, believe me, I know because she almost kicked mine," declares Jake.

General Lionel announces, "Let's get started."

They teleport into the King's Chamber. Bucky, Jumper, and Dance II are inside waiting to train with the warriors in their golden armor. King Leon waves his right hand over the pool allowing the ocean water to rush in.

General Lionel says, "You will practice jumping in and out of the water with your spears in your hand… and you will throw them at the bulls-eye on the wall across from the throne."

Jake boasts, "That should be a piece of cake."

They hop on the dolphins. Athena rides on Jumper, while Francisco and Jake ride together on Dance II.

Disappointed, Francisco asks, "Why didn't I get my own dolphin?"

General Lionel replies, "Maybe one day, but as of right now. You are a junior infantryman. No disrespect, but Jake's more of an infantryman than you."

Francisco frowns. "Why is that?"

General Lionel explains, "Because Jake isn't afraid of the dolphin. You showed a little fear in the beginning. If you show that you're a brave man, the dolphin will respect you. You can never show fear or weakness. You and your sea animal are one… if you show fear or weakness, the sea animal will work harder, making up for the fear and weakness in your heart. This stresses out your beloved animal friend. We Atlanteans do not stress out our sea animals no matter what. They're a part of our lives like dogs and cats are a part of yours."

Francisco nods. "I understand. I feel a little better after hearing that."

Athena says, "Francisco, you have done many courageous things since I've known you. You are very brave."

Francisco hugs Athena. "Thanks, sis. I'm ready, and I am brave, we all are."

King Leon smiles and says, "Good, let's begin."

Athena goes first. Jumper comes up cutting the water in a perfect forty-five-degree angle, and dives down, giving Athena an ideal view of the bulls-eye. Athena snarls and hits the target flawlessly with her double-edged sword. Everyone cheers.

General Lionel applauds. "You were excellent my soon-to-be great-granddaughter-in-law."

Jake and Francisco are up next on Dance II. The dolphin flies in the air before coming down, giving Jake and Francisco a chance to throw their spears before landing into the water. Jake screams like a lion roaring, he throws his golden spear but hits the mark below the bulls-eye. Francisco pitches his spear seconds after Jake, but it lands above the bulls-eye.

General Lionel says encouragingly, "You two will need a little more practice."

Allen is up next riding on Bucky. The great white shark does an incredible vertical leap with Allen holding the reins in one hand and spear in the other. He throws the spear flawlessly into the center of the red mark as Bucky glides down into the water. Allen jumps off the shark doing a backflip towards the bulls-eye. He hangs on his golden spear and does a twirl like a gymnast, then leaps on the middle of the spear and springs off. He comes down pulling the weapon to him before landing in the ocean pool and onto his shark.

The Chamber roars with cheers and applause.

"Whoo Allen!" Athena screams. "You go, babe!"

King Leon looks at General Lionel, at a loss for words. Allen rides his shark toward the edge of the ocean pool and leaps off yelling a Zulu tribal chant while doing the warrior's salute. Everyone's in awe. They continue applauding. "Bravo, bravo!"

General Lionel says very proudly, "I think that was good for today. Tomorrow, we will work on it again, and we'll make it harder. You will practice with the lasso, and you will rope the spear, and pull it from the bulls-eye after you've thrown it into the target."

Francisco scratches his head. "How in the hell are we going to do that?"

King Leon says, "Practice, practice, and more practice. You must not have any doubt, Francisco. You can do it."

Francisco does the warrior's salute, yelling, "Yes, sir! Hail Atlantis!"

Everyone does the warrior's salute as they shout, "Hail Atlantis!"

The first training day is over.

Time flies as a few more training sessions are completed, turning the warriors into a well-oiled machine. Francisco and Jake are becoming more muscular from carrying the spears and shields while riding the dolphins. Athena looks enchanting and powerful as ever, and Allen is pure perfection.

General Lionel feels satisfied and finally says, "You are ready for battle."

CHAPTER TWENTY-FOUR

ATHENA'S GRADUATION DAY

Athena grabs her mortarboard and puts it in front of the mirror. She adjusts the angle, so it tilts slightly and plays with the yellow tassels, flipping them from side to side. Satisfied, she slips her black graduation gown over her jeans and T-shirt and steps into a pair of red high heels.

Allen and the family wait patiently for their soon-to-be-graduating socialite. Uncle Zadok and Allen have their cameras ready. Athena appears at the top of the stairs, and Allen yells from below, "Athena, pose on the staircase before you walk downstairs."

"Okay," says Athena smiling gleefully.

Uncle Zadok remarks, "By the Elders of Zion West, you look like you should be in the Miss Universe Pageant. You're not even wearing an elegant dress. You're absolutely gorgeous, Athena."

She blushes. "Thank you, Uncle Zadok."

Jake and Francisco also take pictures with their camera phones. Jake says, "You look wonderful, sis. You're most definitely a Goddess."

Francisco agrees. "You sure are, sis. We're so proud of you."

Aoki meets Athena at the foot of the stairs and hugs her. "I never had a niece or a sister. I feel like you're both to me, and I couldn't be any happier than I am right now. I'm so proud of you!"

Athena smiles with joy. "Please, Aunt Aoki, you're going to make me cry."

Allen kisses her on the cheek. "Are you ready to go, beautiful?"

Athena glances at her brand new diamond-encrusted watch, and says, "Yes, let's go." She holds up her bejeweled wrist and says to everyone, "Thank you all for this amazing gift."

Everyone nods and smiles at her. Allen offers his arm. "Shall we." He escorts Athena to the stretch limo. They all pile in and take off with Athena's bodyguards on motorcycles leading the way.

As everyone takes their seats at the ceremony, Jake sees Becky Honeycomb who looks very pregnant. Jake feels like it's been years rather than months since Becky tried to baby trap him in her web of lies. They make eye contact, and Jake gives her a warm smile to let her know that he wishes her the best.

Allen is sitting in the audience looking around when he notices Josh sitting six rows behind Athena. Josh has a look of despair in his eyes. He looks like he hasn't slept in days and is wiggling in his seat like a little kid. Allen turns his attention to the band playing on the football field.

A few minutes later, Principal Jenkins walks to the podium and says, "As you all know, we lost one of our own this year. Tyrone McCoy would have been part of our graduating class. He was a fine and talented young man who had a real chance of fulfilling his dream of becoming a star wide receiver in college and the NFL. As a tribute to this young man, let's all take a moment of silence."

The graduates and their families and friends bow their heads as a photo of Tyrone wearing his football uniform appears on the jumbotron. The only person who doesn't bend his head is Josh who gazes at the giant screen with a puzzled look. After the moment of silence, everyone stands and applauds for Tyrone.

Principal Jenkins introduces the valedictorian who launches into her speech: "Good evening friends, family, and faculty. We are all here today to celebrate our graduating seniors. Some of us will continue on to universities, while others of us will join the armed forces, choosing to protect our precious freedom, our beautiful country and our way of life."

Allen and the warriors listen intently as the valedictorian continues speaking. "Some of us will enter into the workforce, some of us will travel the world and explore different cultures, and some of us will start families of our own. However, I know that all of us will talk about the good old days when we were students at South Beach High. I hope we will all continue to strive to be the very best at whatever we choose to do, no matter what obstacles come our way. I know we're all resilient and capable as individuals, but as a group we are indestructible!"

The crowd scream and cheer.

The valedictorian concludes, "We must learn to love our enemies because the enemy is sometimes within ourselves. Also, we must never forget the loved ones we lost from senseless gun violence in this country and around the world. We survived the deadly pandemic. The mental health issues are devastating to our peers and climate change is becoming worse across the globe each year. We control our destiny, and the old regime will listen to our voices. We are not voiceless. We are the new leaders of this world. We must love one another and make the commitment to make this world a better place! Thank you."

The crowd gives the valedictorian a standing ovation. Principal Jenkins walks back to the podium, and announces with great joy, "I'm proud of this year's senior class! With young people like ours, this country will continue to succeed and thrive even during tough times. There will always be hope... Ladies and gentleman. I present to you this year's senior class!"

The music starts again as Mrs. Ramirez calls out the names of the graduates, who walk up to the stage to receive their diplomas. Allen squeezes his way through the crowd so he can get a better view of Athena as she waits in line to walk to the stage.

He telepathically asks Athena, *How are you feeling?*

Athena replies, *It feels like forever... like I've been at this school for decades. I can't wait to graduate.*

Well, now it's time... this is your moment to shine, says Allen.

Mrs. Ramirez calls, "Athena Dranias."

The seniors and other students in the crowd gleefully chant: "Athena! Athena!"

The socialite smiles at Allen before he takes the perfect shot.

Uncle Zadok shouts with great pride. "That's my niece!" A couple behind Zadok pat him on the shoulders and say, "Congratulations."

Jake and Francisco stand next to Allen, and Jake exclaims, "Allen, this is exciting, bro! This will be us in a few years, you know?"

Allen smiles and looks at his fiancée with adoration. "It will, guys… but right now, I couldn't be any prouder of Athena than I am at this moment."

Francisco nods. "I concur. I'm with you on that, bro. Athena's smart and she's an incredible girl. She's one of a kind."

Allen gazes at Athena, waiting for the last senior to be called. "Yes, she is an amazing person, Francisco, she is indeed."

The last senior receives his diploma, and the new graduates throw their caps in the air as they scream in celebration. Everyone applauds.

Athena takes pictures with the senior class who are big fans of hers. Josh is not interested in being around Athena. He leaves immediately after the ceremony with his mother. Detective Wringer, who was at the graduation, said to Josh before he left, "You'll be fine, I've witnessed this before. It seems like you don't have control, but you do." Detective Wringer is worried about Josh. He knows that the monster wants complete control of Josh and usually, the beast wins. The Detective is still confident Josh will beat the Gargoyle, but he must continue to fight the evil urge that wants to control his body. Once Josh's spirit is out of his body on an open plane, he'll think clearly and hopefully defeat the Gargoyle.

Meanwhile, Athena's having a great time celebrating with her family and the twins back at the mansion. "I want to thank all of you for being here and celebrating this incredible day. I definitely feel more like an adult now. The thing I'll miss the most is seeing my honey at lunch and my brothers doing jumping jacks during PE."

Francisco asks in a tender voice. "Do you think you're going to miss not being in high school anymore?"

Feeling a little sad. Athena replies, "I really don't know, Fran. I just know how I feel right now. I appreciate each one of you for being here and always being by my side when I needed you the most." Suddenly, Athena's demeanor changes. "Okay, enough with the sad face. Let's celebrate and party!"

Francisco says, "I was hoping you would say that. I talked to Jake about it, and he decided with me. We thought what would be better than having you go to a high school party. When the high school party could come to you?"

Confused, Athena and Allen look at each other and reply at the same time. "What?"

Jake opens the front door, where half of Athena's senior class is waiting, ready to party. The teenagers stream in carrying kegs of beer and bottles of alcohol. They are all ushered out to the pool area where they begin partying and dancing to The Party Boys latest summer mix. Allen and Athena have a great time. However, Jake and Francisco spend the entire party keeping guys away from the twins.

Irritated, Jake says to Francisco, "I didn't think a surprise graduation party for Athena would make us want to handcuff our women next to us."

"These punk-ass dudes are in our home disrespecting us," says Francisco, almost ready to fight, the way he would have just a short while ago before he became a part of the ASB.

Jake grimaces and says, "What do you mean, Fran? There are also chicks trying to have relations with our girls."

Francisco replies, "It's all good, Jake. This is the last time we'll see any of these jerks, unless they didn't graduate…"

Jake nods. "Yeah, you're right, bro. It's a one-time-only event for Athena. So we'll just have to deal with it."

Francisco shrugs and replies, "I agree."

The twins are courteous to everyone who asks for an autograph and photo. Suzy says to Samantha, "This really isn't that bad. If we don't get a real job after college, our music career is great."

"You said it, sis," says Samantha with a big smile.

Allen and Athena dance close to the pool. Allen says, "Just a couple of more days and you know it's on. ASB game-face time."

Feeling anxious, Athena says, "I'm looking forward to it."

Allen gazes into Athena's eyes and twirls her around. "I know we'll be fine. We practiced hard last week."

Athena declares, "Did we ever! I can't wait to be married to you. I know we've mentioned it about as many times as Uncle Zadok gets stuck on saying something. I really can't wait to be your wife."

Allen smiles and replies devotedly, "I can't wait to be your husband, my love. We'll be a supernatural teen couple."

A few days go by, and it's time to do what the Atlantean Superhero Ballers have been training for. It's time to travel to Hawaii and find Allen's crown, which will officially make him The King of Atlantis.

It's early Saturday morning, and Uncle Zadok is happily singing and preparing the feast of all feasts for the ASB before they leave for battle. Zadok has made a buffet of every meal the warriors like to eat for breakfast, lunch, and dinner. He doesn't ring his golden cowbell; he lets the Teen Warriors slowly rise out of bed at their leisure. They've been used to getting up early every morning for school. School is out, and they will have the battle of their lives.

Allen and Athena wake up in her bed. He opens his eyes, seeing Athena lying on her side staring at her soon-to-be king. The Goddess smiles and whispers, "Good morning, handsome, you look so peaceful when you sleep. I could watch you all night long if I didn't have to sleep."

Allen grins and teases, "You say the most beautiful words with your accent. If I weren't your fiancé, I would think you were stalking and watching me through a window as I sleep."

Athena grabs her pillow and hits him in the head, laughing. "You say the craziest things when I'm having an romantic moment."

Allen grabs Athena, rolling on top of her. He gazes into the Greek Goddesses' golden-brown eyes. "I have said this a million times, and I'll say it a million more. I love you, Athena Dranias."

She touches Allen's face, saying softly, "We will love each other from this world to the next."

Allen kisses Athena, then whispers, "It will be a long time before we go on to the next world. We'll watch our children and grandchildren grow into great men and women on Earth."

Athena wraps her arms around Allen and confesses happily, "Yes, we'll raise an attractive brood of new Atlanteans."

Allen says, "We have plenty of time for that." He raises his nose sniffing in the air. "What is Uncle Zadok cooking? It smells so good. I can smell it from here."

Athena jumps up energized, rubbing her belly. "Let's go eat and then I'll show you the surprise I have for us today before we find your Atlantean Crown."

Allen replies with a sly grin, "I can't wait to see it after I race you to breakfast... last one downstairs is a rotten egg."

Athena displays a conceited smile. She pushes Allen off the bed. "You're a slow poke."

She runs toward the staircase, but Allen catches up to her. Athena says, "Okay, Mr. King, you want a challenge? I'll race you sliding down the banister. We'll see who's the fastest!"

Allen brags, "Sweetheart. I'll give you a head start."

Athena nods as she giggles. "No way... on three."

Allen gestures with his right hand. "On my mark, one, two—"

"Three!" shouts Athena, sliding down a second before Allen.

He laughs. "Okay cheater." And slides down after her.

Athena looks back, blowing him a kiss. She flies quickly down.

Allen stands on the banister sliding down like a surfer. Athena gets to the bottom first, but Allen teleports himself into the dining room and is sitting in his chair waiting for his fiancée when she arrives.

"Hey, you cheated, mister!" yells Athena with a playful frown.

Allen grins. "No different than you getting a head start on me."

Uncle Zadok laughs joyously. "Well, well, my favorite soon-to-be king and queen, already happily arguing. I love it!"

Francisco and Jake are about to dig into the huge buffet. Jake says, "Thank you for the lovely buffet, Uncle Zadok. I'm surprised you didn't yell through your speaker and ring your cowbell this morning."

Zadok replies, "Well, this morning I figured you should get up when you wanted to. This is the biggest day of your lives. I wanted all of you to have the feast a warrior should have. You're going to need your strength today."

Francisco says, "Thank you, uncle. We all appreciate that."

Aunt Aoki starts to cry.

Allen says in a comforting voice, "Aunt Aoki, there's no reason for you to cry."

Aoki wipes her tears. "I can't help it. I'm trying to be strong. I don't want to think anything bad, and I want to keep a positive vibe before you fight. I love all of you so much."

Allen hugs her. "Don't worry." The rest of the teens also hug her.

Aoki says, "I feel a little better now." She blows her nose. "I want you to kick some ass today!"

Zadok looks at Aoki, stunned. "Wow, honey! I knew you had a little spunk in you. You're on fire right now, my little tiger."

The family laughs.

Allen stares at Francisco who is overeating on lobster, pancakes, sausage, and hash browns. "Slow down, brother… all that food will give you heartburn."

Francisco talks with a mouth full. "I'll be all right. Don't you worry about me, bro. I got this under control, and if one of those goons tries to sneak up behind me. I'll just"—Francisco lets out a humongous fart—"kill them with the loud and deadly."

Jake jumps up from the table holding his nose, while Zadok and Aoki laugh out of their chairs.

Athena declares, while holding her nose, "You definitely brought the deadly." She grins and says, "Here's mine." The Goddess farts a petite fart as she shyly covers her mouth with two fingers. "Oops! Sorry."

Allen announces. "Okay, everyone, I think we got"—he makes a strange face, farting out loud—"the picture."

Jake walks up to Francisco and says, "Hey, Fran." Francisco turns around as Jake moons Francisco farting in his face. Francisco falls out of his seat covering his nose and mouth. The Atlantean Superhero Ballers are not thinking about what they'll have to face in the next few hours.

Uncle Zadok does the warrior's salute. "Hail Atlantis!"

The rest of the family follows Uncle Zadok's lead. "Hail Atlantis!"

Everyone has been eating for the last forty-minutes in delight.

Athena says merrily, "Okay, boys, are you ready for the surprise before today's battle?"

The guys nod. "Yes!"

Athena teleports a large box out of her bedroom closet, sending it next to Allen's chair. "Go ahead, open it."

He opens the box and pulls bubble wrapping out. He stares in awe at three pairs of black warrior's boots with ASB engraved in gold.

Allen yells with excitement, "Wow! Warrior boots!"

Athena smiles grandly. "Yes, and these are specially designed to withstand heat up to ten thousand degrees Fahrenheit."

"Wow, Athena! I love these!" shouts Francisco with joy. He jumps out of his seat and tries them on. "You have my exact size. Thanks, sis."

Jake says, "These are way better than those ancient sandals. No offense, Allen or Uncle Zadok."

Allen winks. "No offense taken, warrior. This is what we need for the new generation of warriors."

Uncle Zadok says, "I love them as well, Athena. It fits the look of you warriors. If I had a fresh pair of legs, I would try a pair on."

Allen replies with assurance, "One day, Uncle Zadok. I'm pretty sure the elders of Zion West have advanced technology to restore your legs."

Zadok asks, feeling hopeful, "You really know this, like you said before?"

Allen nods confidently. "Yes, Unc."

Uncle Zadok grins and says in a commanding voice, "Then I think all of you warriors need to get your behinds ready for combat!"

Francisco says in a funny way, "I'll be ready after I shower and wash an accidental stain in my shorts."

Zadok looks at Francisco thinking, *You can take the orphan out of the orphanage, but he still has a little orphan in him.*

Zadok laughs and says, "You just do that, nephew."

Everyone's happy with the new boots as they walk upstairs to get ready for their voyage to Atlantis and Hawaii.

Allen teleports the Teen Warriors downstairs after they've showered and dressed. They're mentally preparing themselves to fight. The ASB communicate on their crystal necklaces as if it were the first time they ever used them.

Allen says, *Come in, Francisco. Check one, two…*

Francisco responds with a thumbs-up. *I hear you loud and clear.*

The teens talk telepathically amongst themselves.

"Let's go to the entertainment room and say good-bye to Uncle Zadok and Aunt Aoki," says Allen feeling eager to be king so he can marry Athena.

The guys wear matching red-and-gold sweat suits and sneakers in honor of their warrior's costume. They hold their ASB gold-initialed warrior boots in their hands. Athena has her Glam Girl makeup on and wears a white and gold sweat suit. She's planning to change into her Glam Girl Warrior Princess attire in the Warrior's Room with the guys. Athena's brand new upgraded white thigh-high boots with ASB engraved in gold are heat resistant just like the guys' boots. The Greek Goddess holds her shoes in her hands, ready to teleport. They enter the entertainment room.

Feeling sentimental, Zadok says, "I don't want to say anything. I'll see all of you when you come home."

The Atlantean Superhero Ballers smile and wave at their uncle and aunt as they teleport through a majestic rainbow cloud of red, yellow, blue, green, black and white.

As they pass through the wormhole, they look up and notice the moon. Francisco says, "Wow, that's an eerie-looking full moon during the daytime."

Jake stares and says with a grin, "It's not going to be as scary as when those goons see us kicking their ass and making them lick the shit stains off our boots."

Francisco cracks a smile, and fist bumps Jake. "You got that right."

The warriors land in the war room, where they are greeted by General Lionel and King Leon and the rest of Allen's spirit family. The spirits of the Atlantean warriors who've fought in many battles salute the new warriors. The African drums beat hard roaring with Zulu tribal rhythms while Spanish harps and Mediterranean flutes delicately play in the background.

"You know what needs to be done. There's nothing else to say," says General Lionel.

Allen replies with a stern stare. "Yes, great-grandfather, we will prevail, but first I must look at the chessboard one last time before we leave for battle."

King Leon agrees. "As you should."

Before going to the chess room, Allen looks at Francisco and Jake. "Sorry, guys, we have no time to waste. I have to change you two out of the sweat suits and into your warrior gear."

Francisco smiles and says, "Go ahead, Allen, I'm ready to go kick some ass and find your crown."

Jake nods. "Yeah, I second that. Let's whoop some ass and help make you king."

He changes them into the warrior gear. Francisco and Jake pick up their sweat suits on the floor and they fold their outfits properly before placing it in their designated spot inside the Warrior's Room.

Allen smiles. "Thanks, guys."

General Lionel says with an astonished look, "I'm impressed… nice boots. We could have used those when we fought with the Centurion Army against wild, fire-breathing Dragon Demons. Deadly Grim Reapers eventually tamed them."

Allen displays a puzzled look.

General Lionel shrugs. "Never mind that. That's nothing compared to what you have to do."

Allen, King Leon, and General Lionel teleport to the chess room. The chessboard lights up as Allen sits down and ponders. *I see nothing has changed, except that Josh has moved two squares closer to Destroyer, and he's pointing at me. It looks like Josh is commanding his pawns to attack me and my team.* Allen whispers to himself, "Josh, I hope I don't have to end it like this."

King Leon says softly, "Whatever move you make, it's your decision only, and if you make the wrong move, the kingdom will be gone forever."

Allen sighs. "I understand, grandfather, I will not fail you. I will see you two soon."

He teleports back into to the Warrior's Room with his game face on. "Okay, guys, this is it, huddle up. Who are we?"

"ASB," the Teen Warriors reply.

Allen repeats, "Louder. Who are we?"

The Teen Warriors yell, "ASB."

Allen thunders, "Who are we!?"

The Teen Warrior's scream out, "ASB!"

Allen lets out another loud echoing roar shaking the floor in the Warrior's Room. The battle to become King of Atlantis has begun.

CHAPTER TWENTY-FIVE

The Battle For The Crown

Allen leads his troops through the golden doors in the King's Chamber. Jake and Francisco have their retractable golden spears, shields, wrist guards, headgear, black golden lassos, and black masks. Athena carries her white golden sword and shield on her back, and the black golden lasso on her hip.

They greet their sea animals and fasten the golden headgear on the dolphins and Bucky, the great white shark. Allen leaps into the air as Bucky jumps to meet him. Allen straddles him, and they fly straight up and then dive back down into the pool. When they surface, Allen has the reins wrapped around his hand. His golden shield, mining pitchfork, and spear are attached to Bucky's side.

Athena runs and does a mid-air somersault, landing gently on Jumper who leaps up to greet her. Jake runs, yelling out a warrior's whoop as he jumps on Dance II. Though he isn't as agile as Allen and Athena, he courageously lands on the dolphin. Allen and Athena let out a warrior cry, acknowledging his accomplishment. Jake holds onto the reins, waiting for Francisco to jump as he encourages himself. "What the hell, let's do this… must show no fear!"

Francisco runs and whoops landing softly on Dance II. He attaches his shield and spear behind Jake's.

Everyone applauds Francisco. "Yeah, Francisco!"

Allen says in his Atlantean baritone voice, "We're ready." He summons a crimson rainbow cloud and says, "No more colorful rainbows today. This is the day there will be bloodshed. We will fight and kill all villains working under Drogan and the Gargoyle, Destroyer!"

The teens scream out a battle roar.

Miles above, the ASB teleport to Hawaii. Allen's Atlantean eyes see the undiscovered island located between Kaho'olawe and Maui in the area where the active volcano is located. He smiles a little and says, "The King's Crown is ready to show itself."

He teleports them closer, and everyone notices the fiery red-hot lava spewing out the side of the crater.

Francisco asks, "Do we have to go inside of that crater?"

"No… not yet at least," replies Allen. He holds the mining fork in his hand. It instantly starts ringing, letting him know that the golden crown with the black crystal is near.

Allen says, "I'll be right back." The golden prongs turn black, indicating that the crown is miles beneath him.

Allen dives with Bucky as he says to the ASB telepathically, *Let me know if anything seems wrong, I'll be back before you know it.*

Allen's gills appear on his neck allowing him to breathe like a fish in the ocean. He dives closer to the red-hot lava lake flowing in the ocean depth. The Atlantean's pitchfork rings louder as a yellowish-black laser beam shoots out the prongs showing where the crown is located. Allen notices that the Earth's crust is separating, displaying the golden crown glistening and the black crystal glows a bright white light illuminating the ocean floor. The soon-to-be-King watches the headdress slowly rising and moving toward the magnetic pitchfork.

He simultaneously hears Athena telepathically screaming, *Allen!*

He's so close to it, but he has no choice but to leave. Allen throws his pitchfork into the Earth's crust, attaching it to the crown and teleports back to the surface with Bucky. As soon as he surfaces, he sees ten helicopters with machine guns surrounding them.

One of Drogan's goons sits next to him in a helicopter. He yells through a loudspeaker, "Put your hands up!"

Allen smiles as a reddish glow appears from his eyes. He swiftly teleports the warriors into the volcano. Drogan and his henchmen see the red rainbow lead onto the edge of the volcanic crater. The volcano is calm at the moment. It hasn't spewed out its volcanic lava on the other side of the peak.

A couple of henchmen take ropes, climbing down to the edge of the crater. The sea animals safely wait in the ocean for Allen's command. The Atlantean General gets into his warrior's stance holding his shield and spear. He extends his spear as he throws his shield up, cutting through the ropes of fifty henchmen rappelling down the crater commando style.

Allen's golden shield returns to him like a boomerang. The ASB watch the henchmen flailing to their deaths into the lava flowing below the crater.

Athena yells as she grabs her lasso and cracks it like a whip grabbing one of the henchmen by his neck. Glam Girl Warrior Princess drags him down and smashes his body against the jagged rocks. He slides down into the lava below screaming.

Athena roars, "Is that all you've got, Drogan?"

More henchmen descend. Jake punches one in the face and kicks him into the lava pit.

Francisco smiles as he brags, "I got this one, bro." Francisco approaches a massive seven-foot henchman landing on the crater.

He looks at Francisco, laughs, and bellows in a deep voice, "I'll kill you easily, midget."

"Oh yeah," says Francisco with eyes narrowed in hate.

The large henchman lumbers toward Francisco. Francisco runs and slides underneath him slamming the edge of his shield into his groin. The henchman grabs his crotch as Francisco runs into him with his shield. The henchman doesn't budge.

Jake telepathically says, *Let me help you, Franny.* He grabs his lasso and wraps it around the henchman's neck. Jake swings around the henchman, binding him and then pushes him to the ground.

Francisco telepathically says, *Okay, let me roll out the trash.* He grabs the henchmen from the middle while Jake yanks his rope, making him roll faster. Francisco continues to move the villain like a huge rug until he falls into the crater. The former teen orphans turned superhero warriors high-five each other.

Drogan yells through a loudspeaker amplifying his loud hissing voice, which makes the warriors grab their ears. Allen looks at Drogan as he raises his shield toward him. Allen projects his thunderous voice through it. The vibration cuts through Drogan's hiss like a knife and knocks the loudspeaker out of his hand.

Enraged, Drogan lets out a monstrous roar. "If I can't beat you, then the Gargoyle will," Drogan screams as he turns into the Destroyer.

Allen sighs with a little relief. "Well, at least it isn't Josh."

Destroyer lands with a thunderous thump onto the crater, forcing everyone to fall. He stares intently at Allen and walks toward him. The Gargoyle briefly turns to Athena and licks his lips. "We meet again I see, good-looking." He taunts her by making his face morph into the image of Drogan's face just for a moment.

Allen lets out a thunderous roar and rushes the Gargoyle. His mortal enemy raises his arm and clotheslines Allen, who falls and drops his shield. Destroyer looks at Athena, then wraps his long tongue around her neck. She tries to loosen the grip, but the sticky, red-hot muscular organ continues to tighten against her neck, which is starting to burn.

Allen slices the tip of the tongue off with his spear. The tongue immediately retracts into Destroyer's mouth. He screams out an anguished cry before he sticks it out again. Destroyer's tongue is whole again. He looks at Allen with a sinister grin. "As you can see, Atlantean, I'm new and improved."

Athena yells as she sticks her sword into Destroyer's back. "You remember this, asshole!"

Destroyer lets out a roar that shakes the volcano, forcing lava to spew out. Athena pulls her sword out of his back and sees that the Gargoyle's back begins to heal instantly.

Athena looks at Allen, horrified. "What can we do? This Gargoyle is invincible."

Destroyer grins menacingly. "Because I am Invincible. You thought you destroyed me, didn't you, Atlantean? I'm stronger and better than ever. I can look like my old master, Destroyer." Drogan shows his face and smirks. "Science has prevailed. I took over Invincible's DNA and my dead brother's genetic material. I can be the Gargoyle you killed thanks to my brother's blood. I will avenge him." He shapeshifts from the Destroyer and shapeshifts into Invincible. He says, "I wish Destroyer were here so I can finish him off before I kill you and become King of Atlantis and the true King of the Gargoyle Brotherhood."

Suddenly, Josh appears. He climbs onto the crater yelling, "Here's your chance!" Allen and the Teen Warriors stare at Josh as the Invincible Gargoyle commands the other henchmen to shoot at them.

Josh says to Allen, "I got this. Keep your friends safe."

Allen quickly teleports the warriors together, they kneel and extend their shields into a cocoon, protecting themselves from the rapid gunfire coming at them.

Josh turns into Destroyer. Shocked, Invincible yells, "How can that be? You control Destroyer?"

Josh says, "Yes. I defeated him in the open spiritual plane. I was stronger." Josh/Destroyer walks closer to Invincible. "You can clearly see that I was victorious!" Josh hits Invincible with an uppercut, sending him flying closer to the edge of the volcano. Invincible looks at the perimeter and swiftly backflips, kicking Josh down.

Allen says to the ASB, "You see, Josh is on our side after all. He fought, and now he controls the Gargoyle."

Invincible grabs one of his henchmen and throws him at Josh's gargantuan body as he does a supernatural vertical leap. The henchman flies into the crater.

Allen whispers, "I want to help him."

"No, you can't, Allen, we need you!" shouts Athena.

Invincible looks at the henchmen and commands, "Kill him!" The remaining seventeen henchmen circle around Josh, shooting at him from all directions. The bullets bounce off his body. However, Josh weakens every time a projectile ricochets off him.

Allen insists, "I can still protect you. Stay crouched in our battle position."

Athena screams, "No, Allen, please don't!"

Allen teleports out of the cocoon, leaving his warrior family exposed to open gunfire.

Allen's superhuman speed knocks out seven of the armed villains. He yells, "That only leaves ten of you."

Athena roars, "We'll get them!" She telepathically instructs Francisco and Jake, *I'll handle four of the bad guys, and you two can take out three each.*

Francisco gripes, *Why do you want to be so greedy?*

Athena jumps on one of the henchmen's neck from behind, flipping him like a wrestler.

She materializes her sword into her hand and plunges it into his back. Athena then emerges her shield into her hand and deflects one of the goon's bullets. She angles her shield, and the deflected bullets hit the villain in the head. He's killed instantly.

"I want some of this action," says Jake. He whips his lasso out and wraps it around a henchman's legs, pulling his feet out from under him. The goon's gun flies up in the air.

Francisco grabs it and shoots him. "You want to go to war with me... Okay!" he says in his gangster persona. Francisco riddles his body with bullets.

Allen takes care of the rest of the goons.

Josh yells to Allen, "Go get what you came for and take care of your friends. I'll see you soon."

Allen yells back, "No! Josh, we're in this together."

Josh screams, "Go!"

Allen teleports the ASB back to the sea animals. He says to his shark, "All right Bucky, it's our time to shine," teleporting with the great white shark directly to the pitchfork. The pitchfork is cold in the hot molten lava. Allen pulls the crown out of the molten rock as if the lava were soft mud. The King's Crown flashes as Allen touches it. His golden crystal necklace, emerald ring, and crown glow in unison.

Allen puts on the crown. He instantly sees his Alien Elders on Zion West smiling and happy with relief. He feels their love and warmth. One of the Elders telepathically says, *The Zion West crystals embedded in the necklace, ring and King's Crown told us who you are. Atlantis has returned.*

Another Elder telepathically declares, *Allen, you will be King as soon as you're back in Atlantis sitting on the throne, wearing the crown on your head. Go and be prosperous for your people.*

Allen smiles with gratitude and telepathically replies, *Thank you, Elders. I will.*

Allen immediately teleports with Bucky above the water. Athena sheds a tear smiling with joy seeing Allen wearing the enchanting golden crystal necklace, ring, and crown.

Francisco and Jake scream at once, "Hell yeah! Hail to the King!"

Allen isn't satisfied yet. He telepathically says to Athena and the guys, *I will see all of you soon.*

He teleports them back to Atlantis as he teleports back into the volcanic crater. Allen says to himself, "My powers are complete. I'm more powerful than any Atlantean King that's ever lived."

Allen ponders. *I hope my powers will defeat my foes.*

He sees Invincible is overpowering Josh. The Gargoyle stands laughing over the edge of the crater with the wounded star quarterback, about to throw him into the lava lake below. Allen grabs Invincible by his neck. He throws him hard against the other side of the wall. The Gargoyle bounces back onto the jagged crater.

Allen asks Josh, "Are you okay?"

Josh shakes his head. "Yes." He feels a slight surge of energy when Allen touches his shoulder. He's able to absorb some of Allen's strength. Josh looks at him with ominous red eyes, and declares, "I will be King." Josh punches Allen in his stomach knocking the crown off his head. The Atlantean slides closer to the edge.

Allen's head throbs and Athena feels his pain. She telepathically screams, *Allen! Let us help you!*

Destroyer has taken over Josh's body. He stares at the crown grinning. "It's mine." The Gargoyle leans down to pick up the crown as it is hit to the other side by a rock thrown by Invincible. He screams with Drogan's Reptilian hiss, "No! It is mine!"

Invincible runs toward it. Destroyer tackles him as Josh's face appears and yells to Allen, "Take your crown and get out of here, now!"

Allen slowly stumbles to the crown and grabs it. He teleports and tries to grab Josh, who has jumped with Invincible into the lava lake. Allen teleports through the rainbow cloud screaming, "Josh, no!"

Allen returns to Atlantis where he hears cheers. The Atlantean spirits appear in human form. The Atlanteans bow down to Allen. He looks at everyone on bended knee.

Athena, Jake, and Francisco all bow down to him. Athena smiles and gestures with her head. "Go, sit on your throne, Alien King."

Allen winks at his soon-to-be Queen as he walks up to the throne. Allen is about to sit when unexpectedly a lasso knocks the King's Crown off his head and onto the floor near his feet. The flesh and blood Atlanteans instantly turn back into spirits. Invincible shapeshifts back to Drogan, who somehow got into the rainbow cloud and followed Allen. Athena rushes Drogan and tries to strike him in the face with her fist.

Drogan swiftly whips out his long tail and grabs the Goddess by the throat. He laughs with a hiss. "For some reason, you love being choked. Is this some kinky fetish of yours?" Drogan throws her to the side.

Infuriated, Allen gets ups and shouts, "This is between you and me, Drogan!" The King's Chamber is silent except for the low monotone tribal chants of the spirit warriors cheering for their new king: "Allen… Allen…"

Allen approaches Drogan as he throws his shield and spear to the side. "I don't need any of this to kill you. You have some nerve coming into my family's kingdom after what your ancestors have done!"

Drogan looks around and boasts, "There will be some changes made around here soon. I'll make this city a shrine in honor of my grandfather, Damius!" He rushes Allen, swiftly kicking him across the room.

Francisco yells, "Get up, Allen! Get up!" The Atlantean quickly gets up and picks Drogan up over his shoulders, throwing him towards the open pool. Drogan almost slides in where Bucky is eagerly waiting with an open mouth ready to devour him. He gets up and throws a jab and an uppercut at Allen, which sends him flying across the room. He hits the chamber door.

"Enough with this nonsense," hisses Drogan. "When I wear the crown and sit on the throne, I'll rule this kingdom and the spirits of your ancestors, forever."

Allen cries out in anger, "No!"

Drogan grins as he strolls to the throne with the crown in his hand.

Athena telepathically says, *Allen, I'm going to teleport your spear to you. It slid close to my hand.*

Allen slightly nods his head, and telepathically replies, *I know what to do.* He remembers his grandfather, King Leon, stopping Damius from trying to rule the kingdom. Drogan lowers his body onto the throne with a conceited grin as he holds the crown above his head. Athena teleports the spear into Allen's hand from across the room.

Allen yells out, "This is for my grandfather, King Leon, and my Atlantean family!"

Allen throws the spear with high speed and accuracy. The spear goes into the middle of the crown, shooting it up into the corner of the chamber wall. Drogan screams as he leaps onto the wall, climbing up to it. Allen regains his strength and throws the shield (just as his grandfather did) into the wall breaking the spear in half. Drogan falls to his death.

Allen picks up the crown as Francisco and Jake hold their spears over their shoulder ready to strike their enemy. They walk towards the dead Hybrid's body. Jake turns the body over, but it's not Drogan. He's teleported out of the Atlantean city the same way his creator and grandfather Damius had done. The lifeless body is the descendant of Navian, the half-Reptilian that died before. This time, it's Josh's body in place of Navian's body.

Allen runs to him yelling and pleading, "You have to live!" Allen instantly throws sparks of electrodes into Josh's body. He coughs a little, gasping. Josh is still alive but faint. Josh breathes heavily. Allen falls to the floor as Athena runs to her king. She holds him in her lap smiling.

She whispers, "Allen King, you never gave up on Josh. Maybe you were right about him."

Francisco and Jake crouch around Allen, announcing at the same time, "You did it!"

Allen asks with bewilderment, "What are you talking about? My name is Josh Stone."

Athena stutters in shock, "Wh-what… No! You're Allen King, my fiancé."

The body of Josh Stone rises up and says, "Athena, my love, I'm here."

The ASB turn around when they hear Allen's voice in Josh's body. Athena unexpectedly faints. She wakes up several minutes later and sees General Lionel and King Leon. She screams out a horrific cry. "What happened to Allen!? Why is his voice coming from Josh's body?"

General Lionel says, "Somehow with Allen's will, he healed Josh so rapidly, his spirit switched places with Josh's spirit."

Athena cries, "No! We're supposed to be married soon. How could this happen? Can we change Allen back?"

Athena has flashes of memories going through her mind about the dream wedding they dreamt together in Australia. It has now become her greatest nightmare. She hates Josh Stone with all her heart. The Nomadic Indian's spirit is in her King's body.

King Leon sighs with sorrow. "I'm sorry, Athena, but Allen isn't a King yet since he's in Josh's body."

Athena continues to cry as she thinks. *Even the great Zeus didn't predict this would happen.* Her Godfather was against her marrying an Atlantean until he realized they loved each other very deeply and they would die for each other's love.

Feeling helpless, Athena asks, "What must be done to bring my love back?"

Trying to hide his sadness, General Lionel says, "Unfortunately, you will have to wait until next summer and try to be friends with Allen's spirit in Josh's body. You must give him hope and encouragement until Allen is back to normal. The Elders of Zion can't help. There isn't officially a King declared yet in this matter. Next year is a rare occasion within a thousand years.

There will be a summer equinox occurring instead of being between fall and springtime when day and night are of equal length meeting in unison."

King Leon avows, "There is only one person on Earth who can help my grandson now."

Feeling heartbroken, Athena asks with urgency, "Who can help Allen? I will go there immediately so we can be married."

King Leon gasps, still feeling hope. "She is the Queen of the Dragonflies, and next summer during the summer equinox, Queen Lourdes will be in great spirits and will help you without challenging you to a duel. It may still cost you something depending on your timing. Lourdes' culture is similar to ours. They're very beautiful and strong, like Atlanteans, mixed with many races. She used to live deep in a hidden jungle close to where she mined for diamond rocks filled with gold. The enchanting Queen now lives in a spellbound city filled with carnivals and samba music. She is dressed as a mortal and does not reveal her wings."

Athena screams, "Just tell me, please!"

King Leon takes a deep breath and replies, "Okay, it's a place with the second largest population of Africans outside of Africa. It also has some of the most striking exotic people in the world. They greet you by saying, 'Tudo bem,' which means, 'Hello' in Portuguese."

They both say at the same time, "Rio de Janeiro, Brazil."

Meanwhile, in the cemetery where Tyrone is buried, Barrington, the evil scientist pours the liquid re-animator he created into the soil. The liquid penetrates into Tyrone's coffin. The teenager awakens from his dead sleep. The ground shakes as Tyrone bursts out of the casket with a roar. He jumps through the hallowed ground and stands in front of Drogan.

The badly bruised and battered billionaire says with a hiss, "Tyrone, my zombie friend... I am not sure if our common enemy is dead... If he's not. It is time to avenge the death of the one who killed you."

Tyrone stares at Drogan with blood-red eyes. "Josh Stone and anyone dear to him will die... except for Mercedes. I will make his girlfriend my bride."

I stop watching everyone as I shed a tear, still feeling hope for my granddaughter. I return to Mount Olympus and report to Zeus. He sees me and asks, "Andromeda, what news do you have on Athena and the Atlantean?"

I say, "Athena is an honorable young lady, and she's a warrior. Many things have happened, but I am confident Athena will prevail in her quest to save the Atlantean kingdom."

To Be Continued...

END OF BOOK TWO

ACKNOWLEDGMENTS

I thank God for molding me into the man I am and living my life as a global citizen. I wrote The Last Prince of Atlantis Chronicles to inspire kids of color to see themselves represented positively in the young adult book world. I am happy to see young people reach out to me and letting me know that they are proud to see themselves represented in the Sci-Fi young adult book genre from my perspective. I will not stop doing what I'm doing until a movie happens in the future and a franchise so that I can give back and help other young people pursue their dreams and achieve their goals with the foster care foundation I hope to create when everything comes together collectively. I would not have made it this far if it were not for the fans I had on Goodreads when I started to market the original book in 2012. Thank you for giving me the courage to not stop writing the three book series, and I appreciate every person who bought the original novel and loved the story of a young Black Prince (with multicultural roots) and a Greek Goddess. I sincerely appreciate your support. Continued blessings to you all. "Hail Atlantis!"

ABOUT THE AUTHOR

Leonard Clifton Leonard Clifton started as a print model, which led him to acting. His first role was in Steven Spielberg's Amistad. He went on to have roles in several other films like the cult classic Bring It On, television productions, and international commercials. Leonard loves writing, supporting his favorite charities, traveling the world, and is always seeking new adventures. Leonard has five-star reviews on Amazon and Goodreads, he was the first author to have a Barnes & Noble book signing for Black History Month at The Grove in Los Angeles. He has been interviewed about his writing on Los Angeles's KPFK radio and he has given a lecture about The Last Prince of Atlantis Chronicles and how it relates to Afrofuturism at California State University, Northridge.

Follow Leonard Clifton On

You can visit Leo online at www.leonardclifton.com

CPSIA information can be obtained
at www.ICGtesting.com
Printed in the USA
FSHW021304120821
84030FS

9 798653 553271